MIDNIGHT ROUNDS

MIDNIGHT ROUNDS

Richard Greene

RICHARD A. GREENE, M.D.

GADD & COMPANY PUBLISHERS, INC.

Gadd & Company Publishers, Inc.
An Independent Division of The North River Press Publishing Corporation
292 Main Street
Great Barrington, MA 01230
(413) 528-8895
Visit our website at www.gaddbooks.com

Printed in the United States of America
ISBN 0-9774053-0-3

Gadd & Company Publishers, Inc. is committed to preserving ancient forests and natural resources. We elected to print *Midnight Rounds* on 50% post consumer recycled paper, processed chlorine free. As a result, for this printing, we have saved:

5 trees (40' tall and 6-8" diameter)
2,029 gallons of water
816 kilowatt hours of electricity
224 pounds of solid waste
439 pounds of greenhouse gases

Gadd & Company Publishers, Inc. made this paper choice because our printer, Thomson-Shore, Inc., is a member of Green Press Initiative, a nonprofit program dedicated to supporting authors, publishers, and suppliers in their efforts to reduce their use of fiber obtained from endangered forests.

For more information, visit www.greenpressinitiative.org

To Lindsay and Mark

Acknowledgments

Cia Elkin, who exhumed what I tried to keep buried, and for her enthusiasm and encouragement in this project.

My beloved uncle and mentor, Harry Sherman, M.D., who got me started on the road to medicine.

Alan Michelson, M.D., my professor and mentor, who taught me to think like an internist.

Rabbi Dennis Ross for his encouragement and support.

And my family and friends, who cheered me on during the writing of this story.

MIDNIGHT ROUNDS

CHAPTER 1

Sal, not my uncle Sal, was dead.

I was calmly sitting on one of those gray plastic airport seats attached to a long row of more gray plastic seats. The first leg of my flight out of Bradley was so delayed that I had already finished the paperback I had bought for the trip. Being tired and bored, I picked up a section of the Springfield Tribune left behind by some lucky soul whose flight had actually taken off. I scanned the local news, local politics, obituaries and classified ads.

Still bored, I put down the paper and started to people-watch. Something was wrong. I was getting a little anxious, as if I might have left the lights on in the car, or the door unlocked. But I knew I hadn't. What was it? *If I don't concentrate on it, if I think about something else, maybe it'll come to me.* I watched the people go by.

I picked up the newspaper again. The obituaries. Salvatore DiCensi had died. Is it possible he was the guy? Am I sure I remember his name right? Was this the same Sal who darkened my life and nearly killed me so long ago? Could I be sure?

What are the chances that on a random day I'd be in the airport and happen to pick up a newspaper on the day that Sal's obituary is in it?

After I came home from my trip I made sure. The Sal I knew was dead. Our story needs to be told, and with him gone, I can finally tell it. It took place twenty-something years ago, in the early 1980s. It seemed like such a long time ago. Reagan succeeded Carter in the White House; Iran let the hostages go; Prince Charles married Lady

Diana; AIDS was first identified. Argentina and Great Britain fought a war for the Falkland Islands. Few people had home computers, no one had cell phones, and I was living, as I am now, in Berkshire County, Massachusetts, an hour and a half away from Bradley Airport. I was younger, thinner, had more hair, and none of it was gray.

It's the Berkshires, not the Berserkshires, and the county seat is Pittsfield, not Pizzafield, and it isn't the pits. It is Taxachusetts, not Massachusetts. It is the westernmost county in the state, tucked up against the border of New York to the west, Vermont to the north, Connecticut to the south. It is beautiful and scenic, with mountains, forests, fields and lakes, farms and towns and small cities. I like it here. The county might be most famous for Tanglewood, the summer home of the Boston Symphony Orchestra, which holds open-air concerts in the big shed all summer. It is a huge tourist draw. There are also a bunch of summer stock theaters, art museums, history museums and ski resorts. There are not as many dairy farms as there used to be, and there are many more summer homes. More motels too.

There are quaint villages dating to the 1730s with houses that have white clapboard siding and window shutters painted dark green. Norman Rockwell lived and painted here for a while; some places look as if he designed them. We have five seasons here. We have a short spring; a real short, but wonderful summer; a fall that starts early, and a winter that goes on and on and on. Then comes the mud season.

I came here five years ago when I got out of medical school, class of 1978. I was smart enough but not brilliant, and managed to graduate at the top of the bottom half of the class. I made it only because of brute force, hard work and caffeine. It was awfully hard. So much to learn and understand and memorize. Much I memorized, many things I didn't really digest. But then I'm more aware of what I don't know than what I do know.

I came to the area to be a resident at Berkshire Medical Center, the local, large, excellent community teaching hospital. That was three years of eighty-plus hours a week, including nights, weekends and holidays; and overnight meant a thirty-six-hour straight shift. Lots of patients, lots of disease, lots of learning, lots of sleep loss, lots of pathos. A decade of experience in three years, and I felt competent enough but not as confident as I hoped I'd be.

That's all over now. I did my three years, passed my board exams and wondered what I would do next. I could read fiction again, have hobbies again. I took a job working a few shifts a week in the emergency room of Fairview Hospital in Great Barrington. There isn't anything great about Great Barrington, but it is a nice, small town. When the Native Americans lived there they had a big encampment near a place where the Housatonic River could easily be crossed, and the Native Americans called it the Great Crossing Place. The British settlers kept the great and called it Great Barrington, instead of maybe New Barrington.

Fairview Hospital is a cute little seventy-bed hospital. At night there is just one doc on at a time and we did three or four twelve-hour shifts per week, eight a.m. to eight p.m., or eight p.m. to eight a.m. Sometimes skiers from out of town would come to the ER and ask if this was the orthopedics pavilion. Nope, this was the whole hospital. Sometimes it was busy, sometimes slow and sometimes crazy. The staff was great. It was like a big family and we bonded in the coffee room and did some socializing outside of work, too. ER nurses have the best dirty jokes. Everybody hung out in our coffee room; the ambulance EMTs, the respiratory therapists, the cops. It was a nice little society. I would work there until I figured out what I wanted to do with my life.

It had been a long day and I was glad my twelve-hour shift was coming to an end. I was working in Room One on a ten-year-old kid who managed to step on a piece of broken glass while wading in Lake Mahkeenac on the first almost warm day of early spring. That kid was a monster. He had a simple laceration on the sole of his foot, but he wouldn't keep still, or shut up. He was lying on the stretcher on his stomach with his right foot extended. His parents were at the end of the bed giving him moral support. The nurse had rinsed out the cut and set up the suture tray for me. I hoped she knew how to wrestle. ER nurses usually are pretty good at it.

I explained everything to the brat before I did it. The small sting from the small needle with the lidocaine, then the burning for a few seconds, then the numbness. He screamed and screamed and screamed. I couldn't understand it. I used more lidocaine. He screamed. I sweated. He screamed when I injected, he screamed when I stopped. I left the consoling department to the matronly nurse, more experienced with kids than I. I'd never had such a screamer. I also didn't have any kids, nor did I really care for pediatrics. The nurse was great. She could have soothed anyone, but the kid screamed when I scrubbed his foot, when I set down the sterile drapes, when I began each stitch, when I pulled each one through, when I tied them, when I cut off the ends. It was like trying to sew a moving target, but it came out okay.

I pronounced with a sigh of relief that we were done, snapped off my latex surgical gloves and pulled down my surgical mask. I had gotten into the perhaps unnecessary habit of wearing a mask, as my nose always seemed to run at the wrong time, like on dates and while suturing. It didn't seem professional to constantly sniffle. My shirt was soaked with sweat. All that screaming can raise the tension. In retrospect perhaps I should have sedated the kid with all kinds of tranquilizers that would have left him dry-mouthed, glassy-eyed, and in general, out-to-lunch for hours.

"Is it really over?" the kid turned and asked.

"It sure is," I said with a fatigued sigh.

"Oh. That wasn't so bad," he responded. I wanted to break his neck.

While I was out at the nurse's station finishing the brat's chart, Will walked in. Will Connor was the ER doc scheduled for the eight p.m. to eight a.m. shift that night. Will was one of my favorite people. Several years older, he had been my resident when I was just an intern.

"I don't have much to sign out to you. There's a guy in the cast room with a hand fracture that's on ice; he's just waiting for an orthopedist to come. Also there's a lady in the third room who I think has a bladder infection. I was waiting for her urinalysis to come back. That's all I have for you." I belched. I'd been doing that a bit lately, but this was more quiet than if I had been alone driving on my way home.

"Had a busy day?" Will asked.

"Not bad, really. Slow in the morning and it picked up a bit in the afternoon. The after supper rush kept me running."

"Got plans tonight, Charlie? Seeing Patty?"

"Nope. Going home. Goodnight, Will."

I went to the ER physician's room, collected my things, and headed off to the parking lot. Tired. Tense. That kid got me all tightened up.

I got in my car and headed down the hill toward Route 7. It was dark. The air smelled good. It was still mild out. I turned left onto Route 7 and headed north, through downtown Great Barrington.

Spring was springing, mud season was drying up, the days were getting longer. The last snow had melted a month earlier. Daffodils were beginning to pop up in front yards. The trees had little yellow-green leaf buds getting ready to open. The air smelled earthy, not just cold. Lawns were getting greener where they faced south. I was in the early stages of a relationship with a lovely young lady. Life was good.

I drove the twenty-six miles home to Dalton. I wanted to go out for a run before it got too cool. It would help me unwind after the tensions of the day.

I ran upstairs into my apartment, dropped my orange knapsack of medical equipment and paraphernalia in the den and changed into a sweatshirt, gym shorts, running sneakers and reflective orange safety stripe. I went downstairs and fiddled with the doorknob so it would look to anyone like I had locked it. I started jogging down Carson toward Main, slowly, stretching and loosening up.

It was a nice evening. The air was fragrant and it was getting cool. The stars were out and the moon was half full. Turning left I ran down the gradual slope, passing a dignified funeral home on one side of the street and a stately Congregational church on the other. A very pretty New England town, Dalton, where I had been living for just over four years.

Dalton is practically owned by the Crane family, whose ancestors founded the Crane Paper Company in 1802. It is rag paper that they make and no wood pulp is used, so there is none of that pervasive sulfur smell like in wood pulp mill towns. It must be the cleanest, neatest mill town in New England. Crane has a dozen or more mill buildings scattered all over town, all brick, all two or three stories, just like you would envision in a quintessential New England mill town. All tidy, each with a wooden sign hanging in front like "The Old Berkshire Mill," or "The Baystate Mill." Even all their trucks are clean and without rust.

Crane makes the paper that money is printed on, as well as very elegant stationery. A patient once told me that he would give his left thumb to work for Crane. They really take good care of you, he said. Profit sharing, good pensions and wages as well as job security. The

Cranes had been great benefactors of the community, donating a recreation center (the kids call it the "cow house," though no one knows why), building a museum in Pittsfield, donations to the hospital. I had heard someone say that during the Depression, when many Crane employees had their mortgages foreclosed, the Cranes bought the houses from the bank and rented them back to their workers for a song. Needless to say, there are also a number of very imposing Crane family mansions in Dalton.

I'd passed the Dalton Post Office and shifted myself to a slower pace as I started uphill again, passing Kelly's Package Store, where the ever-friendly Mrs. Kelly always warned me "take care so you don't exhaust yourself, Doc," whenever I passed.

About a mile from home there's a small cemetery on the south side of Main Street. Once I stopped and walked amongst the eighteenth and nineteenth century gravestones. Some inscriptions were too weathered to read. But, there was one row of stones, all of the Mooers family, in which the mother, two sons and two daughters perished within two months in the fall of 1849. Good God, how depressing. Life and death was a more tenuous thing then. I wonder what killed them. Smallpox? Influenza?

Another one-half mile and left onto Orchard, down a steep hill overlooking the well regarded Wahconah Country Club golf course, which was of no interest to me except in winter for cross-country skiing, and a long beautiful view of the hills rising up to the town of Windsor. Down a little farther were O'Connell's stables. This part I always enjoyed, running past the horses in the fields, seeing them lazily graze, smelling the hay, animals, and forgive me, manure. Wondering why such huge creatures would allow an animal as puny as a human get on them and tell them what to do.

I stopped running for a minute when I got to the bridge over the Housatonic River. I always stopped here to look for trout in the water below. It was too dark to see any, so I resumed running. In this marshy spot the spring peep toads made a racket that sounded like sleigh bells. Another one-quarter mile took me alongside a large cornfield. On the far side of it, against a hillside, the Lion's Club had their annual autumn turkey shoot. For a dollar a shot whoever gets closest to the bull's-eye wins a frozen turkey.

Turning left on North Street I headed back toward the center of Dalton, past the Legion Hall, past the General Store (which featured

Häagen-Dazs ice cream cones), past the Center School. It's a grammar school built in the 1880s and still used. A very massive stone building, almost Byzantine. The severe look of it alone would've made me want to behave. I really enjoyed living in this town. Quaint, quiet, friendly. "Secure Dalton" is what it said on the fire department float in the Fourth of July parade. It was worth the forty-five-minute commute each way from work.

For me running was pretty boring. I did it because it enabled me to eat anything I wanted. It also was a good stress reliever. It helped me unwind after a shift, it helped me get out of my hospital mode and into the me mode.

On a run I usually got bored before I got tired. Then I could daydream, which worked really well if I had something good to daydream about. And I did; Patty. We'd been dating for a few months and it was looking pretty good.

As I got bored running home along North Street, I selected from my mental menu of daydreams which one I'd replay for myself. I'd been daydreaming a lot about Patty.

The first time I met Patty was just this past March when we still had too much snow. I went to the pharmacy in Great Barrington to pick up some things. As I passed the prescription desk I saw the name sign for the pharmacist on duty. It was Patricia Caine, who must have been the Patty I'd spoken to on the phone so many times in the last year, calling in prescriptions. Sometimes we'd chitchat a little on the phone, me being such a friendly guy. I asked the pleasant matronly middle-aged lady behind the counter if she was Patty. She said, "No, I'm the tech, Patty's in the back, do you want to speak with her?" I thought, I might as well, I'm here, why not meet the lady I've spoken to so many times.

The tech disappeared in the back and a minute later this tall vision of loveliness came to the counter. I introduced myself. What a face. Tall, thin, quietly pretty. Heavy eyebrows that moved a lot when she spoke. Long brown straight hair. "So you're the famous Dr. Davids I've heard so much about. One of the few whose handwriting I don't have to struggle to read. What can I do for you?"

I darted a glance at her left hand. No rings.

7

Will Connor would have said: "Could you order me a medium-sized athletic supporter with an extra large cup?" I couldn't say that. Was she dating anyone? Is she heterosexual?

We chitchatted for a few minutes and I surprised myself at being fairly glib. Then I asked if there was a phone booth in the store. "Oh, you can use this phone right here, just come around the counter." Oh no, I couldn't do that. Not for the call I needed to make. I excused myself and said goodbye, and walked away sheepishly, Patty looking at me quizzically.

I went outside and ran to the first phone booth I could find. I called the ER.

"Can you get me Margaret, right away?"

"Hi, Charlie, what's up?"

"I need some information."

"What do you need?"

"I need to know the scoop on Patty the pharmacist at Brook's on North Main Street. I need to know if she needs me in her life. In other words, is she available?"

"Oh. We might need the network for that one, Charlie. Where are you? I'll call back in ten minutes," Margaret said. I waited by the phone all bundled up in my winter coat, outside by the side of the bank, by the pay phone, by the snowdrift.

The phone rang twelve minutes later.

Margaret said, "My ex-brother-in-law's wife used to work there. I called her and she told me to call Jane, who still does work there. I called Jane but her line was busy. I kept trying and then I called Ruthie, the police dispatcher, so she sent a cruiser over to Jane's house to tell her to get the hell off the phone and to call me. I told Jane what we wanted to know and by now it might be all over town, but she said Patty is real nice, available, and would probably appreciate a nice guy in her life."

"That's what I was hoping you'd say. The network is incredible. Thanks, I owe you one."

"That's small town life, Charlie," said Margaret. "I love this stuff! Go make your move. Let me know what happens."

I went back to the drug store. I had butterflies in my stomach as if I'd never asked a girl out on a date before. I went to the prescription counter. I waited until Patty noticed me. She came over to the counter.

"Did you forget something?"

"Uhm, I know this is abrupt, but would you have dinner with me tonight?"

She hesitated for a second, was very still. "Uhm, let me see." She put her finger on her lip. "Let me consult my cluttered social calendar." She disappeared into the back of the store.

She returned a moment later, her finger still on her lip. "It just so happens," she said softly and slowly, "surprisingly, that I am free tonight."

That was wintertime, now it was spring and I was finishing both my run and my daydream.

I was nearing the end of my four-mile circuit. I was nice and sweaty, feeling my heart pounding, breathing deeply, cruising right along, thinking about how glad I'd be when this run was over and how nice a cold Genesee Cream Ale would taste. When I got to my corner I slowed to a walk and strolled toward home. I lived in the upstairs of a dark red two-family wood frame house. It was built in the 1920s and had a front porch and a big back yard. It was dark, the night was cool and my sweatshirt was suddenly cold and wet with sweat against my skin. The run worked. I felt good. I was relaxed. Invigorated. I climbed the three porch steps, fiddled with the doorknob so anyone would think I was unlocking it, and slowly climbed the stairway into my darkened apartment, one step at a time, easy on my wearied legs. I entered the living room en route to the kitchen for a tall frosty one. I stopped, my breath cut short, my heart suddenly racing again. In the darkness of my living room were two very large men.

Escape. If I kept going straight into the kitchen I could never get the pantry door open, the stairway door open, and down the back stairs without them catching me. I could have turned around and headed out the front. But one of the gorillas had slid behind me blocking my way to the front. Even if I'd miraculously slipped past him, chances are I'd have been killed sprinting across two lanes of traffic on Route 9 to the police station three blocks away.

"Sit down, Doc, we're not going to hurt you," said the man in front of me. He had a quiet, deep voice and a New York accent. The man behind me put his hand on my shoulder and gently pushed, coercing me into the big blue rocker that had been in my parent's home for years.

9

Who the hell are you and what the hell are you doing in my apartment?

The man in front of me turned on the lamp at the side of the sofa. He was big and paunchy and looked to be in his late fifties. He was wearing a worn grayish suit. The other guy stood to my left, looming over me, blocking the doorway that led from the living room to the front stairway. He was younger, maybe my age. Big, but not as big as the older man. But very beefy, like a halfback. He was swarthy, covered with wavy black hair, a tuft of which sprouted above his open shirt collar and almost buried his gold necklace.

I sat there indignant. I hoped they wouldn't hurt me. I hoped they would just leave. The older man sat down on the couch facing me, near the lamp. Then he said quietly, "Lemme get you a beer, doc," and he got up and went into the kitchen. I heard him open the refrigerator, get a bottle; open the cupboard, get a mug; pour the beer into it. I heard the empty bottle put down on the counter. He returned to the living room fully filling the doorway from the kitchen as he entered. He ambled toward me in a fatigued gait. As he neared me, the younger man took a slow step closer and leaned forward, his hands poised in front of him. The older man stopped in front of me and carefully handed me the beer. "Thanks," I said. I took it and held it in my lap. The older man took his seat on the couch. The young man relaxed and stepped back.

I was pissed. I was scared. I wanted them out of here. "So who are you guys and what are you doing here?" I asked, sounding as if I was brave.

"Dr. Davids, we want you to work for us. During your free time, we want you to take care of some medical problems that come up with our employees." The older man was sitting on the edge of the couch leaning forward with his forearms on his knees. He was looking at me. His thinning gray-black hair was combed straight back from a half-bald head. His manner was quiet, serious, maybe even sympathetic.

"Why do you want me?"

"You were recommended."

"Who recommended me?"

"You took care of one of our people during the Great Barrington Fair. He was impressed by you, thought you knew what you were doing. So we checked you out. We spoke to people at your old hospital in Pittsfield. And at Fairview. You're smart, sensible, capable. Just what we need."

"Who is 'we'?" I asked.

"You don't need to know that. I don't mean to be smart, but you're better off not knowing."

"Thank you, but I'm not interested in the job." I put the beer on the floor near the chair.

"Now, Doc," he said with an elongated syllable in the word doc, "with all due respect, you don't seem to understand. You *will* be working for us."

"How? What could you possibly have on me to force me?"

"Doc," he said, sounding sympathetic, "you've been watching too many movies. You see, we don't need to have anything on you. We can use any pressure you like. But we don't want to if we don't have to. You could lose your job. You might lose your medical license. You might break your arm."

'*You can make me an offer I can't refuse;*' that line from the Godfather movie popped into my head.

I was grinding my teeth, my head shaking from side to side, not wanting to hear any of this.

"Oh, man, I can't believe this. I don't want to be involved in any of this kind of stuff!" I blurted out.

The older man looked at me for a few seconds and said, "Better get used to the idea, Doc.

"We'll call you when we need you," he said.

What happens if I just hang up, I wondered.

"See you later, Doc. We'll let ourselves out." He got up from the couch, walked out of the living room. The younger man followed. I heard the front door close behind them.

I stayed in the rocker, vacantly staring at the spot where the large man had been sitting. Holy shit. This was unbelievable. I was alone now in my apartment. My home for four years. Comfortable, familiar, cozy. Just like always. Had I been dreaming? Were those two guys really here? I ought to do something, but I had no idea what.

I noticed my arms trembling. I still had a death grip on the arms of the rocker, like I do when I'm in the dentist's chair. I tried to relax. I felt drained. I picked up the glass of beer the large man had given me. *Thank you.* Sipping it, I tried to go over that whole scenario. Short and to the point. They didn't point a gun at me like in the movies. They must have been mobsters. I was so startled. I'm sure that was intended. I must say, if you were ever going to come home to a dark house and find yourself being accosted by the Mob, these guys were the ones to do it. Polite, almost. As polite as they could be aside from their breaking into my apartment. They'd even offered me one of my own beers. Though the older man was determined and demanding, he was as nice as he could have been. His muscular young friend didn't say a word during the whole affair, just stood around menacingly, his presence suggesting I behave. Maybe he was the older man's apprentice. With luck maybe he could grow up to be like his boss some day.

They didn't tell me their names. The older man looked like a 'Sal'. All he needed were spots of dried spaghetti sauce on his lapels. If he was Sal, the younger one must have been named Tony or Rocky or Vito. At least he wasn't carrying a violin case with a tommy gun inside.

After sitting a while I finished the beer, got up and went to the kitchen phone. It was almost ten-thirty. Michael would still be up. I dialed. He was a close friend who lived a few towns away. I met him when I was in med school. He was then in law school and we lived in the same slummy tenement.

"Hi, Michael, I didn't wake you, did I?" I asked.

"No, you know me, I can't go to sleep until I hear Johnny Carson's monologue. What's up?"

"Are you going to be free tomorrow night after work?" I asked.

"I can be, why?"

"Oh, I got presented with an unusual medical situation today, I guess it's a medical-legal situation and you'd be a good guy to talk it over with," I said, obtusely.

"Sure, I'd be happy to. It sounds serious. Is it?" Michael asked.

"I really don't know yet. It might be. I'm not sure."

"Can you give me some details?" Michael asked.

I paused, "Let me wait until tomorrow so I can sort it out in my mind a little better."

"OK. You want to come to my place around seven?"

"Sure. I'll bring the beer. See you tomorrow."

Michael said, "OK, bye," and we hung up.

I opened another beer and moped around the apartment. A minute later the phone rang. I picked it up.

"Doc, are you nuts? You're supposed to be this smart, young doctor. Tomorrow you call up your buddy, Michael, and tell him you talked it over with the hospital's lawyer and you got it all straightened out. And don't ever do anything so stupid again." Click.

CHAPTER 2

Ugh! The bells in the clock tower of Dalton Town Hall woke me up at seven a.m. and I felt like I'd only just fallen asleep. I was tossing and turning all night, thinking about my predicament. It was so weird, so foreign from any prior experience I'd ever had. Kafkaesque. Did it really happen? Could I have been dreaming?

I set the percolator on the stove and took a quick shower. I dressed in jeans, T-shirt and Adidas, poured some coffee and took it to the bedroom. I worked my way into the back of the closet and finally found what I was looking for. My shotgun. It was a Remington 20 gauge pump that I'd bought secondhand when I was in medical school. I had a classmate who was a farm boy from Wisconsin who got me interested in skeet shooting and bird hunting. We had a lot of fun. He taught me and made a fair wing shooter out of me. The skeet were OK, though you needed to marinate them for a long time. Since he and I had gone our different ways, I'd only taken the gun out once or twice to go to the annual Dalton shoot each fall and hunt frozen turkeys. I unzipped the vinyl gun case and looked at it. No rust, but pretty dry. I took it into the kitchen, spread out an old towel, and managed to find the gun cleaning kit with swabs and brushes and oil and solvent; and gave it a good going over.

"This is a simple, solid, practical pump gun. It'll last forever if you take care of it. It's a classic," said the man who sold it to me. I still remember him. He was colorful. Too old to go tramping through the woods, he'd put an ad for the gun in the Pennysaver, which I had answered.

"Take good care of it, it'll outlast *you*," he said. "I had so many nice times with it." It looked it. Used but not abused. Some shallow scratches were on the well-waxed stock.

"Use butcher's wax every season," he insisted. "Don't ever polyurethane it."

But then it hit me – I wasn't oiling up this gun so that I could spend a sunny autumn day kicking through cornfields with a dog, looking for pheasant; I was doing this so I could kill a human being if I needed to.

Also in the closet was a half empty box of shotgun cartridges. They were loaded with #7-1/2 birdshot and I put one in the chamber and four more in the magazine. I made sure the safety was on and put the shotgun under my bed. I didn't know where else to put it. The little I knew about home defense I'd heard from Dick Cataldo, who was one of the ambulance attendants. When he used to work nights he would leave a loaded double-barreled shotgun under the bed for his wife. He told her that if she ever thought someone had broken into the house, don't go snooping around, just pick up the gun and let one loose into the wall. That'll tell the crook that you've got a gun and that you're willing to use it and if he's dumb enough to keep coming, let him have the other barrel.

Then I went to the kitchen for more coffee and saw a beer bottle on the counter. It was the one Sal had poured for me. I stuck my finger in its mouth and brought it into the bathroom. I took some Mennen Shaving Talc, which I'd bought years ago and rarely used, and lightly tapped it, gently sprinkling dust on the bottle. It looked like a dusty beer bottle. I went and got a camel hair lens brush and carefully brushed off the excess talc. Yes, Sal's fingerprints were there. I didn't know what good they were, but I figured they might be useful later and I needed to be doing something clever. Bay Rum scented fingerprints. I set the bottle down on the desk in the den and tried to lift off the talc, composing each fingerprint with Scotch tape, and then stuck the tape to a piece of paper. I didn't have the technique down. *Where's Efrem Zimbalist, Jr., from the FBI Story on TV, when you need him?* I was able to lift about six prints from the bottle. It would've been easier just to keep the bottle.

Then I took out some paper and wrote down every detail about the men that I could remember. What was said, what they looked like. I wrote on a single sheet, not making the old mistake of leaving an impression of what you've written on the sheet beneath.

I put the talc fingerprints and my notes in an envelope, got in my sedate Subaru sedan, with great traction and good mileage, and drove to the Allendale branch of Berkshire Bank. I deposited my paycheck from Fairview and got fifty dollars in cash for the week's spending money. Then the lady let me into the vault, and we removed my safe deposit box. I went into the little room and put Sal's fingerprints and my notes in the box. I came out, smiling to the clerk, and told her that my new baseball cards were now safe. She chuckled, no doubt thinking I was a jerk, and replaced the box. Then I headed for the hardware store.

I bought twelve window locks and four of the largest sliding bolts they had. To install them I bought a box of big wood screws with hex heads on them instead of screwdriver slots. I charged the bill for $21.42.

On my way home I got stuck in the five-minute wait at the Allendale traffic lights. It is an area where almost a dozen roads converge, no doubt a traffic engineer's nightmare. Nothing to do but not get impatient, put your head down, and relax. WUPE was playing one of my all-time favorites, "Oh Baby, Baby" sung by Linda Ronstadt. That lady can wail. I was unusually edgy sitting there at the light. Even while driving out earlier I'd been impatiently shifting gears, hearing unaccustomed noises from the transmission, accelerating and braking more abruptly than usual. Stuck at the light, I recalled all the times I had sat there on my way home from BMC every day for three years. On days when I'd been at work the whole night before, I would but both feet on the brake, put my head back and close my eyes. More than a few times I was awakened by a honk from the guy behind me. I was glad those exhausting days of residency were over.

I spent the rest of the day installing all the window locks and putting the bolts on the doors. It developed in me a very depressed and almost paranoid feeling. All of a sudden I'd gone from such complacency to feeling so insecure that I had a loaded shotgun under my bed and was turning my apartment into a fortress.

I was trying to figure what this was all about. Presumably mob members occasionally get hurt, and maybe the injuries are too suspiciously felonious to go unreported if they went to a regular doctor or ER. Either that or the men who were injured were wanted, or on probation, or for some reason needed to keep a low profile. Maybe that's why they wanted someone to secretly give medical care. I hoped they realized that the proper care of bullet wounds requires an exploratory surgery, and that my training wasn't in surgery but in internal medicine. I supposed that Sal must know very well what I could and couldn't do – he'd gone through a lot of effort to check me out and he'd certainly have made sure I was capable.

I remembered the bug and I went to the kitchen phone and looked at it. I unscrewed the earpiece and then the mouthpiece, took them apart, and looked for something that didn't look like it belonged. Nothing. Then I did the same thing to the bedroom phone. Nothing. I took a flashlight and followed the phone wires along the baseboards, into closets. I went down into the basement and searched along the joists for the wires as they went along to the big Bell Telephone junction box in the corner. Nothing looked extra to me.

I had to presume that it was just my skills, not me, that were valuable to them. I was not going to be a profit to them, just a convenience. They would have no interest in hurting me so long as I didn't pose a threat to them. *But why me?* Why not someone in New York City, a surgeon with his own office and operating suite? What would happen if I learned something they didn't want me to know? Would they silence me?

My main desire was to have nothing to do with them. All I wanted was to keep my nose clean. I didn't want to become associated with them or risk my career. All I wanted to do was to be left alone and not get sucked into any trouble.

I had only recently gotten my lifestyle the way I liked it, and I didn't want to lose it. I had worked so hard so long in college and med school and residency, and finally I had gotten into a situation where I had time to relax and enjoy myself. I could read National Geographic from cover to cover without feeling guilty about a textbook I should be studying. I could sit on the porch with a six-pack and watch it rain all day if I felt like it. I was in a new relationship with a fine young lady. I was earning a decent living and I enjoyed what I did. The people at Fairview were great, so were the patients (most of the time, anyway) and I saw a lot of interesting medicine. I was in Fat City and I liked it. I wanted to have my own office someday, but I planned to stay at Fairview until the right opportunity presented itself.

But now it looked like I was going to be on call for the Mob. Hopefully they would be merciful and at least not make me wear a beeper. One of the few things I knew of any importance was that I would never make any trouble for them. All I wanted was to get out – not to blow the whistle on them, not to be a grand jury witness, not to do the least thing to antagonize them. I'd read *The Godfather*. I'd seen the movie. The Mob can always get you back. I did not doubt that they could coerce me into doing whatever they wanted.

I didn't know how to go about getting out of their grasp. I had nearly made a bad mistake already by calling Michael last night. It would be tragic if I dragged a friend into this.

For the time being, at least, the safest thing seemed to be to comply and wait to see what happened.

I finished all my chores and errands. I had finished installing the window locks and extra dead bolts on the doors. It was late afternoon and I put some leftovers in the oven to warm up. I took a bottle of beer, put on a coat, and sat outside on the porch. Another nice early spring day. There were little kids riding their bikes up and down the street. I sat in a folding lawn chair and sipped my beer, watching the kids yuk it up as they played on their bikes for the first time this spring.

All day long I'd been focused on this nasty business. Enough. Time to think of nice things, of spring, of Patty. Time for another daydream. Where was I when I last left off? Oh yeah, our first date. She said she'd go for dinner with me that night. We're back in the thick of wintertime for this story.

After making the date with Patty I'd had three hours to kill before picking her up. It was not enough time to go home to Dalton and back. I went to the car wash. I stopped at Jack's Country Squire and bought a cleaner shirt. I went to the hospital and took a shower in the doctor's locker room. I killed some more time in the bookstore downtown.

I picked her up at the pharmacy. We drove to the Elm Court Inn in Egremont, a nice old-fashioned restaurant in a big old rambling wooden building with many small dining rooms. I'd never been there before but had heard about it, and it was as quaint as described. I like quaint. There were big snowdrifts along the driveway, icicles on the roof, a big evergreen wreath still on the front door, piles of firewood stacked neatly on the porch.

The drive over was nerve-racking because I was excited and was trying not to show it, and was more focused on Patty than the road and the speed limit and other cars and my mirrors. I tried hard to pay attention to the road.

I kept her talking while we had dinner. She came from Framingham, she played soccer in high school, majored in chemistry for two years in college, but couldn't see herself being a chemist in some corporation playing with test tubes all day and playing the corporate power games. So she transferred to the school of pharmacy and found she liked it a lot. It took her an extra year but she enjoyed the academics. She found being a neighborhood pharmacist a lot different than she naively anticipated, but had come to enjoy it, and also enjoyed the personal contact she had with patients. She also had her share of whiners who came every month for refills and would moan and groan for ten minutes each time they came. Small town life.

Her parents were divorced, she was in touch with both of them, mother in Massachusetts, father in Pennsylvania.

She had a friend who lived in the Berkshires and that's how she got to know it. She came here after graduation and has been working in the same store for three years.

She was in the process of moving into a little bungalow house she'd rented. She had been renting a small apartment but now that she'd paid off a lot of her college loans she could splurge on a bigger rent and was excited about having her new little home. She was having fun decorating it, putting up curtains, bookshelves. She likes to read, enjoys popular music and concerts, had a pass at the Butternut Ski Area. She drove a Toyota Celica two-door, which she said was really zippy.

What really fired her up was when we began talking about the Three Mile Island nuclear disaster in Pennsylvania a few years before, in 1979. That really angered her and she'd been very attentive to all kinds of nuclear reactor incidents in the news. She talked about it with such animation I thought I was sitting with an eco-terrorist.

I said, "Yeah, that and the Love Canal debacle were awful."

She corrected me and said the Love Canal was not a nuclear, but a chemical, catastrophe, building homes and schools on the sealed dump of a chemical company that didn't stay sealed. She then rattled off the different chemicals they found there, how long they take to break down in nature, and how they can poison you until they do break down. She seemed really up on her toxicology.

It was a great first date, and I enjoyed the memory of it. I finished my beer and finished the daydream and it was spring again.

CHAPTER 3

I drove to work the next morning. I left the house at seven and the roads were empty. I drove through Park Square in Pittsfield, surrounded by stately Protestant churches, the courthouse, the Berkshire Athenæum, and the incongruously modern high rise--the Hilton Hotel. Down South Street, past the Pittsfield Country Club, whose clubhouse had once been the mansion of Oliver Wendell Holmes. Right opposite that was the Berkshire Life Insurance Company, which has a beautiful, big, grassy campus and a large stately Federal office building with a clock tower that reminded me of Independence Hall in Philadelphia. Route 7 continued south through Lenox on a particularly ugly stretch called the Pittsfield-Lenox Road, which is wall-to-wall car dealerships, motels, discount stores and restaurants.

Once past that bit of blight the route got pretty again. I passed The Mount, the mansion that novelist Edith Wharton built in the late 1800s, then past many lovely older homes on my way south into Stockbridge. Stockbridge is quite a place. Especially when not crammed with tour buses at the Norman Rockwell Museum. It is a quaint New England town, founded in the mid 1700s when John Sargent and Jonathan Edwards came to civilize (read, Christianize) the local Mahican Indians. As time went by it became a summer mecca for tourists, and many huge mansions were built, creating the town's high-class flavor. Right on the corner of Main Street and Route 7 is the Red Lion Inn. This huge, rambling four-story wooden building dates to the 1700s and is a very elegant inn and restaurant. Ties and jackets required in the formal dining restaurant. I want to take Patty there some day.

The road south to Great Barrington passed through some swampy forest, then Monument Mountain appears on the right. I meandered my way into Great Barrington, past the fields, the stock farm, the Jenifer House, the WSBS radio tower, across the Housatonic River again on the green bridge, past Patty's pharmacy, down Main Street, right at the Lutheran Church and up the hill to Fairview.

Will had been on overnight and I was relieving him.

Like I said before, Will had been my senior resident when I was an intern. We called him Uncle Will because he took such good care of us. New interns need to be taken care of because they have so little experience they often feel insecure. Some senior residents couldn't care less and were not supportive. But if you were on overnight with Will, you knew he would be there for backup if a patient started to go downhill and you couldn't figure out why.

He started medical school in Guadalajara, Mexico. A lot of American kids went there, perhaps those who didn't have the grades to get into American schools. Then they might be able to transfer into an American school after two years, or after graduation could enter a "Fifth Pathway" program, which would enable them, after passing the exams, to enter an American residency program. To some, being a foreign medical graduate was pejorative. Oh, he's an FMG. Didn't matter to me. Seemed to me, the ones I met were very motivated, interested and capable. I don't think I would ever have the drive to learn a foreign language fluently so I could go to school in a foreign country. I don't have that kind of drive.

Will had done it all, had seen it all, was cocky, confident and very, very funny. Irreverent, too. He loved the ER. It was his playground. He was married and had three kids, and often treated the neighborhood kids in his kitchen before coming to work. He loved the action. And the unpredictability of it. You never knew when it would be slow and boring, or when there would be a multiple trauma and all hell would break loose. I always thought you needed to be a special kind of person to survive long in the ER. I was not that kind; Will was. Some people choose to become Marines, choose to play tackle football, some choose to be firemen, some choose to be ER docs. Will did. I was just doing it until I figured out what else I was going to do.

Will was also a flirt. He tried to give me lessons, but I was not such an apt pupil. At the nurse's station, in the coffee room, in the doctor's room, he was often sitting with his arm around a nurse, if not with her on his lap. He was an equal opportunity flirt; he'd flirt with anyone female, young or old, easy-going or uptight, pretty or not. And he could get away with telling the most silly and vulgar jokes. People would laugh. If anybody else made the same joke, people would groan and think, "what an ass," but not with Will. He'd say outrageous things and people would smile and say, "that's just Will." Once I saw him pull a sweet young thing onto his lap and say, "Let's talk about the first thing that pops up!" And people laughed! Another time he said, "I got up this morning and I thought, if it looks good out, leave it out." And people laughed! That's Will.

He had a great attitude about medicine. He knew his stuff. He loved protocols. He was a great diagnostician, and thrived on trauma and codes. I remember him saying, "I'm in the mood for a good multiple trauma." Great. Someone should have a motor vehicle accident to provide him with an afternoon of entertainment. He loved the adrenaline rush, sorting out injuries, evaluating, stabilizing, starting with chaos and creating order. He was so good at it. The ER was his playground and he was masterful in a medical crisis.

It's not that he wanted people to be hurt. It just gave him a rush to treat them.

I remember relieving him one night at eight. That afternoon something tragic happened while he was on. I don't remember what it was, but it might have been a young patient stricken before his time. I heard about it from one of the RNs who was there, and I went to console Will.

"Gee, Will. That's too bad, that was tragic, that must have ruined your day."

"What was tragic, and must have ruined my day?"

"That big code that Sue was telling me about."

"Why would that ruin my day?"

"Because this otherwise healthy person died tragically, years before his time, and you had to deal with it."

"Oh, no. Hell, no. It would have been tragic if it happened to me. But it didn't, it happened to him. Gotta keep some separation here. Hell no, I've been in a good mood all day. There's a big Celtics game on tonight and I've been looking forward to it all week! Damned if I'd blow a good mood just because some idiot chose today to wrap his car around a tree. You mean this would bother you if it happened on your shift?"

"Oh, yeah. I couldn't not let it bother me."

"How come?"

"I just get too involved. Aren't we supposed to do this with all our heart, all our soul, and all our might?"

"FUCK NO! You're just supposed to control airway, breathing and circulation, and stabilize. If you can, good for the patient. If you can't, tough shit. You can't get personally involved with each patient, it'll kill you. You know everybody's gotta die sometime and sometimes we can postpone it and sometimes we can't. Remember the old saying, 'Don't make your problem my problem.' I gotta get going, the game starts in an hour."

Anyway, that's Will. There were no patients in the ER for him to sign out to me. He packed up and hit the road, and I hung out in the coffee room with the staff, catching up on the latest gossip.

A while later, the secretary came back and said, "Hey, Charlie, there's a guy in the waiting room who just wants to ask you a question."

He was the only guy in the waiting room and through the window there was only one car in the ER lot. A BMW. He looked like he was ten years older than me, had on designer jeans that were pressed, an Izod sport shirt, Italian loafers and the gold neck chain.

"I'm here for the week, and I've been having trouble with my knee. My orthopedist in the city gave me some pills for the pain, but they don't cut it and he told me to come here and get something else."

"Well, I'd be happy to see what we can do. Let's get you checked in and I can examine you."

"Nah. I don't want to go through all that. He just examined me last week. I don't want to be examined again. I just want a prescription."

"I'm sorry, I'm not allowed to do that. I can only give care to a registered patient, and before I prescribe I have to assess. Those are the rules I have to follow."

Reluctantly, he sat down at the counter desk with the secretary, who typed him in, and from a distance it sounded like he was being a little snotty. I went back to the coffee room rolling my eyes.

Around the corner I could hear the nurse putting him in a cubicle and drawing the curtain. I heard him say, "Why are you wasting time taking my temperature when it's just my knee that hurts?"

Reluctantly, I went in to see this guy. He wasn't happy. I thought he was arrogant. I began asking for some history: when his knee started to hurt, if he had ever injured it, did he ever have anything like this before, what did his orthopedist say... He answered each question as vaguely and tersely as he could.

When people are like that my revenge is to be so sickeningly sweet and polite, and to keep a silly smile on my face and speak very softly. I think the word is unctuous.

"Now it's time for me to examine you, sir," I said, "would you please remove your trousers?"

"Why do you have to do that, it's just my knee."

"Because I want to give you a nice thorough exam," I replied very sweetly.

I asked him to take off his socks, too. He grumbled as he did it. His feet were warm, the pulses were good, he had no athlete's foot fungus. The muscle mass on both legs seemed about the same. I moved his ankle through its range of motion, and then stressed the joint a little in its extremes. Then I did the same thing with his knee. I exerted medial and lateral stress on the knee and it did not seem to bother his cartilages or his collateral ligaments. The flesh on either side of his kneecap did not seem puffy, there did not seem to be increased fluid in the joint capsule, there were still little hollows on either side of his kneecap. While he was sitting on the bed with his leg bent down ninety degrees, I did the drawer test to see if I could move the top of the tibia forward in relation to the bottom of the femur. It was tight, his cruciate ligaments seemed OK.

Then I had him lie down on his back and, with his knee bent, had him raise his thigh vertically in the air to check his hip. Then I did the "figure-4" test and torqued the joint by moving his lower leg left and right, externally and internally rotating the joint. That's what hurt.

"Hmmmm," I said.

"Hmmmm, what?" he said.

"Just hmmmm," I said. "You have symptoms in your knee only when I stress your hip. Did the orthopedist take X-rays?"

"Yeah, he did. He said they were fine."

"Did he take X-rays of your hip?" I asked.

"Why would he take X-rays of my hip if it is my knee that hurts?" he said as if I were an idiot.

"Well, there is a thing called referred pain, which means that when one part of you has a problem, it's another that hurts. Like when someone has a heart problem it might be the shoulder that hurts."

"There's nothing wrong with my heart."

"I'd like to get some X-rays of your hips."

"Hips? Both of them? Why do you need X-rays of both of them? Why don't you call my orthopedist in New York?"

"We need both hips for comparison." It was getting pretty hard to stay nice to the guy. And I was not going to call his doc in New York. I wrote the order for the films and went down to the coffee room. I heard the guy bellyaching as the X-ray tech rolled him in a wheelchair down the hall to her department.

"That guy is a prick," said Margaret. "I heard your whole conversation."

"Yep," was all I said.

"I would've given him an Rx for something and got rid of him real quick, told him to check back with his orthopod in New York and get out of here."

"I see your point. But you know how it is. Even if we don't like them, we have to try to give them good care even if they don't want it. 'Dr. Davids, please explain to the jury why you wrote a prescription for the plaintiff without doing a thorough examination.' Have to do it by the book."

One more cup of coffee later, the guy was rolled back to his cubicle and the X-ray tech came into the coffee room carrying a big brown X-ray folder. "You're gonna like these, Charlie." We went over to the view box, out of earshot of the patient, and put up the films. Easy to see, in the medulla of the right upper femur just beneath the joint, below the lesser trochanter, was an egg-shaped density that was slightly bulging out the outline of the bone. There's a bunch of things that this could be and I could only think of some of them. They range from really bad, like osteogenic sarcoma, which is a nasty bone cancer, to not so bad, like an exostosis. A radiologist could probably tell the difference, but there wasn't one here yet. I asked the tech if she would make copies that the patient could bring home. She was back with them in a few minutes. *How am I going to tell this guy about this?*

I rolled the guy in his wheelchair to the room with the view box. I put up the films. "This is your good normal left hip," I said. Then I put up the right one. "This is your right hip. Do you see the difference? There is this oval opacity here, right beneath the joint. And it's not normal. There's a bunch of things that it might be. You can take these films with you to your orthopedist and he can get going on figuring out what you have in there. I'm suspicious that this may have been the cause of your knee pain. I'll give you a prescription for a different analgesic to take the edge off your pain. But you need to see your orthopedist as soon as possible. And I would like to ask a favor. Here's a card with my name and address. Would you please give it to him and tell him that I am very interested in what he finds out? Please ask them to send me a copy of his dictation."

The man was very quiet. He didn't even interrupt me. He was almost sheepish, or was I reading into it?

"Gee, doc, you think it might be cancer?"

"I really don't know. But it's on the list of possibilities. There are both benign and malignant possibilities."

"How come my orthopedist didn't find it?"

"I don't know. I wasn't there."

"He didn't examine my hip."

"I almost had to fight with you to examine it myself," I said.

"Yeah, but you found it."

Now he likes me.

"I just follow the rules. I try to be thorough."

He got dressed, took his films and the prescription, and walked out to his BMW. I charted everything in as much detail as I could.

Margaret came over. "That was a good pick-up Chuckie."

"It was a fluke. It was a hole in one. The next five thousand sore knees will just be sore knees. But you never know."

"You never know," echoed Margaret.

The day puttered along pretty uneventfully, and on my forty-five-minute drive home I got a little sleepy and a little bored. So I went back to my Patty memories and dredged up another one to entertain myself with on the way home. I lost myself in a flashback that I enjoyed with vivid and poignant detail. The next chapter of our dating history. It was easy to lose myself in these daydreams of Patty, and it kept me from thinking about that nightmare with the thugs.

When I was in high school, we always talked about dating strategies. After my first very pleasant dinner last winter with Patty at the Elm Court Inn, I waited the formulaic three days and called her up. It was not very formulaic for me to ask her out the way I did in the drugstore. This early phase of the dating process could be so stiff and awkward, though it also brought suspense, an intriguing hopeful anxiety. Patty seemed like a neat lady. She was great, funny, a little brassy really. Beneath that brassiness, though, I sensed she was also sensitive. I saw potential.

"Hello, Charlie, how are you? Any good major trauma in the ER lately?"

"Not much, really. Saw a lot of sore throats and earaches today. A bunch of orthopedic injuries off the ski slopes. Fill any interesting narcotic prescriptions today?" I asked.

"No, it's mostly been a lot of Metamucil and enemas lately," she responded. "By the way, Charlie, as long as we're on the subject, would you like to come over for dinner on Saturday?"

"Let me see. Let me check my busy social calendar," I said.

"Don't be a smart ass! You'll notice I didn't need the Great Barrington Police Department to help me with this invitation."

"Oh, you heard about that. I'm working Friday night and I'm off the rest of the weekend, so yes, I'd love to join you. What can I bring?" I asked.

"Oh, I don't know, I don't know what I'll make yet. Just bring yourself. And a bottle of wine." She gave me directions to her house.

I had three days to look forward to seeing her.

I remember one time when I was a kid, we went to visit my aunt and uncle who had just moved into a new home. My mother had a bag full of things for them in the backseat. I looked through the bag. There was a loaf of challah bread, a bottle of kosher wine, some Sabbath candles, and a jar of honey. I asked why we were bringing all those things. My mother answered, "It's an old Jewish custom to bring these things to someone in a new home, so they'll have the things they need to celebrate the Sabbath." It always stuck with me.

I drove down to Patty's in Great Barrington. I had with me a bottle of Chardonnay from Mr. Kelly's, a seeded French baguette from Guido's Marketplace, two candles, and a jar of clover honey. And a small bunch of daffodils. I liked the sentiment of bringing these things; I didn't know if Patty would get it.

It was messy driving, the sand and salt spray from the road dirtied the windshield. Snow banks were three feet high on the sides of the road. Lots of cars had skis on their roofs. It was still light out when I left Dalton at four-thirty, it was almost dark when I got to Patty's. She lived off State Road in a small bungalow on a quiet street with big old trees in a nice well-kept working class neighborhood. Her Toyota was in the driveway and I parked behind it. There was a bumper sticker on it that read: "If you don't believe in abortion then don't have one." There was a cute little snowman standing three feet high near the front door. Charcoal buttons, carrot nose. A real one. Made of snow, not plastic.

She opened the storm door, stepped onto the porch, put her arm around my neck and gave me a full two-second kiss on the lips. She took my coat and put it in the closet, took my hand and led me into the kitchen. She took my package and put it on the counter. She kneeled down to get a vase from under the sink for the daffodils. She was wearing a light blue button-down Oxford cloth shirt, dark navy corduroy slacks with a brown belt with yellow stitching, leather and wood clogs with very fuzzy socks. Really long legs.

She set the flowers on the kitchen table, poured us wine, and showed me around her little house. It had some nice Craftsman-style accents and moldings. She had repainted some walls, not finished yet, there were still some cardboard boxes left in corners. There was a wooden cable spool in the living room as a coffee table. Very college. The mattress in the bedroom was on the floor.

We had wine and cheese and crackers in her living room. She made a Chinese meal in a wok. Chicken and broccoli and Hoisin sauce. "I love the shade of green the broccoli becomes as you cook it," she said.

We talked and talked until late at night. It was a long drive home.

I reminisced that winter drive home from Patty's as I now drove home from work in springtime, to my apartment with double sets of window locks and door deadbolts and a loaded shotgun under my bed.

CHAPTER 4

The call came a week later, while I was at work. I was sitting in the ER coffee room and I was paged to a number that meant I had an outside call. I picked up the phone, dialed in, and the line clicked while the connection was made.

"Hello, this is Dr. Davids."

"Hello, Doc, how are you?"

I instantly recognized the drawling voice of the older man who had visited me some days ago. I stiffened reflexively, my stomach clenching, and I felt my face flush.

"I'm OK," I lied.

"Good. We have a patient for you to see tonight."

Sorry, I don't make house calls, I wanted to say.

"I don't get out of work till eight," I said instead.

"I know that. When you get out of work drive to the Price Chopper in Lee and park your car. Go in and buy something. When you come out, look for a light blue Plymouth van that'll be waiting for you. See you later." He hung up.

I hung the phone back on the wall and stared at it, stunned. Well, I thought, this is it. It's actually happening. It really isn't just a dream. And it's beginning now. I had four more hours until my shift was over, and I would drive fifteen miles into the next town on the pretext of going to the supermarket. It would be my rendezvous with the underworld, which would take me God knows where, to do God knows what, to God knows whom. *What if I just don't show up?*

The ensuing four hours were long ones. The knot in my stomach didn't loosen. I kept wondering what was going to happen. I envisioned being taken to an abandoned warehouse, only to find the interior littered with moaning, bleeding, bullet-riddled bodies. Like the St. Valentine's Day Massacre. It's not good to be nervous and to have an overactive imagination at the same time. What kind of supplies should I bring?

Eight o'clock finally came, and I was relieved by the oncoming M.D. I said goodnight to all the nurses. As I was leaving, one of them looked at me quizzically and said I looked a little pale. I kept going as if I didn't hear her.

I drove slowly to Lee. Price Chopper was an all-night supermarket. It was fairly busy now, after dark on a spring evening. I thought it would be wisest to park as close to the store as possible, preferably near a streetlight, to get maximal exposure. I got out of the car, put on a green flannel shirt, as it was getting cooler, and slung my orange knapsack over my shoulder.

I walked toward the front door of the market. I scanned the parking lot looking for the blue van, the same way I used to search the college cafeteria for my current crush without seeming conspicuous. I didn't see it.

Buy something, he said. OK, what kind of food do you buy when you're going to be secretly driven to aid a wounded mobster? What kind of munchies would a mobster like?

I couldn't resist. I bought a box of Ronzoni Vermicelli, a jar of Mama Rosa's meatless tomato sauce with mushrooms, a long loaf of Italian bread with sesame seeds, and a jar of pepperoncini. Even if they turned out not to have a sense of humor, I got a kick out of it.

I got through the express checkout lane quickly and then realized, accompanied by noises from my stomach, that now was the time the story would begin. On shaky legs, I walked out of the store. I paused, looking for the van. It was one of the last cars parked on the farthest row from me. Away from the light. Damn. I hoped, just in case, that there'd be someone to see me, so when the headline came out: "Young M.D. Killed by Mob," the witness could say, "Yeah, I saw him, officer. He was wearing a green flannel shirt, over a yellow shirt with a necktie, had an orange knapsack and a grocery bag, and he got into an old blue van with two gangsters in it, and its license plates were ..."

I walked over to the van. I memorized the license plate. As I got near it, I could see Rocky in the driver's seat and Sal in the passenger seat beside him. Sal got his massive frame out and rolled back the side door of the van.

"Hi, Doc," he droned, "glad you could make it."

As if I had a choice.

"By the way, my name is Sal."

"You're kidding," I blurted, not intending to have said it out loud.

"Huh?"

"What's his name?" I asked, referring to his companion.

"That's Bob."

Not Tony, Rocky, or Vito.

He gestured me in through the side door of the van. I got in. He took my knapsack and the grocery bag. He rummaged around in the knapsack.

"Just doctor stuff, right?"

I nodded.

In med school, we were all given free black doctor's bags from one of the drug companies. They were called Gladstone bags. It was a thrill to have such a traditional symbol of the profession. One night a classmate got mugged walking home late from the hospital, his bag got stolen. That's when we all switched to knapsacks.

Then Sal turned his attention to the shopping bag. He reached in, looked at the contents, and chuckled quietly to himself. Smiling, he looked at me, and rolled the door closed.

The back windows of the van were grimy, fairly transparent. There was a shelving unit along the left side of the van with lots of tools, extension cords, coffee cans filled with hardware. There was a fire extinguisher, a plastic bat and a few Wiffle balls on the floor. Also, seeming out of place, was a canvas army cot. I sat on it. There were no other windows in the back. I looked forward and Sal got back into his seat.

"OK, Bob," he said. We drove off.

Sal turned around in his seat and looked at me. "How ya doing?" he said again, quietly.

"OK," I replied. *Actually, I'm scared shitless*, I said to myself.

"You really don't have anything to worry about. We're just gonna drive a while, have you take a look at a guy, then we'll take you back."

I had a hundred questions to ask. What's wrong with him? Where are we going? Was I supposed to bring supplies? I decided to keep quiet, they'd tell me what I needed to know when I needed to know it. I didn't want to pester them.

Sal told me to lie down on the cot. I did. This way, I wouldn't be able to look out the windshield and see where we were going. Evidently, he wanted me to know as little as possible. I lay there, silently, resigned to whatever would happen. I tried to guess where we were going. After a few minutes of driving, we made a long slow leftward curve. The van stopped and I heard what might have been the click from an automatic tollbooth. I surmised that we were getting onto the Massachusetts Turnpike. Whether the van veered left or right would indicate whether we were going west toward Albany, or east toward Boston. I rolled to the left on the cot as the van accelerated. Toward Boston.

"Would you mind giving me your watch, Doc, just for a while?"

I gave it to him. He didn't want me timing anything either. He was thorough. He'd done this before.

It was silent in the van. I couldn't see the men from where I was lying. Maybe they just didn't want to talk shop in front of me. I was tense, and as I lay on the cot in the dark van, speeding along the Mass Pike, being rocked gently from side to side by the motions of the van, I became even more tired.

"Good morning, Doc."

I awoke with a start. I don't know how, under those circumstances, I could've fallen asleep. The change in motion of the van from smooth freeway driving to the stop and go of the city must have awakened me. I didn't know how long I'd been asleep.

"You were really sawing wood there, Doc, snoring away like that," said Sal.

"Yeah. Sorry."

I felt calmer. I even felt something akin to an attachment, a positive association with the two of them. Like they would take care of me. It was an automatic thing that I felt as soon as I woke up. It made me think of the hundreds of times when as a kid, I would fall asleep in the backseat and later awaken to find my father at the wheel, tirelessly driving through the night.

We were driving in a city, making frequent turns, frequent stops. I could hear sounds of other cars, hear their radios playing through open windows on a spring night. We turned again and the sounds of traffic lessened. The van slowed, stopped, and backed up as it was parallel parked.

Sal turned to me and said, "OK, Doc, we're here. You can sit up now. Bob's gonna open the door for you and then you will face the van, and then you'll walk right behind him. I'll be behind you. Don't look around. Just look straight ahead of you so you can see where you're going, and follow Bob. OK?"

"OK."

"OK. Let's go."

The door slid open and I got out. I faced the van as Bob closed the door. I turned and followed him.

Even though I looked straight ahead as I was told, I could see out of the corners of my eyes that we were on a residential street, lined on both sides by parked cars, with brick one- and two-family houses, each with a small front yard. It reminded me of Archie Bunker's neighborhood on the "All In The Family" TV show. We walked past two or three houses.

My permitted field of view included Bob walking several feet in front of me, the sidewalk with transverse crabgrass-filled cracks every four feet, a fire hydrant, some dog droppings, and someone's unsuccessful attempt to reseed a lawn.

Bob then turned right and walked down the driveway of a house. I followed, along a length of four-foot-high chain link fencing that ran between each house. There was a small forsythia bush in full bloom on the side of the fence. We walked down the driveway toward the side door. As we reached it, I could hear the hum and smell the warm sweet exhaust of the next home's clothes drier. Up three cement steps, holding onto a wrought iron railing that had peeling paint. Bob opened the aluminum storm door and unlocked the inner door. There was a bare bulb illuminating a stairway into the basement. Along the stairway there were pine boards set up as shelves, stocked with quart cans of motor oil, Ajax, Windex, a dustpan, and other items of normal everyday living. A mop and broom hung from nails in the wall.

Sal closed and locked the door and came down the stairs behind me. The basement had been made into a small apartment. From the bottom of the stairway, I entered a large room furnished as a living room to the left and a kitchen to the right. Across the room were doors that I guessed led to a bedroom and bathroom. The furniture was old, but sturdy looking. It looked like the better of the Goodwill line.

Several pipes ran across the room, suspended beneath the low ceiling. But it didn't look lived in. There were no newspapers lying around, no saltshaker or box of crackers on the kitchen counter, none of the accoutrements of a home.

At one end of the apartment, Bob was talking quietly with a man who had nodded acknowledgment to me when I entered.

"Hi, Doc, nice to see ya, my name's Frank."

"Pleased to meet you," I said, not knowing what else to say. I was about to move toward him to shake his hand, but stopped myself to see if he would initiate it. He didn't.

Sal came in behind me. "How's he doing?" he asked Frank. Frank looked to be in his late forties. He had a Mediterranean complexion, dark graying hair, and a five o'clock shadow.

"About the same, except he's a little less drunk."

Sal turned to me and said, "You see, Doc, there's a guy in there who got drunk and got beat up. I think he smashed his hand, and he has a big black eye and a bloody nose. At first, for a couple hours, he didn't make any sense and kept asking the same thing over and over again, like he's got amnesia or something."

The man already there said, "He hasn't been doing that so much now."

"What time did this happen?" I asked.

"A couple hours before I called you," replied Sal.

"So that must've made it in the early afternoon. Right?"

"Yeah."

"Can I see him now?" I asked.

"Sure," he said, and they led the way into the bedroom.

The bedroom was as simply furnished as the rest of the apartment. There was a man dressed in street clothes stretched out on the bed. He was a stocky, short fellow, prematurely balding. More so than me. He didn't pay much attention to our arrival. There was a strong smell of vomit and cheap sweet whiskey in the air.

I went over to him and sat on the edge of the bed. As my weight tilted that side of the bed it caused him to roll a little. Tentatively, I reached out and put a hand on his shoulder, intending to gently rouse him awake.

"How ya doin'?" I asked. He didn't say much but made an annoyed sound.

"How ya doin'?" I said, trying again. One must establish a rapport with the patient.

"Leave me alone," he grunted, as he tried to brush my hand away.

I got off the bed and took a few steps back. From what I could see, he was lying on his side, cradling his sore right hand in his left as he lay there. I could also see a swollen black and blue mark at the side of his right eye. His eyelids were puffed, half closing his right eye.

"You should also know, I think, Doc," said Frank, "that he's been drinking quite a bit."

"Great," I said. That would make it harder to tell if his sluggish behavior was from a head injury or the alcohol. This was a problem we had a lot in the ER; is the patient stuporous just because he's drunk, or because he's bleeding into his brain.

I decided to employ my "tough" approach that I used with drunk and uncooperative patients. Nurses told me it was a riot to see me trying to act tough. I sat down on the bed again, but this time with great firmness and authority. I took him by the shoulder, shook him, and said, "Come on, buddy, let me take a look at you. I didn't come out here for nothing."

"Get outta here, you sonovabitch," he replied, and took a slow clumsy swing at me, which was easy to avoid.

The booze on his breath was ripe. He managed to get his eyes open and looked at me. Then he added, "What are you, a kike?"

I chuckled. Now I could add "anti-Semitic" to this man's lengthening list of character flaws.

From the doorway, Bob said, "Hey, Doc, you had a long day. You worked all day, then you had to ride all the way out here. Why don't you and Sal go into the kitchen and have some coffee. Me and this asshole will have a little talk."

We did, leaving Bob and the patient alone in the room. We filled the kettle and put it on the stove.

"What's Bob going to do?" I asked.

"Probably some attitude adjustment. Bob's pretty good at that," Sal replied. Attitude adjustment. I liked that term. I should use that at work.

Through the closed bedroom door we could here Bob shout, "Now listen, asshole." We heard a "whump" followed quickly by an "oooph" as flesh struck flesh. I flinched at the sound.

I turned to Sal and said, sheepishly, "I hope he's not making any more work for me."

Sal said, "Don't worry about it. A few more bruises won't make any difference."

We finished our coffee and went back into the bedroom. The man was sitting on the edge of the bed and was very, very compliant. I asked him his name to see if he could remember it, but Sal interrupted and said that I didn't need to know.

"Oh, yeah," I said, realizing that there were things I wasn't supposed to know.

He said he'd been beaten up this afternoon. He had not lost consciousness, though after a few knocks in the head he'd seen stars and felt dazed. All too quickly the pain came through his daze and he was well aware of his consciousness. He said he'd taken his share of knocks on the head during his life but he'd never had any significant head trauma, been knocked out, or had seizures.

He was very cooperative after his chat with Bob. Contrite. I asked him what hurt him the most. He looked at his swollen hand for a few seconds while he thought about it.

"Everything," he replied.

"Do you feel confused at all?" I asked.

"No."

"Your friends said that you'd been asking the same questions over and over again, saying the same things repeatedly. You don't seem to be doing that now."

"I was?" he asked.

"That's what they say," I said.

"Well, I feel OK now except for my nose and my hand."

"Why don't you get undressed and I'll look you over."

After he stripped down to his skivvies, I started to examine him. He had a black eye with some swelling of the cheek and eyelid. The eye itself looked OK. I used my ophthalmoscope and could see that the interiors of the eyes were OK. He had a lot of tenderness along the bony rim of the eye socket and I wasn't sure if it was broken.

His nose was swollen at the bridge, though it was symmetrical and not bent over to one side. He couldn't breathe through the left side. I looked in there with the otoscope and saw a hematoma, a blood-filled swelling, on the nasal septum.

I continued on, systematically examining the rest of him, finding bruises here and there. When I got to his right hand, it was quite swollen and had an evident deformity. He was most tender over the pinkie's knuckle, which was probably fractured, and displaced toward the palm. This is classically known as a boxer's fracture.

I stepped back from the bed and looked from Sal to the patient, assumed a professional posture, and prepared to discuss the case.

"We have a couple of problems here. Most important is that his brain is working OK and he hasn't damaged it. It's not uncommon, after minor blunt head injury, for people to have some confusion, or difficulties with short-term memory. This is called post-concussive amnesia. It seems to have cleared up and I don't expect it to be a problem. There are, though, some late symptoms and complications after head injuries that you should be aware of, and think of as warning signs. These include progressive lethargy, stupor, undue drowsiness, continued vomiting, inability to arouse the patient.... If any of these things occur, he'll need to be seen again immediately.

"The right eye itself is OK, though the bone at the edge of the eye socket may be broken and should be x-rayed. His nose needs an X-ray also. He's had enough trauma there to cause a hematoma on the septum, a blood-filled swelling in one nostril that needs to be drained by an ear, nose and throat specialist, or else it'll become fibrosed and he won't be able to breathe through that side. He also has a broken hand that needs to be x-rayed and set."

"But we don't have any X-rays here, Doc," said Sal.

"Can't we take him somewhere to have them done?" I asked.

"No, Doc. That's why we brought you here."

"But it's 1983. I can't take care of these things without X-rays."

"Doc, it's not like he plays the violin or anything. However you fix it will be plenty good for him. Do the best you can. Be innovative. Make believe you're in Vietnam or something," said Sal. "Remember, he's not a nice man and any care he gets from you is better than he deserves."

I stopped, struck. That was a new concept. I thought we had to do our best for everybody.

I sighed. I had never done these things before! At work, I would only put casts on undisplaced fractures. If a bone was broken and out of alignment, I'd stabilize it and call the bone doctor. If a nose were crushed, I'd call the nose doctor. To take care of these things myself, without even having any X-rays, was a challenge I didn't want.

"Do you have any supplies?" I asked.

"Come over here," said Sal, as he proudly opened the door to the closet in the bedroom. It was loaded with all kinds of supplies. Gauze, casting plaster, disposable suture sets, antiseptics, adhesive tape, suture material, disposable sterile drapes, rubber gloves, Xylocaine, syringes, needles. The works.

"Wow," I said. "You've really prepared."

"If there is anything else you think we ought to have, let me know," said Sal.

It was time to get to work. I made an ice pack and had the guy hold it against his eye. I told him everything I was going to do before I did it. I injected some Xylocaine into the skin over the hematoma in his nostril, with Sal shining a flashlight for me. I lanced the hematoma with a scalpel and it collapsed as some dark red blood drained out. He gagged as some of it ran down the back of his throat. Then I packed the nostril with Vaseline-coated gauze to keep some pressure against the injury. I taped the whole affair in place so it wouldn't come flying out if he sneezed.

Now the hand. I tried to manipulate the fracture back into alignment, but it was too painful for him. I held him by the fingertips and raised his hand high over his head. My arms ached while I held him like that for several minutes. In time, the weight of his arm exerted traction on the fracture and eased the bone ends back into place. Then I had Sal hold the arm in the same manner while I applied a plaster cast.

I was satisfied with the results. While the plaster hardened, I wrote down a long list of directions. Patients never remember anything you tell them to do. Better to write it down and let them tape it to the refrigerator so they don't forget it. Poor patient compliance is the biggest obstacle in patient care.

I looked at Sal. "I guess I'm done."

"Thanks a lot, Doc," said the patient.

"Yeah, Doc, thanks. C'mon, we'll take you home," said Sal.

"Thank you," I said, and I went to the kitchen sink to wash the plaster off my hands.

Back on my cot in the van I felt very relieved, relaxed and tired.

We began the drive back to the Berkshires and I lay on my cot, contented. I was satisfied that I'd done a good job. The van went over a bump and I suddenly was jolted by the realization that I was not lying on *my* cot, these men were not *my* friends or colleagues. I had just rendered medical care in a setting that could not possibly be thought of as professional or respectable.

"Well, Doc, that was a nice job you did. You were very gentle and kind to him. Everything I read about you is true," said Sal.

"What do you mean?"

"Dr. Davids is a quiet, competent physician who displays much sensitivity and concern for his patients. He is well read in the medical literature and participates actively in academic discussions. He displays sound judgment and employs logical and practical approaches to clinical problems. In emergency situations he remains calm and deliberate. He is competent and confident in basic bedside surgical and ER procedures. I recommend him highly and without reservation for any position for which he might apply. That was in your personnel file," said Sal, in perfect diction.

I was startled by those words. I was startled by the depth of research he'd done on me. I was startled by his verbatim recall. And I was startled that he was so much smarter than he looked.

"How did you decide to become a doctor?" Sal asked.

"That's a long story. Do you have an hour?"

"Shoot."

Please don't.

"As a kid, I always liked science, especially biology. I always thought I'd end up in some health care field, but I didn't want to be a doctor because I thought it'd be too upsetting to deal with sick people all the time. So, I headed toward veterinary medicine."

"You wanted to be a vet at first, huh?"

"Yeah, it would satisfy my interest in biology, I enjoyed the animals, and it wouldn't be as tragic as human medicine. One summer I worked for a veterinarian. He was brilliant. He was also one of the biggest S.O.B.s I ever met. But I felt that if I had all that knowledge I would want to do something more substantial with it. More meaningful to me."

"So you decided on human medicine."

"Yeah. The next summer I worked as an orderly in an ER I saw a lot of things happen to people there. A lot of it was scary, but I thought with experience it would be less fearsome and that a doctor could really make a contribution there. So I decided to go for it. I did everything I could do to improve my chances of getting into med school. I studied constantly through college, and was lucky enough to get accepted. Then, I spent the four most miserable years of my life in medical school."

"Why were they so miserable?"

"There were so many bastards there. There were so many professors who thought that unless you coupled humiliation with education there'd be no learning. There were some people there with such colossal egos, you know, really pathologic personalities. Emotional brutality. I remember one incident - it was just two or three weeks into our first year and they'd split the class into several small groups to have a tutorial with a professor about some topic. The professor I had would stand us up and shoot questions at us. A kid in the class gave a wrong answer and with scorn in his voice the professor said, 'You just killed the patient.' Now imagine a poor freshman in his first month of school who's scared stiff, studies every waking minute, who's just been told he killed a patient. It wasn't even like he was kidding. There's no reason for that kind of insensitivity. It's destructive as hell. There were lots of people like that there. I had some residents who thrived on making us painfully aware of how stupid we were."

"That's too bad," said Sal, "that wouldn't help you learn any."

There were few things that could get my blood boiling, and med school was one of them. Granted, there were a number of people there who were helpful and supportive, but they were so overshadowed by all the other bastards.

I felt the van move to the left and accelerate, we passed what sounded like a tractor-trailer, and Bob veered back into the right lane.

"Listen, I contribute every year to my college. But I wouldn't give a penny to my medical school. If that place caught on fire I don't think I'd stop to spit on it."

Sal chuckled under his breath.

"Anyway, after I graduated I was lucky enough to get my internship and residency at a real good hospital with a great department chairman. It was as good as med school was bad. I really learned my trade there.

"A couple of months ago I was at my old medical school for a seminar. I was in the elevator and one of my old professors got in. He didn't recognize me. I was looking at him, standing there in his starched long white coat with his name pin with all his titles on it, with his nose up in the air and his chest sticking out. Looking just like he did when I was his student. Only older. Holier than thou. A healer. A medical man. And I thought back about the way he behaved and treated people and how he thought he knew everything. And I wanted to say, 'Hi, I was a student of yours. You know what? You really are a schmuck and you really aren't as bright as either of us thought you were and you certainly can't relate to people.' I didn't say it.

"My friends who went to other schools certainly had their gripes, but they seem to have been in places that were more humane and supportive. I didn't mind studying all the time and I didn't mind not knowing very much, I just didn't like being treated like a lower form of life."

Our discussion continued in the darkened van as we hurtled along the turnpike in the early hours of a spring morning. Sal asked how I'd chosen the specialty of internal medicine. I told him that at first I was attracted to surgery and had enjoyed four months of it as a student, but it got very boring to admit patients to the hospital who said, "Hi, I'm here to have a hernia fixed," or, "I'm here to have my gallbladder taken out," or "Hi, I'm here to have a tune-up and an oil change."

"Then one day a woman came in with jaundice of unknown cause, two months after she'd been operated on for an ulcer. And I had to think for a change. I enjoyed it. It was so refreshing to deal with a diagnostic dilemma, that I realized I ought to go in for internal medicine."

Why am I telling him all this? Why am I chattering on like this? Why am I opening up like this? Probably because I want him to like me. To not hurt me. I'm exposing my throat hoping he won't bite me. Maybe this is like the Stockholm syndrome where the victim tries to get the captor to like him.

"So I did three years as an intern and resident in internal medicine. I worked my tail off eighty hours a week for three years, learned a lot, passed the boards, and decided to take it easy for a year or two and do shift work in an ER. I'm catching up on all the free time and relaxing I missed out on for the last ten years. And while I'm enjoying myself,

I'm keeping my eye out for the right kind of practice opportunity to come along."

For me the real fun in medicine was being able to talk to people and having time to read and think about things. And there are so many practices out there that are like factories, they just crank the patients right through, order lots of tests and make lots of money.

Some doctors with busy practices lose control of their lives. They're constantly torn between an office full of patients and needing to be in the hospital to deal with some problem that unexpectedly sprang up. They spend little time at home, and have a family life unlike anything I looked forward to.

It would take all the fun out of it to practice medicine that way. I wanted to have time to think things out, and explain things to patients and their families. Not just hand them a cryptic prescription and say, "Here, take these..." To practice the way I wanted to I'd never make a bundle, but I'd enjoy it and feel good about it. I wanted control of my life.

We arrived back in the supermarket parking lot. I sat up and got my knapsack. Bob said, "Goodnight, Doc, drive safe." I let myself out of the van and stood in the dark parking lot.

"So long, fellas." It was cool out and I buttoned up my flannel shirt.

Just like they had dropped me off after an evening out with the guys.

I drove home. Safely. The longer I worked in an ER, the slower I drove. I put George Benson in the cassette player and I reviewed the events of the evening. Things had gone well with the patient. He should do well, and I felt good about that. I'd had a nice chat with Sal. If I didn't think about it too carefully, I'd had a nice time. If I thought about it carefully, what did it mean that I had enjoyed myself?

When I got home it was just after two a.m. I wet my toothbrush and brushed most of my teeth. I undressed and got into bed. I set the alarm for six. I had to go to work in the morning.

CHAPTER 5

When the alarm went off I felt as if I'd just gotten into bed. Those first few minutes are always the worst, the agonizing realization that it's time to get up, that I must wrest myself from slumber and climb into reality. After a few minutes, it's not as bad. A shower and a cup of strong coffee seem like an extra hour's sleep. Blue slacks, yellow oxford cloth short-sleeved shirt, and which plaid tie will it be today? I had a plaid tie fetish.

It was a dreary, drizzly, gray day outside. I walked through the puddles to my car and drove to work, listening to the rest of the George Benson tape. That's one of the nice things about a tape deck; you don't miss the rest of the song when you get out of the car. Twenty-six miles on Route 7 in the Berkshires three or four times a week really isn't that bad. Even in the rain. Certainly better than seventeen miles into Brooklyn every day for thirty years, like my father. I was feeling entirely awake by this time; I had lots of practice with sleep deprivation.

I made mental notes about my evening with Sal and his friends. Later I would write them down and put them in the safe deposit box. I'd guess we were on the road last night for an hour to an hour and a half. The only road in the area where you could do that speed for that amount of time was the Massachusetts Turnpike. And the only city I knew of near the pike that looked like that is Springfield.

The rain kept most people out of the ER and it was a quiet day. I got through a couple of medical journals that were full of the latest biochemical breakthroughs, none of which had any usefulness for the doctor in practice. I saw a housewife who cut herself while making an egg and thumb salad sandwich. I saw a little senile lady from a nursing home who'd fallen and fractured her hip.

After lunch a very sheepish teenaged boy came in. He had a towel wrapped around him.

"Doc, you're not gonna believe what happened."

"What's the matter?"

"Well, you see, I accidentally got my dick caught in my zipper."

"You're kidding," I insisted. He didn't look like he was in that much pain, and his voice wasn't high.

"No. I tried to get it out but I couldn't."

"How did you do this to yourself?" I asked in amazement.

"I know this is gonna sound incredible. You see me and my friends have been camping over in Copake. But since it's been raining all day we were just sittin' around in the tent and drinkin' beer all morning. And every half hour or so I had to go out in the rain to take a leak. Well, I was hurrying because it was raining so hard and I started to zip up my fly before I had my thing back in my pants, and it got caught."

"Oh, my God," I exclaimed, "you poor kid. Let's see what's going on."

He unwrapped the towel, and sure enough, the skin on the underside of his penis was caught in the teeth of the zipper of his cut-off denim shorts.

I looked at it in amazement. "You poor kid," I said again, wincing in sympathy.

"This is really pretty embarrassing, you know," he said.

"I can imagine. Think how much worse it would be for you if I was a lady doctor. Look, I love to camp and to drink beer too. I fully sympathize with you. I'm going to give you some Xylocaine in there."

"It doesn't hurt that much."

"Never mind. It'll make me feel better. You know, you almost circumcised yourself."

I numbed up the area and cut across the bottom of the zipper with a bandage scissor. From below I gently separated the two sides of the zipper; the teeth unhooked and released the boy from his predicament. He was very grateful.

The hours dragged by slowly. Around six there was a lull so I went to supper with some of the ER people. We went downstairs to the hospital cafeteria. It's a nice old building. As we walked leisurely down the main first-floor hallway, I admired the way they built things eighty years ago. The walls of the hallway were glazed ceramic tile up to about shoulder height. Then it was plaster up to the tall ceilings. There were moldings where the walls met the ceilings and around every doorway, their fine contours rounded by many years' layers of paint. The doors themselves were a foot taller than the doors in most houses, wider too, and they were heavy frame and panel design with big brass hardware. Even the bathrooms were nice, with big marble slabs separating the stalls, pedestal sinks, and big bulky porcelain knobs on the faucets. The floors were tile.

The stairway had cast-iron balusters that had some detail molded into them, also partly obscured by years of paint. The banister was wooden.

All that nice old detail ended when you got to the steel fire door on the basement floor. This floor had been remodeled. Linoleum on the floor, vinyl mopboard molding where the floor meets the wall, gypsum drywall for walls, ranch molding around modern metal doors, and suspended ceilings with acoustic tile. The old and the new. I liked the old better.

After supper a really cute thing happened. A young man came to the ER with his wife. They were very concerned because they noticed a lump on his side. Naturally they were concerned he might have cancer.

The nurse brought them into the exam cubicle and I went in with them and drew the drape. I asked him some questions and asked him to take off his shirt and show me the lump. It was on his flank.

"You can see it and feel it better when I sit like this," he said. You could.

"Would you please stand up straight and tall, like a West Point cadet, hands out from your sides?" He did.

"Loosen your pants and lower them a few inches for me." He did. I backed up and looked at him from a few feet away. Then I went over and felt the opposite side. "There's one over here on this side too," I said, smiling.

"Oh, no," his wife said.

"Nothing to worry about," I said. "Have a seat, both of you, let's talk." They did.

"Tell me, how long have you been married?" I asked.

"About six months."

I turned to the patient's wife and asked, "Do you like to cook?"

He answered for her, and said, "She's a great cook."

"The technical term for those bumps on your sides is 'love handles', sometimes also called 'beer handles'. How much weight do you think you've gained?"

Sheepishly the man turned and looked at his wife. "You know," he said, "my pants have been feeling kinda tight lately."

We all looked at each other, smiled, and began laughing.

Ceremoniously I tore up the ER admission sheet and said, "You guys can go on home. This hospital visit is on the house. Don't stop at Friendly's." We all laughed again, the man put his shirt back on, shook my hand and patted me on the back as they left.

As I drove home I wondered if I'd ever get to marry Patty, or anyone else, given my situation with Sal.

When I got home I forced myself out for a short, slow run. When I got back I took a long, hot shower. I dried off and stood there looking at myself in the full-length mirror on the back of the door. I was five feet eleven inches. I weighed 158 pounds the last time I'd checked. My hair was dark brown, a little long but still clean cut enough. There was a patch of brown hair on my chest and a vertical stripe of hair that ran down to my navel. There were some curves from muscle but I was not muscular. My legs were hairy. I did not have beer handles.

CHAPTER 6

The following Saturday I was off, and when I woke up I felt rested and calm. It was warm and sunny outside. While the coffee perked, I dressed and went down to the front porch to get the newspaper.

The kitchen was bright with the morning sun. I cracked open the two windows in the kitchen to get some fresh air. The double locks on each window reminded me of Sal.

I listened to the FM public radio station. Robert J. Lurtsema in Boston was hosting his classical music program entitled "Morning Pro Musica." He was playing a set of baroque Telemann pieces with a harpsichord.

I sat at the kitchen table barefoot, in jeans and a sweatshirt. I read the paper and had coffee and breakfast. Breakfast was a toasted poppy seed bagel with low-fat cream cheese.

For the second time that week I did something I promised myself I would do daily. There was a pull-up bar I put in the bedroom doorway long ago. I did five pull-ups and five chin-ups. I did fifty sit-ups on the floor with my toes hooked under the bureau. Then I did forty push-ups, with my hands on the floor and my feet on the edge of the bed.

I changed, and put on my running stuff and sneakers, and went out the door.

Today I was in the mood to suffer a little, and did my usual course through town at my cruising speed. Warm up, speed up until it just starts to hurt a bit, and stay there. For four miles. Usually all I could ever think about during this kind of run was stopping, but once in a while I reached nirvana. I felt great and just had the right attitude. Attitude was my biggest hurdle in running.

When I was a kid I would sometimes watch ABC's *Wide World of Sports* on Saturday afternoons. They had a great introduction, with an announcer talking in deep resonant tones about the thrill of victory and the agony of defeat, while a skier had a major mishap falling off a ski jump and crashing down to the slopes below. What always got me were the faces of the athletes when they finished their events, whether they won or not, you could tell they were 150 percent in the moment, they were mentally focused and had physically given their all. To look at the faces of the sprinters, hurdlers, swimmers, as they finished their events, I was envious of the look on their faces that showed total mental and physical involvement, exhaustion; their effort was there to the max.

There were also other people I'd see who were in it to the max. I remember seeing Percy Sledge sing "When a Man Loves a Woman," and he really belted it out, muscles tensed, feeling all the emotion of the song in his voice, totally in the moment. James Brown was another one. Performers, athletes, those people who had golden moments of such intense focus, supreme physical and mental and emotional energy. How cathartic it must be. I had vague memories of having hard, uninhibited cries as a kid, a total sensory and physical experience leaving me drained yet relaxed afterwards. A maximal personal experience please, don't hold the onions, don't hold the garlic or the hot peppers, I want it all, I wanna really feel it.

Sometimes I get a little of this when I go out for a run. Sometimes, if I were stressed at work and bad things were happening, I would go out for a run with the intention of really hurting myself. Of keeping a pace that would keep me at the limit of my aerobic capacity, on the verge of sprinting, and everything would hurt and my leg muscles would burn, my lungs would burn, my chest muscles exhausted from breathing so hard and fast and deep as I sprinted along, and it would "hurt so good."

Of course there were no fans cheering me on.

Except for once. In the Berkshires there is a famous annual tradition of the Josh Billings Run Aground. Josh Billings is the pseudonym of a long-dead Berkshire humorist who was much in the style of Mark Twain. For some reason they used his name for an annual September athletic event, which consists of a twenty-mile bike race, a seven-mile canoe race, and a six-mile, run. It is a very popular event, and lots of teams of bikers, paddlers and runners enter. Some people do all the events themselves and are called Ironmen and Ironwomen. Anyway, during my internship, or as I called it, my internment, I was asked if I wanted to join a team and do the running. Sure, why not? The other members were a senior resident, one of the hospital secretaries, and another person I can't recall. I trained pretty hard for this race. I knew we weren't going to win, we were just doing it for fun, and to just finish was our goal. The others on the team were not particularly athletic, not that I was a running star myself. Anyway, the bicyclist did her miles and handed off the wristlet to the canoeists, who paddled twice around Stockbridge Bowl. I met them at the shore as they paddled in and they tossed the wristlet to me. Of course I dropped it but picked it up, put it on, and began running the 6.2-mile course. I had been on call the night before, wouldn't you know. It hadn't been a real tough night but still I probably only had two or three hours of poor quality sleep. So I was a little insecure about how I would do since I was sleep deprived, but what the heck. If I could take care of patients sleep deprived, I could run sleep deprived.

It ended up being just great. I ran well, I ran hard, I got in my groove, I was fully involved, my muscles were almost screaming, my senses were full. It was better than a regular training run because the race gave me more motivation. There were lots of spectators all along the route and they were good sports and they cheered for everybody who ran by. Every mile or two there were folding tables set up with Dixie cups of water. I saw runners in front of me pick up a cup in each hand, one cup got dumped on their heads to cool off and the other they drank, all without breaking stride. Very dramatic.

The last leg of the race turned from Hawthorne Street (yes, Nathaniel Hawthorne lived around here for a while), then turned down Route 183 toward Tanglewood (summer home of the Boston Symphony). Here the crowds of spectators were even thicker, and they shouted their encouragement, and I tried to climb into a higher gear. The last few hundred yards, the "chute," was down the Tanglewood driveway, which was two cars wide and bordered by a long split rail fence behind which there were even thicker crowds. It was great, it was like a maximal grand command performance and I was killing myself, sprinting, and it hurt so good. I was flying down this corridor of people, aware of them not individually but en masse, seeing the green foliage of grass and trees, pink faces, multicolored T-shirts all urging me on. There I was, *Wide World of Sports*, giving more than my all, belting it out. But it only lasted seconds and I was through the chute, my wristlet number logged in, my steps slowed and shortened, slowing down over twenty or thirty yards, moving off to the side to recover, gasping, bent over with hands on knees, gasping and spitting and trying to clear the mucus out of my throat, like all the other runners, trying not to vomit. Oh, it was great. That was it. That was my moment in the sun. Ten minutes later I felt much better. My time was pretty good, too.

I don't get many opportunities to have such super maximal experiences that use up my brain, my emotions, my body, like that. It's too bad.   Moments you can lose yourself in.   It doesn't happen in medicine. Sometimes on call at night when I was racing around from floor to floor putting out fires, my beeper going off constantly, each time with another demand from another nurse about another patient with another problem. At first it drove me crazy and I dreaded it. Then I remembered the Hemingway hero who portrayed grace under pressure. I tried to make it a game. On those crazy nights when all hell broke loose, I tried to think of it as an exercise, a trial, a long-distance run that I knew I could do, and kept my clipboard list of calls and scut-work I had to do, and went from floor to floor like a calm automaton. It wasn't as much fun as the Tanglewood race, but I had to endure thirty-six hours of being on the wards, all night, doing what I had to do, drawing blood, admitting patients sent up from the ER, evaluating people with new headaches and fevers and shortness of breath and chest pain, looking forward to seeing dawn's red light on the Taconic Range as I looked west out the hospital's fifth floor windows, knowing my friends would be in soon to relieve me and carry on the battle, and I would no longer be alone.

A few hours later would be morning report, where I would have to present the case of each patient I'd admitted and explain how I came to the diagnosis I did, and why I ordered whatever treatments I did. Sometimes in morning report I was so tired and I would dissociate. That's a psychiatric term for when a person seems to cleave in two, and one part passively observes the other part in action. It was like that. I'd be sitting there with all my notes in front of me, trying to give a good objective intellectual report of whatever patient this was who had presented in mild congestive heart failure, and I would go on autopilot, and the words would just come out as if of their own volition, and I would just sit there passively listening to myself talk, and as I talked I found I could think about other things even though I was presenting the case. I'd be reading off the patient's lab tests and I could think about, say, sex, and it wouldn't even spill over into my presentation at all, which was a good thing or it would have been pretty embarrassing. I could be telling about the guy's EKG and explaining how it had changed since the last one the guy had on his last admission six months ago, and while saying that I could be thinking about what a jerk the guy next to me was. In the back of my mind I could be thinking anything I wanted and in the front of my mind I could see Charlie over there talking about a sick patient and doing a pretty good job of it and sounding pretty convincing, while I was hardly paying attention at all.

The first few times it happened it was pretty confusing and maybe a little alarming. I mentioned it to some of the other residents and some of them said, yeah, they'd had it too, but for them it didn't sound as frequent or as profound as it was for me.

I finished my run.

The mail was in and I shuffled through it as I headed toward the kitchen. Aside from the usual junk mail that doctors get so much of, there was a white business-sized envelope with no return address. I opened it. Inside was a blank piece of typing paper folded around five, used hundred-dollar bills. That was all.

At first I was bewildered. Maybe this was how Sal was paying me for my professional services the other day. And not at a bad rate. But I couldn't take this money (though it was tempting). To do it would put me on the Mob's payroll. It would imply complicity, or collusion, or whatever the legal term was. All I wanted was to not have any trouble. To keep my nose clean. What should I do with the money? I thought of donating it anonymously to some charity - maybe I should donate it to fight organized crime. Maybe I should just keep it in the vault. I had to go there anyway today, to put in the notes about my little trip the other night. And the next time I saw Sal I would tell him that I wasn't interested in the money and that I wanted to give it back to him.

I lounged around the front porch with a Genny Cream Ale and tried to concentrate on last week's New England Journal of Medicine. No luck. I went upstairs and sat down at the piano. My neighbors weren't home, so I could play as loud as I wanted. I banged out some Scott Joplin until my fingers tingled. Then I had another beer.

I was seeing Patty that night and it was time to start getting ready. I showered off the day's exertion, shaved with a new blade, and rubbed on Polo after-shave balm. Patty had told me that once on a slow day she went through the pharmacy smelling all the men's colognes, and Polo was her favorite. I told her it was mine, too, and I used it often. The next day I bought some.

From the ground up, I wore desert boots, Woolrich chino slacks, a navy blue knit sport shirt with one button buttoned. Wet hair. No stethoscope, no beeper. I looked in the mirror and what I saw was passable. Physically I felt good, with a quiet somatic euphoria that persists after good exercise. But I was edgy.

As I drove through Stockbridge, it suddenly became cloudy and cooler. B.B. King came on the radio as I passed the Red Lion Inn, and together we sang the blues as we headed down Route 7 South. It looked like we were going to get a spring storm.

I wished I had someone to talk to about this business with Sal. Amongst my friends I had a whole panel of expert advisors in various fields. Mark answered all my questions about cars and stereos. Eddie always recommended good books and movies. Whenever I needed dirty jokes I'd call Roy. Michael gave me legal advice and I nearly got him into deep trouble when I told him about Sal's first visit. But I knew no expert on extortion.

When I got to Patty's, it was pouring.

CHAPTER 7

Fortunately, Patty had a covered porch, so we were still able to barbecue the shish kebobs she had prepared. Her bungalow was bigger than my apartment. She was almost finished painting it. It looked nice. The house was surrounded by mature trees and I could hear the wind and rain in the branches and feel the breeze through partly opened windows.

Her house reminded me of some grad student friends of mine in college. She had somebody's hand-me-down sofa, and that large round wooden cable spool for a coffee table. There were bookshelves made of cinder blocks and planks stuffed with books like J.R.R. Tolkien, Camus, Hesse, the American Hospital Pharmaceutics Formulary. I explored with my eyes, taking in the plants and books and wall hangings. Held up on the refrigerator by a magnet was a bumper sticker that read: "A women's place is in the house... and the senate..."

It was like déjà vu, I felt like I was in college again. I was excited, anxious, still thinking and hoping that she might be the one, enjoying the suspense of it.

We sat on the porch while the food sizzled, sipping wine and listening to the rain drumming on the roof. She was wearing tight blue jeans with no belt. Tucked into them was a blue and white horizontally striped nautical-looking top with a little red anchor embroidered near the collar. The neckline was high and wide and pointed at the sides. I could see her collarbones and sometimes the top of her bra strap. I think it's called a boat neck collar.

We sat talking on the porch. We could hear thunder a long way off. When she got up to turn the shish kebob on the hibachi I realized how hard I'd been staring at her. She's a long, lean person. Her movements are graceful.

We had met in March, it was now June. I'd had some relationships that were over and done with in this amount of time. I was putting a lot of effort and restraint into developing this relationship with Patty, so as not to overwhelm her. To nurture the relationship but not push it. This business with Sal was probably going to complicate things.

The food was ready. Patty brought the shish kebobs into the house on a big plate. We sat at the kitchen table. The food was delicious. The meat was spicy from the marinade, the tomatoes, green peppers and onion burned just the right amount. We had rice pilaf and more wine.

We talked about our jobs.

"So, how's it going at work?"

"I like it! It's okay."

"Anything else you can see yourself doing?"

"You know, I can't really see myself doing this forever. I'm sure it will get old. In the world of big chain pharmacies there's a corporate ladder and I could be working my way up to being a store manager. Or a regional manager."

"Ugh," I exclaimed.

"That's the way I feel, too. Ugh. That's all business and numbers and money. And personnel and hiring and firing. Oh, excuse me, it's not personnel anymore, it's human resources."

"What else do you want to do?"

"Oh, there's a lot of things a pharmacist can do. I could migrate into research, or industry, or academics. You know how big the drug companies are and how they're always trying to create profitable new drugs."

"Do you think you'd like to be in on the theoretical end or the clinical studies end?"

"Probably the theoretical end, but you know how it is, you can't always write your own ticket. And they're always looking for pharmacists to become pharmaceutical representatives, especially young female ones to sidle up to all you doctors and convince you to prescribe their drugs."

"If you sidled up to me I'd do anything you want," I said.

"Maybe I will, later."

"You know, I meet a lot of those people. I'm told it's a good job, the money is good, they get a company car, they're all nicely dressed. Some are very professional. I feel badly for the ones who have a mediocre redundant product that they have to push."

"It's really just a sales job. I don't think I could do it," she said.

"Do you want to stay in the Berkshires?"

"Maybe. I'm keeping my options open. Speaking of options, I have the option to buy this house I'm renting. The landlord said he'd apply the first year's rent toward the purchase price."

"Incentive for you to buy," I said.

"Yeah, I guess so. I do love it here. This house and the Berkshires. But things change. Life is a path with many branches. Who knows where you'll end up. Sooner or later I'll probably get married and have a family and that'll have a higher priority than my career. You know how it is. Decision tree analysis. Do they teach you guys decision tree algorithm?"

"Oh, yeah."

"But there's other stuff that interests me, too. I'm kinda political. I could see myself getting involved in civil liberties issues, women's rights, freedom of choice."

We were on dessert. Patty was sitting on my lap and we were both eating out of the same Häagen-Dazs ice cream container. Rum raisin. I was in heaven.

"Tell me about your parents," I asked.

"My parents are great. Except they're divorced."

"When did that happen?"

"My second year in college. I think they'd been planning it. You know, I'm the youngest of three. I have two older brothers."

"Was it hard for you?"

"Yes and no. You know, your parents are like your foundation, they're there for you, they're solid and reliable. The cement between them is part of the solidity. When it crumbles you kinda feel insecure. But that's the child in me. I don't know. There are public reasons and private reasons for everything. They just said that when all us kids moved out they had nothing in common anymore. There wasn't a third person. That I know of. They were perfectly polite and amicable about it. They still are. They still speak. They weren't happy together. I guess they hadn't been for a long time. I hope they're happier now. Who knows what other private reasons there were."

"Do you have much contact with them?"

"Oh, yeah, I speak with each of them probably once a week. I see my mother more often than my dad because she's closer."

"Where's your father?"

"He's in Pennsylvania. He's director of purchasing for a manufacturing plant. He started out as a mechanical engineer. My mom was a second grade teacher. They just grew apart."

"That sounds very generous and cerebral of you."

"Thanks."

"How does the kid in you relate to this?"

"The kid in me thinks it sucks. But I've gotten used to it. And I never want it to happen to me."

The phone rang. Patty got up and walked to the wall phone.

"Speak of the devil, hi Mom!" she said into the phone. I motioned for her to stay on the phone and I got up and cleared the table, cleaned the dishes and picked up. I finished cleaning the kitchen, poured each of us a little more wine and followed the long phone cord from the kitchen to find Patty sitting on the couch in the living room.

She was just saying goodbye to her mother. I took the receiver and gave her one of the glasses of wine. As I went back to hang up the phone she turned on the stereo, turned to a classical station. Sounded like Tchaikovsky. There was one lamp on in the living room and it was dark out now. The rain had stopped. I sat down next to her.

"Your dieffenbachia needs pruning," I said.

"Shut up and keep massaging my shoulders," she said.

"You know, it's always amazed me that the shoulder is barely connected to the main skeleton by bone at all. It just has a flimsy bony attachment to your sternum via your collarbone. It's held on just by muscle. And the shoulder blade is also held on only by muscle. A house cat doesn't even have its collarbone attached; it's just a loose little toothpick that does nothing. That's why cats have such a huge range of motion with their front legs."

"How interesting."

"I think it is."

I was massaging her trapezius muscle and working out toward the deltoids. Then I began to knead my thumbs into the supraspinatus and infraspinatus on the shoulder blades, then medially to the rhomboids.

"You know the rhomboids are so important in stabilizing the shoulder blade to stabilize the whole arm. It's like a tug of war of several different muscle groups pulling on the shoulder blade and shoulder to keep it in place, keeping it in position as a braced unit, like guy lines on a tent."

I began to massage her latissimus dorsi but kept well behind her mid axillary line lest she think I was moving in toward the mammaries. I did not want to appear too forward although I was thinking about them a lot.

"You know, this is not very romantic." I took that as a hint.

"Ah, anatomy can be very romantic. It can be very romantic if you try to understand it rather than memorize it. Anatomy can be very beautiful." *Particularly yours.* "It depends how you look at it. Want me to show you?"

She did.

The following week Patty had to go away to a pharmacy convention. She hated those. She'd be away for three days. It was being given by the chain she worked for. She'd get the continuing education credits she needed every few years for her license. There was also a lot about bookkeeping systems for narcotics and other restricted medicines, marketing, sales and promotions, and a lot of stuff that had nothing to do with pharmacology. These courses were usually held in some big hotel too close to a big airport near a big city. She found them tedious and lonely, and after the first clinical part, boring.

I had a mission. I went shopping. I bought a collection of things that I put in a small cardboard box, which I wrapped up in brown paper and tied up with string. I gave it to Patty and told her not to open it until she was in her hotel room the first night. Inside were a few of her favorite things. There was a brandy snifter and a little airline bottle of Amaretto and another one of Drambuie. There was a small bottle of bubble bath and a small scented candle. There was a card on which I'd written out the lyrics to "Bridge Over Troubled Water" to be sung softly to oneself. There were several little rectangular plastic packages with a compartment containing salted crackers and another with spreadable cheddar cheese and a little red plastic spreader stick.

CHAPTER 8

I was standing at the patient's bedside getting ready to sew up her laceration. She and her husband had recently bought their first house, a real fixer-upper. This was during the energy crisis of the early eighties, and she was helping her husband stuff more insulation in the attic. It was awkward working under the pitch of the roof and she bumped against the point of a roofing nail and gave herself a nice two-inch long laceration on the meaty part of the back of her shoulder.

I had already checked her out and explained everything to her and given her a tetanus shot, and she was cool. She was lying prone on the table and I began wiping the wound area with brown Betadine soap. Then I began anesthetizing it.

"Okay. I'm gonna numb this up now. You'll feel a pinprick. It'll hurt a little, but not a lot. I'm gonna use a lot of Xylocaine. Better too much than too little. We have a lot of it and it's cheap."

"Sounds good to me," she replied.

I put down the sterile drape with the opening in the middle to isolate the wound and give me a safe, sterile work area. I dipped a gauze sponge in sterile saline and mopped at the wound itself, scrubbing away the gelatinous blood so I could explore the wound, clean it, check for foreign debris. It wasn't much of a wound. With an iris scissor I just neatened a few sections of the wound edges that were a little ragged.

"OK," I said, "I'm ready to start sewing this up. We have several choices for thread color. We have Prolene, which really is a very pretty, almost iridescent, cobalt blue. We have Ethilon, which is black. As you know, black will match whatever you're wearing. And they say black is slimming. And we have Mersilene, which has a green color. It's a braided thread, not very popular."

"I'd like to have that pretty blue thread you mentioned," she said. "It'll match my eyes".

"An excellent choice," I replied.

The nurse, who had heard all this before, rolled her eyes and dropped a sterile packet of 4-0 Prolene onto the surgical tray.

The unit secretary came over to the cubicle and said, "Charlie, your uncle Sal is on the line."

I froze. "Tell him that I'm tied up. Ask him for his number and I'll call him back." Yeah. Right. She disappeared. In a moment she returned and said he'd call me back later.

Oh, no. I was supposed to see Patty after work. If he needs me I'll have to make up an excuse for Patty. This isn't going to be good.

I threw in eight simple interrupted sutures, each quadruple knotted, approximating the wound edges nicely, with slight intentional eversion of the edges. I snapped off my gloves.

"Well, that's finished. Now we'll clean you up again and put on a dressing. Today we have French, Italian, and Thousand Island."

"Oh. Do you have blue cheese?" the patient asked, taking my bait.

"Yes, of course, we have a lovely creamy Roquefort blue cheese, but that would be fifty cents extra. Would that be alright?"

"Yes, of course. My insurance will pay for it, we have a very good plan. Do you have croutons?"

While the nurse put on the real dressing, I instructed the patient on wound care and when to get the stitches out. I thanked her for being such a good patient and having a sense of humor.

"And for putting up with all your lame jokes," the nurse added.

While I was at the nurses' station writing up the report on the lady with the laceration, Sal called again.

"Hi, Doc, sorry to bother you," he said.

Yeah, I'll bet.

"What's up, Sal?"

"I need to pick you up tonight. Same place, nine o'clock."

Did I hear any magic words? Like, 'please.' Not a grateful request. A command.

"What do you have for me?" I asked.

"I'll tell you when I see you. OK, Doc, see you at nine." He hung up before I could ask him if there was anything special I could bring.

I called Patty and begged off and she didn't sound happy and I wasn't either. I finished my shift and drove to the supermarket parking lot. It was still light out, in late June, almost the longest day of the year.

The van was already there. Maybe I should duck down and sneak over and pop up right in front of the windshield and see if I could startle Sal and Bob. Probably not a good idea.

I approached in full view, from a distance. Sal saw me and got out of the front passenger seat to greet me and open the van's sliding door.

I got in and settled on my cot.

"What does the patient have, Sal?"

"He has a cut on his neck."

"What did he get cut with?" I asked.

"I dunno. Something sharp." Big help.

"Is he otherwise OK? Did the bleeding stop? Is he in shock? Can he talk?"

"Oh. He seems OK except for the cut. Doesn't seem to be in too much pain. He's pretty calm, actually."

"What part of his neck?" I asked.

'I don't know, he had it all wrapped up in a towel to stop the bleeding."

Great. I began reviewing in my head the anatomy of the neck, and the different vital structures I might need to contend with. The posterior triangle of the neck has the external jugular vein, the spinal accessory nerve, a bunch of little nerves to the shoulder muscles; deeper in are the brachial nerves to the arm, the phrenic nerve to the diaphragm. The anterior triangle has the internal jugular and the carotid arteries, the common carotid branching into the internal and external carotids. Under the chin is the branch of the facial artery and the hyoid bone. In front of the neck, below the Adam's apple, is the thyroid gland. A deep cut to the base of the neck could open into the apex of the lung and collapse it.

There's a lot in there to worry about. If one of the major blood vessels were cut he would have bled to death already and they wouldn't be needing me now. If it's a nerve that's cut, there's no fixing that. That simplifies things.

So there I was, lying on a cot in the back of a van driven by two thugs I didn't know, being taken to a patient I didn't know, worrying about what, of a multitude of things, might be damaged by a knife cut to the neck.

Finally I could tell by the movements of the van that we were off the highway and in local traffic.

"We're here, Doc. Same drill as last time."

Bob parks the van. Sal opens the door and I get out and it's beautiful outside. The air is fresh and cool, the stars are out, the moon is almost full, the air is sweet and it's so nice to get out of the van. I walk toward the same house, behind Bob and in front of Sal. Into the house, down the stairs to the basement apartment.

The basement was brightly lit and there were two young men sitting in front of the TV watching baseball. Each was holding a bottle of beer, and there was a pizza box between them.

"Hi, Sal. Hi, Bob. Hi, Doc," said the first one.

"Hi, Sal. Hi, Bob. Hi, Doc," said the second one. He had a bloody towel wrapped around his neck. He kept a hand on it to keep it in place.

"You guys want some food? We saved some for you, there's plenty," said the first guy.

"Not me, thanks," I said, "I'd like to get to work." Sal and Bob looked at me. "Go ahead, don't let me stand in your way," I added. Sal and Bob dove into the pizza box.

"You should eat something too, Doc. I hear you had a long day already," said the second man, the one with the towel.

I paused for a few seconds and said, "Sure, why not," and picked up a slice. It was almost cold but it was very, very good. I always liked cold pizza. Especially for breakfast.

"OK," I said, "what's the story?"

"I got cut."

"Can you tell me how you got cut?"

He turned toward Sal, who nodded, no.

"No." He glanced at Sal.

"Can you tell me if you're hurt anywhere else? Any bangs or bruises elsewhere, on your knuckles or hands or forearms or ribs?"

"Nope."

"What were you cut with?"

"A knife."

"Can you tell me where this happened?"

Silence. "No."

"Can you tell me *when* this happened?"

"About two this afternoon." It was now ten p.m.

"Do you think it was a fairly clean knife, or was it a gardening tool?"

"Probably clean." He went on to say that it bled a lot for a few minutes, then stopped. This was the first and only towel on his neck, and although bloody, it wasn't soaked. Overall he felt pretty well, his neck only hurt a little. He could obviously eat and drink. He was only on his third beer. He hadn't tried to see if he could turn his head left or right, up or down. Good thinking. His voice was fine, his breathing was fine. How badly injured could he be?

I went to the supply closet and collected everything I thought I might need, including several disposable surgical packs; each had one hemostat. I hoped I wouldn't need them. I set up a sterile area on a table in the bedroom, laid out the tools, got bottles of sterile saline and Betadine.

"OK, guys. I'm ready for you," I called into the next room.

"Aw, come on, Doc, can't we wait until the end of the inning?" said the man with the towel. I was glad he was so relaxed.

"Get going," Sal said. "I'll let you know what's going on with the game."

I had the guy lie down on his back with his head at the foot of the bed, where the light and my access were better.

"Don't you wanna have a beer first, Doc, help steady your nerves and relax ya?" he asked very politely.

"No, thanks. Maybe after. Thanks for asking," I said. I couldn't help liking this guy. I took his pulse and blood pressure, and listened to his heart and lungs, and it was all fine.

Very slowly I began peeling back the towel, ready to grab a hemostat real quick if he sprang a leak. I got the towel off and he had a three-inch horizontal laceration on the left anterolateral neck. It was not gaping. There was a lot of dried and moist blood all over the area. I cleaned off most of the blood with a sterile gauze sponge soaked with saline and Betadine. So far so good. I changed gloves and put on a new sterile pair. I put down a sterile drape.

"OK, I'm going to start numbing you up. I'm going to inject some Xylocaine into the skin all around this cut. I'm gonna use a lot. Better too much than too little. Sal has a lot of Xylocaine in the closet here and it's cheap."

"Go for it, Doc."

"OK, you're gonna feel a little prick," I said.

"Sorry to hear about that, Doc," the patient said.

"About what?" I said.

"Your little prick," he answered, in a jovial, funny way, not malicious at all.

I used about six ccs of Xylocaine all around the wound.

"OK. We'll let this Xylocaine marinate into you for a couple minutes and then I'll take a look inside."

From the next room Sal said something about Jim Rice hitting a homerun. "God I wish I was watching that game," the patient said.

"Not me," I said.

"Huh?"

"Not me. There's nothing I'd rather be doing than being right here with you, right now, helping you with your neck," I said softly.

"Thanks, Doc. I'll cut the wisecracks."

I wrapped a sterile gauze around each of my index fingers and gently pulled the wound edges apart. More dried blood. I packed it with a sterile soaked sponge and in a few minutes the blood could be easily wiped away. The skin edges were very straight and cleanly cut. It was a sharp knife. The yellowish fatty tissue beneath the skin was also cut, and as I explored the cut I saw, anteriorly, that the sternocleidomastoid muscle had a little half inch nick in it. No big deal. Doesn't even need to be repaired. I felt no abnormal broken structures like a hyoid bone. As I worked my way posteriorly I spread the fatty tissue on the two sides of the cut and there, all of a sudden, was a dark red vertical tube, perfectly undamaged.

I whistled under my mask.

"What?" the patient asked, urgently.

"Nothing bad. You are one lucky camper. Do you buy lottery tickets? Today is your lucky day," I said.

"What do you mean?"

"Well, this guy's very sharp knife did not cut you very deeply but it went right up to your external jugular vein. I'm looking right at it, it doesn't even have the tiniest nick."

By this time Sal and Bob and the other guy were leaning over my shoulder, looking at the wound as I held it open with my left hand. With my right I picked up a hemostat and used it to point at the jugular. "See it?" I asked. They all grunted, uh huh.

Bob was amazed by how much we all look like a chicken inside.

"What would've happened if that vein got cut?" the patient asked.

"Well, it could've been life-threatening, although if it's just the external jugular you'd have had a good chance of surviving if you pressed on it real hard right away, pressing on it above and below the cut. You know, or if you put a tourniquet around your neck until your eyes bugged out." They chuckled.

"Alright. Time to sew you up. We only have Ethilon thread here, which is black. The last lady I sewed up today chose Prolene, which is a pretty royal blue color."

"No blue today? Aw, rats, blue is my favorite color. My Corvette is blue. I coulda matched."

"Yeah, but black is always in style. Good for formal occasions. You'll match anything," I said.

"And black is slimming," he said.

"That's my line," I said.

"Now, what kind of scar would you like? I can do nice and neat. I can do something real macho, like a dueling scar Errol Flynn had in one of those swashbuckler movies. Right here on your neck I can sew in an auto tire valve stem like Frankenstein's monster. Which would you like?"

"How about nice and neat?"

"OK, you got it."

In ten or fifteen minutes I had it all sewn up. I had him sit up on the edge of the bed. He was still smiling.

"Now I'll put on a dressing."

"Blue cheese," he said, "please, if you have it."

"Dammit!" I said, smiling.

"What?" he asked.

"You're stealing all my lines."

I got it all bandaged up. I took a clean towel and wrapped it around his neck and taped it closed just to act as a neck collar and stop him from moving his neck too much.

"You're a lucky guy. That was a sharp knife and a shallow cut. This could've been real bad. You should say a prayer, light a candle, kiss your mother. Buy a lottery ticket."

"Thanks a lot, Doc. You're a good guy. You ready for that beer now?"

"Oh sure, why not. It's only midnight and I don't have to work tomorrow."

Bob handed me a Budweiser Light in a long-neck bottle. It was cold. It was good. We sat around and I told them about wound care and when to get the stitches out.

The patient said, "You really love your work, huh, Doc?"

I took another swallow and thought about my answer.

"Yeah, I really love my work. When things turn out well and there's a happy ending. Like with you tonight. But when there is a bad ending, a sad ending, it really eats me up inside and I feel sick for days."

The four of us chatted a little longer and then they drove me back to the supermarket parking lot where I'd left my car. It was almost two a.m. and I was exhausted.

I thought about calling Patty in the morning, but I wouldn't know what to say.

CHAPTER 9

I was hoping for a quiet night at work. Thursday nights usually were, and I looked forward to sitting around in the lounge catching up on some reading, and getting some sleep later on. Unless some mill worker got the itchies with the week's paycheck, couldn't wait for the weekend to start partying, and wrapped his car around a tree. Or he might come in sick drunk and expect me to cure him of the effects of his indiscretion. I always wanted to say, "Throw up, you'll feel better," but I never did.

But I was due a quiet night. I hadn't had one in a long time and it was my turn.

By ten o'clock I'd seen a bunch of minor problems like an earache, two sore throats, a sprained ankle, a broken finger, and poison ivy. And a partridge in a pear tree.

The chart on my next patient stated he was forty-nine years old and his chief complaint was, "I want to talk to the doctor in private." Which meant he had V.D.

Much to my surprise he did not have V.D. The reason he wanted to see me was to warn me that his mother-in-law was going to sue me. He said he told her she was crazy, that it wasn't fair, but she'd already gone to a lawyer. He began to tell me the details of the story and suddenly I remembered as if my mind just changed to the right channel. A skinny, sixty-year-old lady came to the ER with symptoms of a cold that persisted for a week. She told me she was a heavy smoker, and she had nicotine on her fingers and breath. She was probably skinny because you can't chain smoke and eat at the same time, and she'd probably rather smoke, I thought. She was a horrible historian, unable to express herself, let alone give a clear answer to a simple question.

"Have you been coughing much?"

"I cough enough."

Dumb. I remember examining her and finding nothing, but got a chest X-ray and blood count just to make sure she hadn't already grown a bleb of the lung cancer that she was heading for. Concern for total health care. Get the big picture. Assess the patient's health status in general, not just the presenting complaint. Both tests were normal. I'd given her my usual schpiel about care for colds, urged her to stop smoking and to take care.

Her son-in-law told me that a week later she had "double pneumonia" (a term I never heard in med school), that she was admitted to another hospital, had to have a breathing tube in her throat for a few days, almost died, but is better and at home now. And wanting to sue me because I didn't stop her from catching pneumonia.

I thanked the man for coming to tell me. When asked why he did, he said he thought it was the only decent thing to do.

I went into the coffee room and told Margaret what had happened. She couldn't believe it either, though she'd seen it happen before. Stupidity and greed is a bad mixture.

"You know what'll happen, don't you?" she asked.

I was standing in the middle of the small room, fidgeting, restless, mad, looking around at the walls and shelves. Just looking. Margaret was great. She was a heavyset buxom lady who'd been a nurse for decades, had great intuition, lots of experience, and could always see through the crap to the meat of the matter. When I was a student, I was told to keep an eye out for that kind of nurse. There are some nurses who never learned another thing since they got out of school thirty years earlier, and there are those, like Margaret, who never stop learning. Look for those, I was told, they can really help you.

It was wise advice and I took it. In the past, I always sought out a Margaret when there was something funny going on with a patient that I couldn't get a handle on. Margaret. Basic unyielding values, honesty. Horse sense. The wisdom gained by going through life with open eyes and an open mind. Not only did she have medical wisdom, she had life wisdom.

"Do you know what'll happen?" she asked again.

"No, what?"

"Her insurance will call the hospital's insurance. Ours will say, 'Y'know, your case really has no merit.' Hers will say, 'Yeah, I know.' Ours will say, 'Y'know, it'll cost us both a couple of thou for legal and court fees and in the end you'll still lose.' Hers will say, 'Yeah, I know.' And then ours will say, 'Look, if we give you five grand will ya drop this whole thing?' And hers will say, 'Sure.' And then, you know what?"

"What?"

"Our insurance will pay her five thousand dollars. And even though you didn't do anything wrong, the fact that she got money says to everyone that you did. And you didn't."

"Shit," I said. "You know what really bugs me?"

"The injustice of it? Her greed?"

"Well, that too, but in a bigger sense, it's just the whole climate of health care today. And everything else. If things don't go right, people are unwilling to accept it - unwilling to just say something like ...well, that's the way the ball bounces. There aren't any guarantees and they want one. And if they can't get one, there must be someone around that they can sue."

"Ah, so young and so naive," Margaret said, smiling sarcastically. "It's fascinating to observe the dawn of your enlightenment."

I thought I would just ignore that.

"And you know what else, I hate this doctor-patient adversary relationship. I went to school for a long time, I paid a lotta tuition and studied like crazy and did all my residency and stuff, so that I could do good medicine, do what's right for what the patient has and needs. I get no kick out of not giving patients Penicillin when they want it for a cold. I didn't go through all that to not do what's best for them. And they come in here and I try to teach them about strep throats and smoking and things, try to teach them the hazards of using antibiotics and drugs unnecessarily, and they look at me like I'm not on their side."

I was getting pretty worked up; for me, this was quite a tirade.

"And you know what, Margaret, it pisses me off. I must've ordered tens of thousands of dollars of unnecessary lab tests and X-rays just because the patient insisted on getting a dumb little black and blue mark checked out, and I couldn't talk them out of it, or to cover my ass for the lawyers, just so some stupid greedy lady like this can't sue me. And then you pick up the newspaper and see a string of editorials and letters about the horrible rise in the cost of health care, all those damn doctors who can't take care of people without all those tests ... I tell ya Margaret, I'm fed up."

"You know what you need..." Her advice to me was interrupted by a tone on the HEAR radio - the emergency communication system that links the hospital with the police and the ambulances. A policeman was calling for an ambulance to be sent to the scene of a motor vehicle accident some seven miles south. What worried us was he sounded anxious. Usually they don't. And when they do, that's bad.

The next transmission was from the ambulance crew at the scene. They wanted another ambulance dispatched to the scene as soon as possible. They would be bringing the most serious victim; the others would be routed to another hospital. More to follow.

Margaret and I went into the trauma room and got everything out and ready and accessible and tested for any eventuality. It sounded like a bad one and we alerted the lab, X-ray, and respiratory care. I buttoned all the buttons on my long white coat.

The next transmission informed us that the patient was an unconscious male in his twenties, involved in a head-on MVA at high speed, who had bleeding from the right ear, slow gurgling breath sounds, and elevated BP at 195/130. We were waiting for them in the trauma room. I felt nervous in my stomach.

The phone rang at the ER desk.

"It's for you, Chuck," Margaret informed me. When I first met her she asked if I preferred Charlie or Chuck. I told her Charlie. So, from then on she called me Chuck.

"Hello, Davids here."

"Hello, Davids there, this is Patty here, how ya doing?"

"Oh, good, how're you?" How could I say that, I felt like a matador about to enter a bullring. What we say for the sake of cordiality.

"I wanted to tell you that you managed to be good company the last time I saw you," she said.

"Thanks, you were, too," I said, automatically, wanting to pay more attention but being preoccupied.

"Listen, Patty, thanks for calling, but the ambulance is coming with a real bad one and I'm standing by on the radio. I hate to, but I've got to go."

"Big deal. Have fun. Don't get any blood on you, and I'll see you around. By the way, shit head, I think I'm falling in love with you."

She hung up before I could say anything.

If it weren't for the ambulance, I would've been elated.

Finally, the ambulance drove up and they rolled out a stretcher with a great big beefy linebacker, with poor color and lots of blood on his face. I felt tense, but controlled.

Faked practice calm is better than natural panic. I began to assess him. A simple approach has been developed for the critically ill patient that even a terrified doctor can remember, even if he has skid marks in his shorts. It's as easy as ABC. Airway, breathing, circulation. His airway was questionable, he had a lot of gurgles when he breathed, which wasn't often enough. His skin was bluish. His lungs sounded poor. His pulse and blood pressure were too high. I tried to safeguard his airway by passing a flexible plastic tube from his nostril into his trachea. Doing this usually causes a small nosebleed, but with his high blood pressure it gushed like a red geyser. The same thing happened with the other nostril. To put the tube in through the mouth you need to tilt back the head and you can't do that in someone who might have a neck injury or you'll finish breaking it. So. Not through the nose, not through the mouth. I'm going to have to cut open this kid's windpipe. Oh my God. I was afraid I was going to have to do this some day. Being afraid of it kept me thinking about it, kept me reviewing the procedure.

"He needs a tracheotomy, Margaret," I said in a quiet voice. I said it as a statement, but meant it as a question, wanting her to agree with me.

"Here are your gloves, I'll bring over the instruments," she replied. True to form, she had everything ready. She wheeled over the stand with the trach tray on it, all set up. Then she picked up a gallon jug of Betadine, unscrewed the top and sloshed the brown antiseptic on the kid's neck. It was then that he began to seize, probably from lack of oxygen.

It took all the ambulance crew to keep him from convulsing off the stretcher while the guy from respiratory care kept methodically squeezing the clear green plastic oxygen bag attached to the mask on the kid's face.

When the seizure stopped, I made a midline incision through the skin on his neck below the Adam's apple and it just gushed blood. I wiped it off with a gauze so I'd be able to see which tracheal rings to cut between, but the hole filled up with blood so fast I couldn't see. It wasn't like this the hundreds of times I put myself through nightmares about it.

For a nightmare, I was doing well. I was hot and tense and my heart was beating fast, but I wasn't rushing. I was in control.

I'm OK with my hands, though I'm no surgeon. Doing a tracheotomy is not a technically difficult procedure. But in a life or death situation when seconds count and you need to do it right the first time, it isn't easy. It isn't the procedure that's difficult, it's the situation.

It wasn't this hard when we did it to dogs in the advanced trauma life support course.

I couldn't see through all the blood. I put my right index finger in the top of the bloody wound and felt for the big V notch at the top of the Adam's apple. Then I followed it down to the groove beneath it. I put my left thumbnail next to my right index finger and the end of my nail slipped transversely into the groove. This was the cricothyroid membrane I was trying to find. Holding the scalpel with a #10 blade in my right hand, and using my left thumbnail as a guide, I incised the membrane and the tip of my glove. There was a whoosh, a spray of air and blood that coated my glasses and face. Like when Moby Dick got harpooned. I took a curved closed hemostat and inserted it into the slot and elevated the trachea so the slot opened up into a hole. The trachea looked like a miniature vacuum cleaner hose. I slipped in the #6 endotracheal tube and inflated the cuff. The respiratory therapist connected his ambu-bag to the trach tube. With my stethoscope I could hear that he was ventilating well with both lungs.

Outwardly I did my "all in a day's work" routine, that is, if you look calm and confident, your staff will too. Keep up the morale. Inwardly I was saying, *Charlie, you're the kid who wants to lead a nice, quiet life, have a quiet little medical practice, have a family, play piano and kick back. What the hell are you doing here?*

With the tube in place, he started to look a lot better, his color pinked up, he had no more seizures. The rest of his exam checked out pretty well, except he was out cold. I ordered some blood tests and basic X-rays of his neck while I got on the phone to arrange to transfer him to Berkshire Medical Center, where they had a neurosurgeon and a CAT scanner.

The details got taken care of, we quickly photocopied the reports and lab results, put the kid in the ambulance, which then went screaming up county to BMC.

All the staff and I looked at each other and had a big sigh of relief. "It's Miller Time," I said, and everyone laughed. They complimented me on my deft hand, said they were impressed (so was I), and no doubt by tomorrow the story would be all over the hospital.

I helped Margaret clean up the trauma room, which she told me was not in my job description. A good way for a neurotic compulsive to burn off energy. Besides, why go to sleep and have nightmares? It had not been a quiet night. The kid was transferred at about two-thirty and I must have plagued BMC with hourly phone calls for status reports. It didn't sound good.

At about five-thirty a.m. a rotund lady came in complaining of vaginal bleeding. I went into the room, introduced myself. She had a thick Southern accent and was missing a lot of teeth.

"Hello, I'm Dr. Davids. I'd like to ask you some questions about your flow."

So it went. I got out at eight a.m. and on my way home I stopped at BMC to check up on the kid. He was still in a coma. The CAT scan was normal. There was nothing to be done operatively, nothing for the neurosurgeon to do. It was up to the kid now.

As I drove home I looked forward to tuning in *Morning Pro Musica*, having a nightcap, and relaxing in my sun-filled living room before turning in.

Sal was there to join me.

"Good morning to ya, Doc," he said.

"Oh, no!" I said.

I was going to ask how he got in despite all my new locks and bolts, but decided against it. Instead, I made a mental note to buy a burglar alarm. I returned his greeting. I hadn't seen him for almost two weeks, and my reaction was again one of ambivalence. *Sal, I don't like people breaking into my apartment and making me do things I don't wanna do, nice to see you Sal, you're a nice guy, almost fatherly, how's it going, can I get you a cup of coffee?*

"I take it you have some work for me."

"Yeah, Doc, I'm afraid I do. I thought it was urgent so I came right here to get you," he said apologetically. "You look tired, Doc, you been up all night?"

You know I was, I thought.

"Well, why don't we get going," I suggested. The sooner we got done, the sooner I could go to sleep. I was curious about what was waiting for me, but I thought Sal probably wouldn't tell me anything until we got there.

When we walked out my front door I saw the blue van pull away from the curb a block down and cruise over to pick us up. Like a trained cow that goes to the right stall when the barn is opened, I got in the back, said hello to Bob, got on my cot and went to sleep.

We drove to the same nondescript street that was probably in Springfield, up to the same everyday house, in the same commonplace side door, down the same stairway cluttered with the same mops and brooms and accoutrements of everyday life, and into the same ordinary basement apartment.

My patient was a middle-aged lady and she looked like hell. She wouldn't talk to me. She would moan, utter an occasional monosyllable, and point to the places where she hurt. She'd been beaten to a pulp.

I looked at her, absentmindedly shaking my head, biting my lip, outraged at the disgustingly obscene violence of it all. I turned to Sal. "What the hell happened?"

"C'mon Doc, you know we can't answer questions like that." But there was pain in his voice too.

She wasn't going to tell me anything. He wasn't going to tell me anything. In front of me was the epilogue and I would have to make up the story. All I could do was examine her and do what I could.

The eye that wasn't swollen half-closed looked at me, red and tearful. Every time she tried to say something to me, her composure would weaken and her sobbing would resume. Every time I found another spot that hurt, another silent flood of tears would run down her cheeks. It was not just her body that had been devastated.

I had seen battered wives before. At my best, I could understand, in the heat of an argument, wanting to slap someone once, but how someone could just go on beating someone, I couldn't understand. Nor could I understand why these victims would almost always go back. Often, for more.

So what had happened? Was she a hooker who had been beaten up? Was she a wife whose husband thought she needed a lesson?

Certainly if she were brought into my ER I would be legally obliged to report to the police.

Mostly she just had a lot of bumps and bruises. And three ribs that were either badly bruised or cracked. She would be OK. Then Sal suggested that I check out her, ah, privates.

When she removed the pads, I saw a vaginal tear that looked like someone had just performed a sloppy episiotomy. There were many shallow linear lacerations. My God, what had they rammed her with? I was stunned.

Hastily I got up from my seat at the end of the bed, snapped off my gloves, motioned Sal out of the room as I followed, pushing him from behind. When we were out I closed the door and pushed Sal further into the next room.

"Whatsa matter, Doc?"

"Who did this?" I wanted to know.

"A bad guy," Sal answered.

"I know that. Who did this?" I asked again.

"You wouldn't know him," Sal replied.

"Sal, you've gotta take care of the guy who did this."

"Settle down now, Doc."

"He needs to be punished, Sal." *Did I just promote vigilantism?*

"It'll be taken care of, Doc."

"Are you just saying that to humor me?"

"It'll be taken care of, Doc," Sal said again. "If it hasn't been already," he added.

I didn't really want to know what he meant. I went back into the room to take care of her.

My reaction must have scared her even more and she sobbed hysterically. I tried to calm her and assure her that though it was a big cut, it could be closed easily and should heal up just fine. It just looked worse and scarier than it was, they always do, and in time it would be fine. She would be sore for a while, but it would be fine.

What kind of barbarian could do something like that? What kind of animal? No, no animal. Animals don't get off on malicious mutilating violence. Only human animals.

I would have preferred a gynecologic surgeon took care of this, but I knew what Sal would say. Do the best you can. I found everything I needed in Sal's magic closet of medical supplies. I cleaned everything up, trimmed off a ragged edge here and there, and pulled the thing together with chromic catgut sutures that would dissolve in one or two weeks. She would have to take a lot of Penicillin and sit in the bathtub a lot. She would be OK. I wished I had a tetanus booster to give her. But she would probably be all right.

Normally I'd want to get some lab work to see if there were red blood cells in her urine from trauma to the kidneys. To see if her blood count was dropping from internal bleeding or a ruptured spleen.

Sal and Bob took me home. We didn't say much in the van. Maybe they were depressed and disgusted also.

I told Sal I didn't want the money he sent me.

"Money? What money?" he replied.

I kept thinking about that poor lady. I'm glad I didn't know what really happened, that enabled me to assume that she had been innocently victimized. I felt an anxious sorrow. Like when I see a dead animal on the side of the road. Or an ambulance screaming down the highway, lights flashing, carrying some poor guy in mortal distress. Or envisioning Mr. Mooers, in Dalton in 1852, throwing a shovelful of earth in his wife's grave, after already burying three of his children earlier that fall. Or seeing a comatose eighteen-year-old boy from a car wreck get a hole cut in his throat. Take me home. Let me go to sleep. Don't show me any more tragedy. If I want some, I'll go to the movies.

CHAPTER 10

I needed advice. I needed someone to talk to about this. I got home late after Sal's case and slept restlessly. When I awoke I wrote down all the details as best as I could remember, to put in the vault. I was bummed. But then I remembered I was seeing Patty that night and it put a grin on my face for a minute.

I finished breakfast, washed the plates, and put them in the drain board rack. I showered and painfully shaved off two days growth. I made the bed, and while doing it, remembered the shotgun I'd stashed under it a few weeks before. I pulled it out and looked at it. I checked the breech, and it was empty. I thought I had put a shell in there. The magazine was empty, too. I guessed what had happened when I saw a rolled up piece of paper protruding from the muzzle. A note from Sal.

"Now, Doc, what's a careful guy like you doing with a loaded shotgun in the house? You ought to know better than that."

The shotgun got zipped up in its case and angrily stashed in the far corner of the closet.

Maybe I should just get tough with them, stand my ground, give them back their money and tell them to get lost. No, that'd be dumb.

"Yeah, me," I said, "real tough." An easily exploitable cream puff. They say you can tell a lot about a person from their home. I looked around my apartment. With a piano and stacks of sheet music. A recording of "Brigadoon" on the turntable. A book of poetry by both Brownings on the nightstand that I'd been trying to finish for months. A Japanese watercolor. I bet Sal was just scared to death of me.

Tough. He knew about tough. He was so tough he didn't even have to try.

I hastily folded my pages and stuffed them in my back pocket. I got in the car and headed for the bank. The lady at the vault asked me if I'd gotten some new baseball cards. At first I didn't catch on, then I realized she was teasing me with the same line I'd given her a few weeks ago. I got two rolls of quarters from the teller.

From there I went to my favorite luncheonette, ordered coffee and a danish. As soon as I ordered I went into the phone booth near the rest rooms. They still had one of the old fashioned wooden phone booths with the seat inside and a bifold door that turned on the light and the vent fan when you closed it. I called information for Grand Rapids, Michigan. I was going to call Matt, whom I'd met in college. I was a nineteen-year-old sophomore at the time and he was a twenty-four-year-old freshman. He'd been in Special Forces in Vietnam before going to college to study psychology, on the GI Bill. If anybody knew how to take care of himself, he did. After graduating he floundered for a year or two looking for a job in his field, but there isn't much you could do with a B.A. in psychology. So he went to New York City to become a cop, one of New York's Finest. The NYPD. He did well, and advanced to detective. But he grew to hate it, and in last year's Christmas card he told me that he was packing up his wife and two kids and moving to Grand Rapids to sell life insurance and live without fear. It made sense to me.

Five dollars and twenty five cents later the Aetna secretary said she would transfer my call to his office.

The phone clicked as he picked it up. "Good morning, this is Mr. Adams, can I help you?"

I was excited; it'd been a long time since we'd seen each other. We were close friends in college. Unfortunately our communication had dwindled down to little more than season's greeting cards.

"Matt, how the hell are you? This is Charlie!"

"What? Is this Dr. Charles Davids?"

"The very same. How the hell are you?" I asked.

"Superb."

We filled each other in on the news. He and his family were nicely settled in, his kids liked their new school, his insurance business was growing nicely and he didn't miss the NYPD at all.

Then I told him the real reason I'd called. He stopped kidding around. As I told him the whole story of Sal and his gang, he rarely interrupted me, and only for clarification. His words were clipped and efficient. His interrogating skills were obvious. I told him the whole thing from the beginning, as if I was reading it from the notes safely tucked in the vault. I told him about the way they found me, the way they let themselves into my apartment, the bug on the phone, the way we rendezvous with the van. About the house in Springfield, the money in the mail, the poor lady from a few days ago, the shotgun.

"Matt, what should I do? Matt, please, please tell me what the hell I should do about this mess?"

"Call me back in a few days. I'll make some calls about this and do some thinking. But for the time being, keep playing the good little boy. Quiet, polite, cooperative. OK?"

"OK, Matt, thanks and I'll call you."

"Take it easy Charlie. Speak to you soon."

I hung up. The operator called back and wanted another fourteen dollars. It took a long time to feed in all those quarters.

I went back to my table in the restaurant, had a sip of cold coffee, a bite of stale danish, got up, paid my bill and left.

I felt better having spoken to Matt about it. If anybody could help me, he could. He'd been through a lot of hard knocks, growing up, in the army, as a cop. He'd had his share of scrapes with death. He had great intuition. He could size up a situation. He had confidence in himself. He knew what he was and what his limitations were. They probably kept him alive in Vietnam and in New York. He wasn't big, but he was strong and fast. In the service he'd been a MP for a while and it baffled me how a smallish guy, who'd rather be reading Jung or Freud, could quell an army base barroom brawl.

He explained, "Charlie, when I walk in there holding my .45 I'm the biggest man in the room."

We used to live in the same dorm in college. He had graduated from the college of hard knocks and I had just gotten out of high school. We horsed around, I helped him with chemistry and he taught me about Heineken Dark and Glenlivet Scotch. We both grew beards together, and vowed that the first guy to shave would owe the other a six-pack of premium beer. I had an Abe Lincoln beard before I shaved for medical school interviews and I dutifully paid up. I meant to ask if he'd had to shave to fit the clean-cut insurance salesman image, but I'd forgotten.

I went to Radio Shack and looked at their burglar alarms. The salesman wasn't much help. He only wanted to sell me a home computer. I finally decided on a unit called Perim-A-Tron. It consisted of a bunch of little wireless transmitters that get mounted on all the doors and windows you want to protect. If a transmitter is tripped it signals a console unit that looks like a big clock radio, and horns start going off all over the place. The console has a little computer in it and you can set a delay so you can get in the house, punch in your secret magic number and turn it off before the horns blow.

I spent the rest of the afternoon wiring up my apartment with the alarm, drinking Genny Cream Ale, thinking about Matt, and about my upcoming date with Patty. I tested it many times with just the test lamp. Just once with the horn. It was loud. For $250.00 it better be loud.

I borrowed a canoe from a friend, picked up Patty after work. It was a beautiful early summer eve with a sweet smell in the air. We drove to the Goose Pond boat ramp, unloaded the canoe, put in my knapsack and the meal I packed. We put on our life jackets and started out, going east along the northern shore, which was quite rocky and had a strip of small cottages along the shore. Then it became just forest with a lot of mountain laurel growing thickly right up to the water's edge. I had not been on this lake before but had heard that it was lovely, and one of the few in the county that was not fully encircled by summer cottages. I also heard that at the eastern end there was a channel that would bring you to another lake, smaller, called Upper Goose Pond, said to be undeveloped and serene. It had a small island, and that's where I planned to picnic with Patty.

As we paddled along, Patty was talking about acid rain and how it wiped out a lot of the aquatic life in the Adirondacks. So far it hadn't affected the Berkshire watershed much, but in time it was bound to. The Housatonic River, which runs through the whole county, is thickly polluted, she explained, especially from Pittsfield south. She said that the General Electric factories had dumped chemicals including polychlorinated biphenyls into the river for decades. Those chemicals stay in the riverbed and don't break down at all. The girl knew her chemistry.

"The Hudson River has PCBs in it, too. Also from the GE plant. And if that's not enough, there's a concrete manufacturing plant on the river, in the town of Hudson, that's planning to quadruple its size. They want to build a thousand foot chimney that'll spew all kinds of ash and particles into the upper air streams that'll affect people for hundreds of miles."

I was impressed. I tend to focus on the health of the person in front of me. She's concerned with a much bigger picture – the eco-environmental impact of man's nuclear and chemical mishaps upon the population at large, now and for decades into the future. She's committed to it, she writes letters to congressmen and everything.

Being a weeknight, the lake was not very busy, and as we paddled along we saw only a few fishermen in boats, and one motorboat pulling a skier. Pretty early yet for waterskiing. The water must have been cold, it was not really swimming weather yet. It took a half hour or so to get to the channel and it wasn't hard to find. It was maybe two hundred yards long and heavily forested, and in the evening light it was fairly dark and mysterious as it wound sinuously along. And then the channel opened up to the next pond, a beautiful hundred-acre pond surrounded by woods, and farther in the distance, low mountains. It was like entering Brigadoon.

We paddled to the small rocky island, clambered out and stretched. I set our life jackets at the base of a boulder that would be our backrest. I retrieved my knapsack. First I took out two wine glasses that I had packed in empty tennis ball cans to keep from crushing. Then I took out a nice half loaf of French bread from Guido's market that I had also packed in a tennis ball can to keep from crushing. Then a bottle of Chardonnay from Mr. Kelly's. Then I unwrapped a little rotisserie chicken with a fragrant herb coating. I opened a small can of eggplant campanata, a small container of tabouleh. We had a little feast on that little island. I still had dessert hidden in the knapsack. Twinkies.

I enjoyed watching the amusement in Patty's eyes as I brought out each item.

"I want to ask you some questions, Charlie," she said as I was stuffing my face.

"OK."

"If you were stranded on a desert island, which ten record albums would you want to have with you?"

"That's easy. Any ten Beach Boys albums," I replied.

"No, really. Ten different artists."

"Is there electricity on this desert island?"

"Make believe there is."

"Is this a sandy desert island with the wind blowing around?"

"Yes."

"Wouldn't it be better to have a tape player to keep the sand out?"

"Make believe there is a dust cover on the turntable."

"OK. Are you with me on this island?"

"That depends on what albums you pick."

"OK. I'll make believe you're with me on my make-believe desert island with make-believe electricity. Would it be like this little island we are on now?"

"Oh, no. Much bigger. Less rocky. More tropical. Warm all year. Palm trees."

"Is this a desert island like Aruba, with hotels and casinos?"

"No. It is a Robinson Crusoe island."

"Will you be my Friday?"

"Depends. What music?"

"OK. Have to have a Carole King album. *Tapestry*. Crosby, Stills, Nash and Young, *Déjà Vu;* Santana, *Abraxis*. Good driving music."

"You won't be driving anywhere. There's no car on this island."

"Can't I make believe?"

"Sure. What else?"

"Something by Janis Joplin. Either *Big Brother and the Holding Company* or *Pearl*. Something classical like the Brandenburg Concertos or Vivaldi's Four Seasons. Or Beethoven's Moonlight Sonata. Gotta have a Beatle's album. *Abbey Road*. Maybe a Peter Paul and Mary record. Jackson Brown, *The Pretender*. Simon and Garfunkel's *Bridge over Troubled Water*."

"I think you're over ten."

"There's one more I have to have."

"What's that?"

"The sound track to *South Pacific*."

"Do you mean the musical? Because you're on a desert island?"

"No, because it is such a wonderful show, it has such great music."

"I guess I don't know it so well."

"One of the songs, called 'Some Enchanted Evening,' has to be one of the most beautiful songs ever. We'll have to find a VCR recording of it and watch it some cold winter's night."

While we were having this discussion we were eating. The chicken was delicious and moist, and the pieces easily pulled apart. The wine was good. Patty was nice. The sun was starting to go down and the oranges and pinks began to light up the clouds on the horizon. It started to get a little cool, and Patty put on my sweatshirt. I pulled the Twinkies out of the knapsack and gave her one. She looked at me with a funny smile.

"I would have expected something a little classier."

"I think Twinkies are classy. They're delicious. Don't you think they're delicious?"

I leaned my head back against the rock behind us and watched the colors. Patty leaned against me. Before I knew it my eyes were closed and I was half asleep. The wine did it. A little while later I felt Patty move against me and felt her kiss the side of my forehead.

"C'mon. We should get going. It's getting dark. This was fun."

After we loaded up the canoe, I said, "Excuse me for a minute. I'll be right back," and I turned and began picking my way through the rocks and brush to the other side of the island.

I hadn't gone six feet before Patty said, "Gotta take a leak?"

I turned to look at her, a little embarrassed, and nodded.

"Yeah," I said. She had a big grin on. I turned again and began walking away.

Another six feet later Patty said, "If you shake it more'n twice you're playing with it!"

I stopped. I turned around, shaking my head, my hands on my hips. We looked at each other, she was grinning mischievously.

"Remember, I grew up with brothers," she said.

We packed up and got in the canoe. It was a little hard to find the channel in the oncoming darkness. I had a big three-cell flashlight and we found the channel. We paddled through. She could pull a pretty good stroke. I could feel the canoe give a little surge with each of her paddle strokes. The girl had some shoulder.

"So, how did I do? Would you join me on this island with this music?"

"I might. I just might," she responded quietly.

We paddled along for a few minutes. Then Patty said, "Books."

"What books?" I asked.

"What ten books would you want if you were stranded on a desert island?"

We both started laughing.

"Is this the same island as before, without the hotels and casinos?" I asked.

"Patty, why are you asking me these questions?" I asked quietly, without annoyance in the tone of my voice.

"I don't know. It helps me get to know you better."

We talked about books all the way as we paddled in the almost dark back to the car. She, too, loved Steinbeck, especially *East of Eden*. She also loved *To Kill a Mockingbird*, liked English mysteries, took a Chaucer course in college, and we both disliked Kurt Vonnegut. I would need to bring Sir Alexander Cope's *The Early Diagnosis of the Acute Abdomen*, one of my favorite medical books.

By the time we got back to the car it was past dark. The moon was coming up so you could still see where you were going. We put the canoe on top of the car and lashed it down. I threw the paddles and gear in the back.

I drove Patty home. She invited me in. I really wanted the evening to continue but I was pooped after the previous night's activities. I begged off. I had to be in the ER at eight in the morning and it was now almost nine-thirty at night. I made sure I apologized enough to Patty that I really needed to get going.

CHAPTER 11

At noon I called Matt from work. I didn't think Sal would be tapping the hospital phones. What did I know? The WATS line was a valuable unwritten fringe benefit of my employment. It stands for Wide Area Telephone Service. Big businesses had them if they made lots of long distance outgoing calls. They paid a pretty hefty flat rate and could make all the long distance calls they wanted. Of course, it was supposed to be for business and not personal use. Right.

I called Matt and he picked up on the second ring. He was his usual jovial self. I was eager to hear his perfect solution to my dilemma. He had to have one. Because if he didn't, no one would, and I'd be stuck.

"Hello," he said.

"Hi, it's Charlie, what can you tell me?"

"Well, first I went to the university library and tried to look up some things on microfiche, but it was too general and wasn't very helpful. Then I called one of my old associates on the NYPD and discussed it with him. He made some calls to the Springfield Police and to the FBI office in the Springfield Federal Building. He was careful not to tell them too much, so he wouldn't pique their interest and suggest something was up. We have to keep them out of this Charlie--the police. They would not be able to properly and safely help you. It's not the kind of situation they're good at."

I listened attentively.

"So, Charlie, here's what I found out. As you know, there are families of organized crime, and branches of families of organized

85

crime all over the place. Everybody knows there's a lot in New York. There's also a lot where you are, in New England. In New England it's centered in Providence, Rhode Island, run by the Patriarca family. But that's just the center of it, they're in all the big cities, including Springfield. In Springfield, I found out, they're involved in a lot of the usual stuff. You ready for the list?"

"Sure."

"Bootleg, black market, stuff that fell off the truck. Trucking and teamsters. Extortion for protection, payoffs, loan sharking, gambling, money laundering, some drugs and prostitution, but not a lot."

"Anyway, as you have unfortunately found out, they have needs for medical services. People get injured in those lines of work and sometimes they want to keep it quiet. As you know, if someone comes to your ER shot or beat up, you've got to report it. If someone comes in with gonorrhea, you know the Board of Health will get on the case and track down all the contacts and all that stuff they wouldn't want to be bothered with. If someone welches on a loan and they break his leg or his thumb, they don't want the guy to be questioned about how it happened; stuff like that. Probably they had a doc who was connected. You're not."

"Yeah, but why me? Why me over in the Berkshires. Why not someone closer?"

"Good question. I was asking myself that one, too. They probably did have someone closer. I tried checking obituaries on the microfiche but that was too time consuming. I called the Hampden County District Medical Society to ask about any local doctors passing away. There were some, but how could I tell who might've been the one? It's irrelevant, anyway. That's old history; we don't want you to be history.

"So, whoever they had doing their medical care was no longer available, for whatever reason. They needed someone new, they had knowledge of you as you explained, and you were obviously their easiest, most convenient choice."

"How could I be convenient if I'm an hour, an hour and a half away?"

"You have to realize, Charlie, that these guys are not busy people. They don't have stuffed appointment books. They don't put in long tedious days in the office. Having to go for a drive is not a big deal, it's not an imposition for them. Hopefully they will develop someone else more conveniently located. A doctor with local contacts who could bend some rules, get some people hospital care. But then, as you described, with that well-equipped basement apartment they take you to, maybe not."

"Do you think they'll ever let me go?"

"Maybe. If they develop someone else more convenient."

"Would they have to silence me if they let me go? Kill me?"

"They'd probably threaten you heavily about keeping quiet, but it's not like you're their bookkeeper and privy to the ins and outs of their dirty business and could get them into trouble. Or, they might keep you and relocate you."

"I wouldn't want to do that. I like it here."

"I don't think they'd really care too much about what you'd like or wouldn't like, do you?"

"No. Why me?"

"Why is irrelevant. They've got you. You have the skills they need. You're abusable and exploitable. You're young, you're single. You're not a prominent person in the community. You're convenient as hell for them. You're at work three or four times a week, and when you're off, you're off. You aren't tied to making rounds every day at the hospital. You're available."

"Remember, you're a convenience to them. They want you for what you can do for them. They'll look out for you to a reasonable extent. They won't bond with you. You, yourself, don't matter to them. Only the convenience of the skills you provide. They'd kill you in a minute if they decided that was the thing to do. No, not in a minute, they don't think that long; five seconds."

"So what do I do?" I asked despondently, still hoping for the magic answer.

"Don't make trouble," Matt said. "It's their game and they didn't even deal you in. You haven't got a card. To them, your rights are immaterial; they don't exist. You simply suit their needs. They have to be very cautious, taking in a doc from the outside. They must've gone through some trouble to check you out..."

"That's what he said," I confirmed.

"Don't get too impressed with yourself now. They went through a lot of trouble to check you out, bug your place, search it. Don't underestimate them. Don't trifle with them. They're probably having you watched, at least part of the time. So be careful. Don't do anything you don't want them to see."

"Like what?"

"Like going to the safe deposit vault the day after anything happens. Don't go putting your diary in there the day after each case you go on. It's suspicious. They can probably get in there easier than you can, anyway."

"Aw, come on!"

"I have four ideas and the first two aren't very good. The first is to take some of those C-notes they've been sending you and go find a good, New York criminal lawyer who knows about the Mob. Tell him you represent somebody in a bind. Use a pseudonym. Tell him the story. I would give you names, but it's better with no connection back home."

"That's a good idea," I said.

"He probably won't be able to tell you anything useful. You know what my general opinion of lawyers is anyway. But it might be worth a try."

"OK, I'll try it. What's number two?"

"If you can't beat them, join them, if you don't find it ethically unacceptable."

I thought about it for about two seconds and said, quietly, "I don't think I can do that." Actually, I'd almost rather work for Sal than for some of the Health Maintenance Organizations that interviewed me.

"I didn't think so, but if push comes to shove, you might remember it as an option," Matt said.

"OK, I will. What about the good ideas, number three and four?"

"Three is to hope for the best, and four is to prepare for the worst. Tell Sal that you plan to keep being a good little boy and cooperate and not make trouble, that you respectfully would rather not be involved in this sort of business, and as soon as your services are no longer needed you would appreciate being let off the hook. That's the best you could hope for."

"The worst that could happen is that they kill you," he added.

"C'mon, Matt, you said that before. You don't know Sal, he isn't gonna kill me."

"Listen, shit head, you don't know Sal, either. In fact, you don't know anything. That's why you called me, remember? You're playing hardball, not tiddly winks. You're in a serious, potentially deadly situation. Do you realize that? This isn't a TV program, you know. You better get that through your head!"

"So what should I do?" (In college I could always count on Matt to kick me in the ass and set me straight when I needed it. He'd say, 'I'm your buddy, if I won't do it, who will?')

"First, get a will."

I choked.

"If there's anything you own that you care about, arrange for it to go where you want it."

"Next, I have to ask you a vital question. Could you kill someone? To avoid being killed?'

I thought about that for a second. 'I guess so, if I had to."

"You're dead," Matt said.

"What?"

"You're dead. What do you mean, 'I think so'? Do you wanna survive this thing? Do you wanna die next month, or when you're an old man? Charlie, you may find yourself in a situation where you don't have time to get metaphysical and decide *if you had to* or not. You may have to act in a second. And the threat to you may just be intuitive. They're not gonna post an announcement beforehand, y'know.

"Charlie, if you wanna survive, you must decide *now* that you will kill if it gets to that point. And be resolved and committed to that decision. So you can act, when the time comes, and act fast."

All I could say was, "Shit."

"Do you have a gun license?"

"What?"

"Do you have a handgun permit?"

"No."

"Go to the chief of police of your town. Tell him you want to apply for a handgun permit for target practice and personal protection. Tell him you're a doctor, you work in an ER, and bad ass people come in wanting drugs all the time who get mad at you because you won't give them any. Tell him that you've been getting some nuisance phone calls. Tell him that as a physician you do keep some emergency-type drugs and syringes around, have prescription blanks and other medical instruments of interest to addicts and pushers, and that's where your interest in personal protection comes from. When you get the permit, go to a sporting goods store in a town where they don't know you, and order a Smith and Wesson Model 459. Don't get talked into anything else. It's expensive, but you're a rich doctor now and can afford it."

"What is it?"

"It's a lightweight alloy semiautomatic pistol in 9 mm caliber."

"What's so special about it?"

"It's a fine weapon. Made with precision. Never jams. Very powerful. And it holds fourteen rounds."

"Fourteen? What do I need a machine gun like that for?" I asked with agitation.

"Well, if you want to be sporting, just put one or two bullets in it. Really, Charlie, wake up, get real. We're trying to maximize everything we can in your favor, and firepower is real important. Take it from me, I've been there, when you need more ammo, you really need it. What you may lack in accuracy you can make up for with quantity."

"OK. I'm sorry. You're right," I said.

"When you get the pistol, get a good holster and some targets and shells. Take it somewhere and shoot it. Get used to its noise and kick. At home, tape a penlight to the barrel. Look at a doorknob or something, close your eyes, and then point the pistol where you think the doorknob is. Open your eyes and see how close the penlight is shining. Practice it till you're good at it. Remember, you won't have to shoot far. Aim for the biggest part of the guy, and keep firing until you're sure he's nonfunctional. OK?"

"OK."

"Charlie, good luck to you. I can't leave my family and my job to help you. And there's really nothing else I could do. Take care."

"Thanks, Matt, I will." I paused, wanting to say something else, but I didn't know what. I was on the verge of tears.

"Goodbye."

I hung up and stared at the phone. There were patients to see.

CHAPTER 12

So the little old man had finished dying. It was his time. But could we just let him go? Oh, no. His wife made the mistake of calling 911 instead of the funeral home, so the EMTs, as required, charged in, did CPR, crushed his ribs like pretzel sticks, brought him to me in the ER where we had to go through the obligatory arrhythmia protocol with IV drugs, electric cardioversion and defibrillation, knowing that it was futile, and that if we revived him he would not be happy with us.

After a respectable twenty-minute attempt at resuscitation, I "called the code" and thanked everybody for their efforts. The nurses pulled out all the tubes and things and cleaned him up. Then they left and called the guy from the morgue to come get him. I was alone with him in the curtain-enclosed part of the room. I took out of my pocket a little card printed with a prayer, which I began to read quietly.

Will came in. "What are you doing?"

"I'm reading the Kaddish."

"What's the Kaddish?"

"It's the Jewish prayer for the dead."

"Why are you saying it?"

"Because he's dead, stupid. I don't have anything else to do for him."

"I don't think he's Jewish."

"Tough. It's the only one I know."

"Do you think it does anything?"

"How the hell do I know? Couldn't do any less for him than the CPR did. Don't you have anything useful you could be doing?"

"Is that Yiddish?"

"No, you moron, it's Hebrew. You don't pray in Yiddish. Make like a tree and leave."

"Do you always do this after a code?"

"No." *Only if I feel like it and I get around to it.* "Go take a long walk on a short pier."

"I didn't know you were religious."

"I'm not. Make like a hockey player and get the puck out of here."

Finally he left and I started the Kaddish from the beginning again. It only takes two minutes.

One night when I was a brand-new intern I got paged to a floor and a nurse said I needed to go pronounce a patient. That meant to declare him dead. I didn't know anything about this, so I called my senior resident, who told me what to do. I went up the stairs to 5-West where they usually had the people from nursing homes who were too sick to stay there. I went to the patient, shone my flashlight in his eyes, and saw that the pupils were fixed and dilated. I held my stethoscope to his mouth and nose and heard no breath sounds. I squeezed a fingernail hard, and then a nipple (he told me to do this), and there was no response to deep pain. There were no reflexes at the knee or elbow. I went out to the nurses' station and wrote all this down in the chart, included the time, and signed my full name. Done. I sat there for a minute. Something was missing. Then I went back to the patient's bedside and sat down on the edge of the bed. I held his hand. I said the Kaddish from memory in my sloppy and awkward Hebrew. It wasn't a big deal. It was the least I could do to say Kaddish for a stranger when he died. I didn't know if other people did this, and they might think I was corny, so I tried to do it when no one was around.

Will came back later to start in on me again.

"I didn't know you were religious."

"I'm not. I don't even go to temple."

"Do you believe in God?"

I was annoyed. "I don't know, how am I supposed to know? Go away."

"What do you mean, 'How am I supposed to know'? What kind of answer is that? Either you do or you don't."

"Well, I do and I don't."

"You can't say that. It makes no sense."

"I'm getting used to not making sense."

"I can't figure you out."

"I can't figure me out, either. I gave up trying a while ago. Make like a shepherd and get the flock out of here."

"Do you believe in God or not?"

"Who the hell knows? I'd like there to be a God. I've chosen to live my life as if there is."

I shook my head and walked over to the doctors' room and sat down at the desk. Will followed me. He sat down on the couch.

"Hey, Will, you were in Vietnam, right?" Maybe he could give me some information I needed.

"Yeah, for eleven months and nine days."

"If you don't mind my asking, what did you do there?"

"I don't mind. I was with the quartermasters. I was on a base and we supplied stuff, and fixed equipment."

"How far from the front line were you?"

"Hard to say where the front lines were, they were moving around all the time. At least five miles anyway. We could hear shelling sometimes."

"What went on at the base?"

"Everything. There was a big helicopter section, they were always coming in for repairs. And to replace their gun barrels."

"What was with the barrels?"

"Well, every helicopter had a door-mounted machine gun. Those things would be fired almost constantly sometimes and they'd heat up, burn out, and need to be replaced."

"What else went on at your base?"

"Well, they warehoused a lot of supplies; it was a staging area. There were lots of infantry recon units that would come in, get geared up and choppered out. There were hundreds of trucks and Jeeps and tank trucks coming and going and needing servicing."

"Were you involved in any nasty stuff?"

"No, I wasn't out in the jungle, just on base. We had to patrol the perimeter, but it was pretty secure. I didn't see combat."

"How familiar were you with the way medics took care of injuries in the field?"

"Pretty familiar. Corpsmen. We called them corpsmen, not medics. I was interested in medicine even back then and I hung out with some guys who were corpsmen. They had a small medical unit, but any halfway serious injuries were taken to MASH units."

"What would a corpsmen do in the field if a soldier got shot?"

"Well, you know, the usual. Airway, breathing, circulation. Advanced trauma life support." I had taken this grueling course at UMass Medical Center the year before, which is where I learned to do the tracheotomy, put in chest tubes, do arterial and venous cut downs on anesthetized dogs. But that was in a modern facility, not on the ground in the jungle. "They'd stabilize them the best they could and they'd MEDEVAC them out."

"What's MEDEVAC?"

"A helicopter."

"You could radio for a helicopter to pick up a wounded guy?"

"Yeah."

"What about your location? You could guide a helicopter to a clearing? How long would that take?"

"Hours. If the weather was bad, days. If you were in a place that was safe enough and the Viet Cong were not all over the place."

"What if they were? What would you do for the poor guy while you were waiting for the pick up?"

"Give him lots of morphine. Give him IV fluids. They usually carried lactated Ringer's solution, but how many liters of that can you carry? They usually had some volume expander they could give, like IV serum albumin. They'd give millions of units of Penicillin IM."

"Would they do anything for the wound?"

"Hell, no. Other than control the bleeding, clean it up and try a primary closure. You know you can't probe for a bullet, it hits some hard tissue or bone and it could skittle around in any direction, you'd never find it without an X-ray."

I hadn't dealt with any bullet wounds for Sal. Yet.

"What if you had a penetrating abdominal wound, like from a bayonet? I don't suppose you could do peritoneal lavage."

"Not much point in doing that unless you have an OR to go to in ten minutes. Just MEDEVAC him out. Give Penicillin and MEDEVAC him out."

"What about a sucking chest wound?"

"Put in a chest tube and MEDEVAC him out."

"What if you couldn't get him out for a few days?"

"More morphine, more penicillin, and pray."

"See!" I said. "You're religious, too."

"There are no atheists in foxholes."

"Would you try doing anything operative in the jungle."

"Other that what we talked about, no. Infection happens so fast in the jungle. You gotta get them out."

"If you thought someone had a subdural hematoma on the brain, would you innovate a way to do a burr hole? What if you weren't in a jungle with helicopters? What if you were the doc at an Antarctic Research Station and there'd be no plane for months? Would you try it then?"

"Try what, a burr hole? Why are you asking all these questions, Charlie?"

"What if you were a medic on a big nuclear sub sitting on the continental shelf with all your missiles for three months and you had to deal with all the trauma and illness of 150 men with no MEDEVAC to bail you out? What if someone broke a bone, an arm or a leg or an ankle?"

"You would just do the usual. Like we do here. Without the X-ray. Splint it."

I wasn't really getting the answers I was hoping for, to help me with my work for Sal. In the ER I had all kinds of backup. In Vietnam they had MEDEVAC. Sal did not give me those options.

Later that shift a really funny thing happened. It was hard to take seriously. I know I'm supposed to comfort the afflicted and all that, but I couldn't keep a straight face. I wished Will was there because with his steely sarcasm and wit, his remarks would have been hysterical.

The ambulance called in to say they were en route with two teenage girls. There was another ambulance coming with two more. The tone of voice of the EMT was unusually relaxed and cheerful. All four were being brought in from the Roller Rink on Housatonic Street in Lee, and they had been in an altercation. All were stable.

As it turns out these four girls were trying to learn how to be tough, but they weren't very good at it, and they tried to duke it out and got all upset and started hyperventilating.

It seems there were two pairs of friends, and each pair didn't like the other pair. So here they are at the roller rink. There had been some popular movies in the theaters lately about roller derby queens, and the pastime was getting popular again. While they were skating around there must have been some words exchanged. One of one pair said something to one of the other pair that she chose to take as an insult, then the second one shoved the first one, then the friends joined in slapping and smacking and giving each other puppy punches, and rolling around on the hardwood floor in their roller skates with spit and swear words flying in an otherwise nice sleepy little New England mill town on a Friday night.

The EMTs rolled in with big grins on their faces, shaking their heads, and the first girl was a skinny little teenaged girl on a stretcher, sitting up, whimpering with one cold pack against a shiner on her right eye, and another cold pack on her left elbow.

The second stretcher had a bigger, beefy girl, twice the size of the first, hyperventilating with a small brown paper bag held over her mouth and nose, which was alternately expanding and contracting rapidly as she hyperventilated into it.

The third girl rolled in with a cold pack on her nose, and there was blood on the front of her sweatshirt. As this third girl was rolled past the cubicle of the first girl, the first girl shouted, "You fuckin' bitch, you broke my fuckin' nose!" and flipped her the finger.

At that we couldn't keep it together anymore and all of us, the EMTs, the nurses, me, respiratory therapy techs who had all gathered in the ER for the show burst out laughing, and the more we laughed, the harder we laughed, some of us bent over double. Amy squeaked out between guffaws that she thought she'd wet her pants, it was hard to breathe and I knew we were gonna get into trouble for this, and I could just see myself in the hospital president's office tomorrow saying, "I know it wasn't professional to laugh like that but it was just so funny!" At that point they rolled in the fourth girl, who had a big fat swollen bloody lip, and we all looked at her and started laughing all over again. This fourth girl looked at us indignantly and said, "What's so funny?" and one of the EMTs said, "You all are," and we continued shrieking. One by one each of the girls started laughing with us, and in a minute people from way down the hall were running to the ER to see what all the noise was about.

I hadn't laughed that hard in years. When we all finally settled down, we were exhausted; our sides hurt; faces were wet with tears of laughter; I was sweaty. The atmosphere was all different; the ice was broken and the girls who had been so snotty and arrogant were no longer taking themselves so seriously and were relaxed, giggling despite their bloody noses. It was a transformation like you'd see on a TV sitcom.

CHAPTER 13

Just before I finished my shift at eight p.m., I called Patty to ask if she wanted to get together for a drink or something. Hopefully something. She wasn't feeling well but wanted a rain check. I offered to make a house call, but she said no, my rates were too damn high.

I left work and drove home. I was looking through the mail when a loud, blaring noise startled me and rattled the apartment. I'd tripped the alarm, and the sixty-second delay was up. My neighbors were going to hate me.

I sipped my way through two bottles of Genny Cream Ale and unwound with my piano, trying to play along with some Beatle tunes on the record player. *Rocky Raccoon* isn't a very funny song when you're half drunk, thinking about a dying patient, and a hood who's putting the screws to you.

The next day, Sunday, I worked the eight a.m. to eight p.m. shift. I called Berkshire Medical Center to find out how the kid who I had trached was doing. "Not much change," the intern said. "His lungs are clearing, probably reabsorbing all the blood he inhaled. Nice job on the trach, sir." I thanked him. So far, I'd saved a vegetable.

In the afternoon they brought in a kid from one of the many local summer camps. The camp nurse sent him in with one of the counselors. She thought he had a strep throat and wanted a throat culture and a prescription for Penicillin.

The kid was adorable. He was nine years old. He had brassy brown hair, hazel eyes, cinnamon colored freckles on peach pink cheeks. He wore denim shorts and a cute colorful striped T-shirt. He was a skinny little thing. Fragile looking. His shoulders looked eight inches apart. I introduced myself. We spoke. He gave very quiet one-word answers and avoided eye contact. He did not look happy. He did not look sick. His throat was not that red. His glands were not swollen. His eardrums looked normal. He didn't have a cough or a runny nose. His temperature was normal. His lungs sounded clear and his heart sounds were normal.

I hoisted myself onto the stretcher and sat right next to him. I took an alcohol prep pad out of my pocket and tore open the wrapper. He was watching me. I wiped off the little rubber ear cushions on my stethoscope. I threw the pad and wrapper into the garbage, but I missed. I could feel him giggling next to me. I turned to him and slowly put the earpiece of the stethoscope in his ears. He let me. I held the stethoscope diaphragm in front of my mouth like a microphone. I looked at him.

"Am I coming in loud and clear?" I whispered.

He grinned and nodded his head vigorously.

"Do I have your attention?" He nodded.

"What camp are you at?" I asked.

"Mohawk," he said.

I recoiled. "You don't have to shout!" He giggled again.

"Where's home?" I asked.

"New Jersey," he said.

"How's camp?" I whispered.

He paused. "OK."

"How many more weeks of camp do you have left?"

He held up two fingers. Poor kid. Two weeks is a long time when you're nine years old and homesick.

"You like camp?" I whispered with the stethoscope. He shrugged.

"What do you like, swimming? Softball? Arts and crafts?"

"Arts and crafts," he said softly.

"You miss home?"

He nodded slowly, looking at me. He looked funny with this big stethoscope on his little head.

"You know what?" I asked. He shrugged.

"You're supposed to say 'what?'"

"What?"

"You can do more than one thing at a time." He nodded. Two nurses were standing side by side across the hall from the cubicle, watching us, grinning at us. "You can walk and eat an ice cream at the same time. You can do arts and crafts and talk to your friends at the same time. You can have a sore throat and fool around with your doctor at the same time, right?" He nodded.

"You can miss home and still go swimming. You can miss home and still enjoy arts and crafts. Are you trying hard to not miss home?"

He nodded.

"Don't. Don't try hard to not miss home. It doesn't work. It's OK to miss home. It's fine to miss home. What happens if you try not to laugh? You laugh harder, right? The kid next to you in school says something funny and you start laughing, but you better stop or you'll get in trouble with the teacher, right? It doesn't work. In fact, it works in reverse. Know what I mean? You try to not laugh and you laugh more. You try not to miss home so you miss it more. It's backwards. Just do two things at once. You can miss home and you can laugh with your friends. You can miss home and have fun at camp. You can do two things at once. Right?" He nodded. "You'll try?" He nodded. "You promise?" He nodded. All this, whispering into the stethoscope.

"OK." I got down off the stretcher. "Can I have my stethoscope back?"

"No," this little kid said, grinning.

"Aw, come on, I have to work for hours yet," I pleaded. He handed it to me, grinning. I picked him off the stretcher and eased him to the floor. He weighed nothing. I walked him to his counselor in the waiting room and said goodbye. I wanted to hug him. What a cute kid.

I walked back to the nurses' station to finish my paperwork. One of the nurses came up and asked, "What were you two talking about?"

"I was teaching him how to pick up chicks," I answered.

The rest of the shift was uneventful. Patty was feeling better and her mother had come by to visit.

I drove home. It was a nice summer evening. I went for a walk in the neighborhood. I wondered who I would see next, Patty or Sal. I wondered what the future had in store for me. I meandered home and went upstairs to my apartment.

I loved my apartment. I had the upstairs of a barn-red, old, wooden frame house. On the front porch were two doors, the left one was mine and opened to a small foyer and a flight of stairs up. At the top of the stairs was a landing, and right in front was the small second bedroom where I had my desk and books and stuff. Around the landing toward the front of the house was my bedroom. It was a nice room, with two big windows facing front, and one on the side. I had a full-size bed on a box spring and frame, no headboard or footboard. There was a dresser and a rocking chair. I had a calico print comforter on the bed. The night table had a lamp and a pile of books.

Past the small bedroom was the living room. There was a couch, an easy chair, my old stereo system, a bookcase of records, and a TV. This, of course, is the room where I first met Sal. The small spinet piano was tucked into a corner.

Beyond the living room were the bathroom and the kitchen. The kitchen was pretty sizeable, had lots of windows and a view of Tully Mountain. I had a pretty gaudy kitchen table and chairs I'd picked up cheap, years ago at a yard sale. There were art prints tacked up on the walls.

It was home. It was cozy. I liked it better when Patty was in it, and less when Sal was in it. I could smell his cigar smoke for days after he'd been here.

The next morning, Monday, I visited the Dalton chief of police. A very nice, portly, middle-aged man with salt and pepper gray hair. Very relaxed, he'd been a small-town cop for years. I'd met him four years ago when I first moved to Dalton and I needed a Firearms Identification card for my shotgun. I was in a much different mood then. Then, I was registering a sporting firearm, with visions of crisp, sun-filled autumn days in the fields, a brace of grouse falling with each pull of the trigger, landing directly in my oven, to brown succulently. But now I was there to ask for a license so that I could carry a concealed fourteen round lightweight alloy semiautomatic 9 mm pistol so I could blow away any goon who might cross my path. Not an idyllic sporting way to spend an autumn afternoon.

I was perspiring as I sat in his office. Knowing how tough Massachusetts is about gun laws, I expected difficulties and red tape. He was very sympathetic and had his perky, pretty clerk type up a certificate that would serve as an interim license until the laminated one came in from Boston. Then he fingerprinted me and had me sign in several different places.

With the certificate in hand, I went next door to the library. A beautiful old building it was, built with a donation from the ever-generous Crane family at the turn of the century. It had high ceilings with oaken beams, a beautiful hearth, and above it, a large framed watercolor of pink and purple peonies. The children's section had some adorable murals done by a local artist. There was also a large moose head named Charlie on the wall that had been shot by one of the Cranes on an Alaskan hunting trip around the turn of the century. Most surprising to me was that such a small, small-town library with limited space, and no doubt limited budget, could be so current and up-to-date, have so many best sellers, current textbooks, magazines, and so on. They also had a Boston phone book from which I copied down a long list of firearms dealers. I went home and almost began calling them, then I remembered the phone tap. I called from the luncheonette, one by one, until I found one that had a Smith & Wesson #459 in stock. There was a store in Lawrence, a Boston suburb, that had one. Sure, they'd put it aside for me. I told them I'd be there in four hours.

Then I called my old buddy Catherine. She used to live downstairs from me when she worked at Berkshire Medical Center as a pediatric nurse. She had married a nice guy named Barry, also an internist, and they had moved to Boston. Luckily she was home. I invited myself over for the night with the premise that I missed them, and that I needed a Chinese food fix.

"Sure, c'mon over, we'll be glad to have ya," was the answer that I expected, and the one that I got.

I went home, threw some things in a valise, and hit the road.

Three hours later, I was in the store in Lawrence. It was in a rundown neighborhood. I felt a little nervous as I entered the store.

"Hello, my name is Davids," I said to the salesman, "I called before and asked to have a Smith & Wesson set aside for me."

"Oh, yeah," the guy said, "I got it in the back." He went away through a door in the back of the store. He had a big beer belly, covered tightly by a white short-sleeved shirt cinched under his gut by a belt. His gray hair was combed straight back. He was smoking a Hav-A-Tampa cigar.

While I was waiting for him to come back, I looked around the store. It was your basic sporting goods store. Salt water fishing stuff. Lots of guns. Lots of knives; jackknives, sheath knives, throwing knives. Dartboards. There was one other guy in the store, looking at the knife counter. A young Hispanic man, chubby, in a tank top. Long black curly hair covered by a red bandana knotted in the back. A straggly beard. A homemade tattoo on the left deltoid. Blue jeans that looked like he'd once sat down in a puddle of crankcase oil. Leather belt studded with brass rivets, a Buck knife scabbard on one side, and the keeper for a trucker's wallet in the other. A foot-long length of chain drooped from the keeper to the leather wallet stuffed into the back pocket. Grungy.

So much like the buccaneers of old, I thought. Complete with unshorn locks, naked arms, scarf tied on the head, tattoo. Wide leather belt complete with sword and chains. All he needed was an earring. He probably had one on the other side.

The salesman came back carrying a small blue cardboard box. On the edge of it was a white label that said #459.

"That's a fine weapon," the man said with satisfaction as he set it in front of me on the counter. "You one of them survivalists?"

"What's that?"

"You one of them survivalists?"

"No, I mean, what's a survivalist?"

"You know, them guys that are stockpiling lots of food and guns and ammo and such, in case there's a nuclear war or somethin', you know, breakdown of civil order. Been selling most of my merchandise to them lately, y'know?"

Goddammit no, I'm not buying this in case of war, I'm buying it so I can survive peace.

"No, I'm not one of those," I answered, more seriously than I'd intended. "I don't wanna be around after the bomb goes off. I plan to drink a bottle of Jack Daniels and not worry about waking up with a hangover."

He chortled and probably thought I was funny. But I was much more serious than he might have thought.

He showed me the gun. It was a big, mean, ugly-looking bastard. Just looking at it gave me the creeps and made me want to behave. He showed me how to operate it, load it, clean it, clear it in the unlikely event that it jammed. He was a good salesman and he knew his merchandise. I asked him about a holster and he brought out a lined nylon "Slimline" model. I asked for some targets and shells. *What am I doing here?*

"Solid or hollow?"

"Huh?"

"Two kinds of 9 mm shells - solid point and hollow point."

"Whatsa difference?"

"Solid makes a nice hole, hollow makes hamburger. Solid chamber's easier, hollow more apt to jam."

"Solid."

I gave him the letter from the Dalton chief of police. I came with plenty of cash. I doubted Sal could trace my credit card, but why chance it?

I thought about bringing some of Sal's cash. But then I thought, if I'm really trying to keep my nose clean, why should I use dirty money?

He filled out the forms, took the money, and packaged things up. It was a lethal and evil-looking device. I stowed the package in the trunk of my Subaru and drove to meet my friends at Joyce Chen's Restaurant in Cambridge. A wonderful place.

It was great, as always, to see them. And to be at Joyce Chen's. As usual I burned out my mouth on Szechwan hot and sour soup at the beginning of the meal, and could taste little of the moo shu shrimp that I ordered afterward. It didn't matter. It was all great.

We went back to their apartment after dinner, and Barry and I stayed up late drinking beer and telling hospital stories. In the morning, they had to go and work for a living while I slept in. At nine I got up, showered and made coffee. I went out, locked their apartment securely, and cruised around Haymarket Square, looking for something for Patty.

I listened to a Julian Bream guitar tape twice while cruising westward on the Mass Pike. I got home to Dalton around six. I took my overnight bag and lethal bundle out of the trunk, emptied my mailbox and headed up the stairs. I was thumbing through the mail when I suddenly remembered the burglar alarm, and I raced to disarm it before it gave the neighborhood another migraine.

When I got back to the mail I found another envelope, without a return address, stuffed with hundred dollar bills wrapped in a blank sheet of typing paper.

The phone rang. I walked into the bedroom to answer it.

"Hello."

"Doc, where've you been? I've been calling you for two days now." It was Sal, and he was practically shouting. He didn't have his usual, lazy laconic drawl.

Be a good, polite little boy, Matt had said. "Oh, I'm sorry. I had a few days off from work and I went to Boston to visit some friends."

"You can't do that. I had some work for you to do. You can't just get up and go outta town like that!"

"I'm sorry, Sal, I didn't know. It won't happen again. Is there a way I can reach you to get my plans OK'd in the future?"

"No, Doc, you know I can't give you a phone number." The drawl was back.

He liked me again.

"How about if I keep a beeper with me all the time so you can always find me?"

"That's a good idea, Doc."

"Do you need me now?" I asked.

"No, it's all taken care of." Good. They could manage without me.

"Sal, I want to tell you something. I have every desire to cooperate with you and not make any trouble. I'm not interested in doing it for the money, and I'm not interested in doing it any longer than you insist that I do. If a time comes that you don't need me anymore, I would very much appreciate being let off the hook. Until then you can expect my cooperation. I just wanted to be straightforward and let you know how I feel about this whole thing."

"Thanks, Doc, that's very nice of you. Get yourself that beeper. I'll call you to get the number. Goodbye. I'll be in touch."

CHAPTER 14

I decided I would annoy Sal to death. I'd try to be so whiny and unpleasant and demanding that he would hurry to replace me. Whenever he calls next I'll run down to the cafeteria and have a big bowl of chili. I'll whine about how cold it is in the back of the van, can't they get some decent heat back here? "Don't drive so fast or turn so fast, you're making me carsick." Maybe I could make myself vomit in the van; that's an awful image.

I'd gripe about everything. Can't you get me some goddamn decent instruments? These disposable stamped steel instruments stink, the scissors I had in kindergarten were sharper than these. How the hell do you expect me to do nice work with these crappy instruments?

Most of my work for Sal was in the basement of that house in Springfield. The light was not very good. I could whine about that. How do you expect me to probe that laceration, I can't even see what I'm doing here, that light throws nothing but shadow. I might as well demand new instruments from him, like nice German Miltex Adson forceps, and Webster needle holders, and carbide serrated curved iris scissors. I might as well get a real good autoclave to sterilize it all in. Better yet, a Chemiclave. That might not be such a good idea; it could make a lot more work for me. It'll be me that has to stay and clean and bag the instruments and run the sterilizer and wait around until it cycles and then vent it. I couldn't see trusting one of the goons to turn off the autoclave and vent it when the buzzer goes off. "Hey, Vinnie, don't forget to vent the sterilizer when the buzzer goes off." "Right, Doc. I'll take care of it. Don't worry." The sterilizer would probably still be on the next time I was there, all the fluid steamed out of it, all the bags inside brown as toast, all the cutting edges dull as butter knives.

"Hey, Sal, you're gonna have to get me some textbooks. You can't expect me to keep all this in my head. Get me a *Harrison's Principles of Internal Medicine*, a PDR, and since you're bringing me all these junkies to detox, I ought to get a book on that.

"Hey, Sal, what do you think I am, an octopus? In the ER I have nurses to assist me and they're all better looking than you. I can't do all this by myself. You know I only have two hands. How many do you have? Put on a pair of gloves and get in here. Don't you know how to put on a pair of sterile gloves properly without contaminating them?" Maybe one day he'll bring in a guy with a big boil that needs to be lanced. I could whine, "Why do I have to make a three hour round trip just to see this joker with a boil to lance. How is this a criminal case? Don't you realize I have to be at work at eight a.m. tomorrow? How do you expect me to do all this traveling to take care of this joker and still get a decent night sleep? Why don't you just take these guys to any walk-in center or any of those new doc-in-a-box places that are popping up all over? I probably won't get home now until two or three in the morning."

I could just hear Sal, in his laconic drawl, say, "Gee, Doc, you could sleep in the van." Or, "Gee, Doc, those textbooks were real expensive." *Tell me about it.*

So, about the guy with the boil, I could say, "Hey, Sal, give this guy a bullet to bite while I open this sucker up." I could imagine him reaching back under his suit jacket and producing a big Colt .45 automatic, working the slide to rack a round out of the chamber and giving it to the guy to bite on. No, really, I'd numb up all around the perimeter of the boil, and then the top of it. Maybe I'd also inject some Xylocaine right into the middle of it to make it nice and tense so it would really spurt when I opened it. Like a custard-filled donut at Dunkin' Donuts. Except they smell really gross like overripe Stilton cheese. Maybe I could position Sal at the right spot to help me, and if I angled my incision right and gave a little squeeze, too, I could get it to squirt him and give him a shirt full. Oh, would that be fun.

Fun to think about. But I'd never do it.

CHAPTER 15

It was time to see what the story was with this gun. I had the day off; Patty was out of town. Good. I wouldn't want her to know what I was doing. We were liberals. Liberals don't do things like this. About gun control, someone once said: a liberal is a republican who didn't get mugged yet. But I was in an extenuating circumstance.

I took my box of recent purchases from its hiding place above a ceiling panel in my bedroom. I opened the blue plastic case and looked at the ugly black weapon lying there in the rust-inhibiting wrapping paper. It wasn't the familiar benign-looking little toy revolver Jack Webb used to carry. The gun had a smooth black finish. The grips were hard black plastic with slip-resistant, sharply cut checkering. The handle itself was long and thick, large enough to accept the huge magazine. The muzzle was an ominous gaping maw, so wide you could stick your finger in it. The gun's geometry was all angles and planes. No curves at all, this big, black, merciless killing machine. What was I doing with it?

I read through the owner's manual a few times. I was wearing running shorts, and put the holster on a belt and put it around my waist. I put the gun in the holster. No bullets, no magazine. I ran up and down the stairs a few times, but without pants with belt loops, the heavy gun flopped all over. I found some cut-off denim shorts and tried it again. Big difference. I threaded the holster on the belt a number of different ways without really finding one that was comfortable. The best way seemed to be just behind my right hip with the handle of the gun tucked against my ribs. I posed with it in the mirror. It would go well with my black stethoscope. To get used to it, I tried nonchalantly to go about my everyday routine.

I wore it all morning as I cleaned the breakfast dishes, drank coffee, read the paper, played the piano. When I sat at my desk to balance my checkbook, the muzzle of the gun hit the arm of the chair. As I went down, the gun didn't, and the holster yanked up my belt and the grip gouged my armpit.

I wanted to go out for a run with this thing on my hip, but I didn't want anyone to see it. I put on my biggest, bulkiest sweatshirt. It was much too warm out to wear a sweatshirt, but I did anyway. I took the gun's empty box and other accessories and hid them in case Sal came sneaking into my house while I was out. I went out the door and started jogging down the street toward Pine Grove Park. I kept reaching down with my right hand to make sure my sweatshirt was low enough to keep the gun fully covered. It was awkward to run with this two and half pound chunk of steel on my hip. With each step it would swing forward, then swing away, then slap back where it started. It was chafing me. As I pumped my arms running, I knocked it with my funny bone and it hurt like hell. From then on I ran swinging my arms wide but the grip was still trying to get me. I ran on with no sense of grace with this lopsided thing slapping around. What's it like to run with two breasts flopping around? They would be softer than this gun. They're not made of steel. A brassiere is like a holster.

I kept running with this thing, trying to get used to it. How much heavier would it be if it were loaded? How the hell do cops run with their belts full of guns, handcuffs, radios and other gear. I'll have to ask one next time I see one at work.

I circled around on High Street at the far side of the park. After another quarter mile I found I could adjust my pace to the movement of the gun and keep the beat with it so I didn't swing so wildly. That was pretty good, but it was only a jog. Then I sprinted, and the gun jiggled like crazy again. I hit my funny bone again and my wrist tingled. I did not like this at all. I circled around Curtis Avenue, heading home. I couldn't wait to take this evil thing off. Whenever a car passed me or I passed someone on the street, I was self-conscious and made sure the gun was hidden. I felt so awkward that I was sure it must be conspicuous. Maybe if I carried another gun on the other hip I'd feel more balanced and natural.

What if I tripped and fell and landed on this thing? That would hurt. What happens if EMTs are picking up a guy and they find he has a gun on him? Then when you get to the ER the police are there and everyone might wonder why this civilian was making believe he was Dirty Harry. "Did you know that when they brought in Charlie he had a gun on him?"

I slowed to a walk because my side was burning from the chafing. I tried to hold it through the sweatshirt to keep it off my skin, but it must've been very conspicuous looking to anyone who saw me.

When I got home I took the thing off and looked at my side. There was a big red patch with little peelings of skin like after a sunburn. I found some moleskin in the bathroom closet and stuck it on the raw spot.

I sat down at the kitchen table and looked at the gun. I passed it from hand to hand. I supposed I should shoot the damned thing. I looked around the house for something to shoot at. I got an empty Special K box from the trash. I took a full can of Campbell's tomato soup. I looked in the fridge. There was a cantaloupe. I grinned.

I vaguely remembered an old novel that I think was written by Frederick Forsyth. Was it *Day of the Jackal*? In the story, some mysterious assassin was hired to kill Charles de Gaulle. He secretly had a special rifle made for the job, and to test it he used poster paints to make a melon look like de Gaulle's head. Then he took it out in the woods and shot it from a great distance. He killed the melon. It exploded.

I put all these things in a duffel bag and drove to Anthony Road off North Street, to the Dalton Rod and Gun Club. The place was empty, as I'd hoped. I went to the range area and set the Special K box against the bottom of the big sandpile backstop. I inserted some bullets into the magazine, inserted the magazine in the slot in the handle and it clicked into place. Just like it said in the instruction book, I gripped the back of the slide in my left hand, pulled it back, released it, and the slide sprang harshly forward, pushing a live bullet into the chamber. It was ready to shoot. I looked at it. The hammer was back like a big open jaw waiting for me to twitch my finger so it could slam forward, hit the firing pin which would hit the primer which would detonate the gunpowder which would fire the bullet which would leave the barrel at about 1300 fps with about 350 foot pounds of energy to destroy, irreversibly, whatever it hits. In a millisecond.

I walked ten feet away, raised the gun in my outstretched arm, sighted across the sights down at the cereal box. I slowly increased finger pressure on the trigger till the gun went off with a huge roar, the gun jumped up and twisted slightly to the right, and my ears were ringing. I looked at the cereal box. It looked OK. It was not bleeding. It had a hole in the bottom middle. A big hole.

My ears were still ringing. I had to work that night, I needed to be able to use a stethoscope. I needed to be able to hear subtle heart and breath sounds. I needed some earplugs. I packed everything back up, threw it in the car. My feet were not making the right amount of noise on the gravel. I drove to O'Laughlin's Pharmacy and got some wax earplugs. While I was driving I felt the same rushing water sound in my ears I used to get after going to a rock concert. When was the last time I went to one, anyway? Years ago. I think it was Schaefer Stadium in Foxboro. It was Fleetwood Mac, the Eagles and Boz Scaggs. Yeah, I remembered that. It was a good time. Boz was the warm-up band. Great concert, but my ears were buzzing for a day.

I bought the earplugs and drove back to the shooting range. I was still the only one there. Good. I put out the cereal box and shot it a few more times. Now it was dead. The earplugs worked well. The gun was easier to shoot with two hands but I had to be careful my other hand didn't get in the way of the slide moving back after the shot. It moves back real fast and real hard and can hurt you.

I took out the cantaloupe and looked at it. I had bought it four or five days earlier. The blossom end was just getting a little soft. I smelled it. It was faintly fragrant. I looked at it. I put it back in the car. The cantaloupe did not deserve to die.

I set the Campbell's tomato soup can on the wooden support of the target rack. The can cost forty-four cents. The label had the familiar red on top and white on bottom with a gold seal in the middle like a belly button. This was going to be an experiment in hydrostatic force. I stepped six or eight feet away and sighted very carefully at the gold seal in the middle of the can and slowly increased pressure on the trigger until the gun went off.

When I finished cleaning the tomato soup off my eyeglasses and wiping it off my face and arms, I put the gun in the car and went searching for the can. I finally found it in the weeds, about ten feet behind the target area. There was a bullet hole near the gold circle. Both the top and bottom of the can were bulged out and rounded and the seam in the back of the can was split wide open. There was no second bullet hole. The bullet must have exited through the split seam. The impact of the bullet must have caused such a huge pressure wave of soup moving away from the bullet that the top and bottom of the can bulged out, the seam split, and the bullet passed through the open seam. That had to be fast. If the bullet goes about thirteen hundred feet per second, how long does it take to travel three inches through a soup can? And in that amount of time the top and bottom bulged out and the seam split even before the bullet exited. Amazing.

I pulled out the earplugs, packed up and went home. I brought the stuff into the kitchen. I looked at the gun. I got a sponge and wiped off a little more soup from it. Kinda like blood. A sick thought. But that's what it's for. I went into the bathroom and looked at myself in the mirror. Good thing I didn't bump into anyone on the way home. I was speckled with droplets of tomato soup that looked like blood. I washed up.

I looked at the box of bullets. Six bullets gone, forty-four still left. A pro already. I filled the magazine with its maximum of fourteen rounds. It was heavy. I put it in the gun and holstered it. It was still heavy. It was better to wear it when not running. My side felt better with the moleskin on. Probably it was going to hurt when I peeled it off.

I had errands to do and I was going to carry a loaded gun with me all day, instantly accessible, hidden under my windbreaker, to get used to its presence. But first I went back to the kitchen and ate a big wedge of the cantaloupe whose life I saved from an ugly, brutal death.

I got in the car. The seat pushed up the bulky gun, which pushed my belt, which made my pants uncomfortable. How did cops live with this? It was hard to force the seatbelt tab into the buckle around the gun. I drove into Pittsfield. Every time I made a right-hand turn and leaned into the gun, it pinched me in the ribs. I drove up to the bank to make a deposit and visit my safe deposit box. As I got out of the car I self-consciously fluffed my windbreaker to make sure the gun was covered. I walked into the main entrance of the bank. I felt so unnatural, so self-conscious, so guilty with this thing. I felt as conspicuous as if I had had a blender on my belt. As I walked, I tried to keep a normal arm swing, but I needed to swing my right arm wide so I wouldn't bump it. Was that noticeable? Is a wide arm swing a tip-off to security people that a guy has a gun? I waited on line for the teller. I looked around the lobby. Thick Plexiglas in front of the tellers, closed circuit TVs all over the place. No guard. Why was I casing the place? I was just there to transact legal business. With a licensed firearm hidden on me. I made my deposit and left.

Getting into the car again was a nuisance and I wasn't any better at it yet. As I was slowly driving out of the parking lot, some obnoxious jackass in a souped up car with a noisy exhaust honked, cut me off so he could get to the light before I could. Idiot. I wondered if he'd do that if he knew I had my big gun. I had a sudden instant of anger when he honked and cut me off. Good thing I had good impulse control. Good thing it would have taken me five minutes to extract the gun from under my jacket under the seatbelt without banging myself in the ribs with it. It would have been too much trouble anyway.

Next stop was the supermarket. I got a cart and started to go up and down the aisles. I started at the produce aisle. I kept checking to make sure my windbreaker was all the way down. What would happen if, say, I was reaching up to a shelf for a big jar of Skippy extra crunchy peanut butter and as I did, part of the gun was exposed and some little girl saw it and said, "Mommy, that man has a gun," and she told the manager, and then in a few minutes I would be spread-eagle on the floor surrounded by three nervous cops with their guns pointed at me; me explaining to them that I have a gun license in my wallet in my back pants pocket and I really wasn't planning to rob or hurt anyone and I'm not a fugitive on the run.

I turned down the next aisle and there was a half-full shopping cart right in the middle of the aisle and I couldn't pass left or right. The lady it belonged to was way down the aisle trying to decide which box of crackers to get. I hate it when people do that. *Maybe I should shoot her.* See, having this thing on me made me think crazy. I stood there, glaring, waiting for her to notice me. She was oblivious. Maybe if I sent a few 9 mm rounds whizzing past her I'd get her attention. *See, there I go again.* She finally looked up when I cleared my throat, and she rushed to move her cart out of the way and said, "'scuse me," as I rolled past. I ignored her.

What am I doing with this gun? I went home, carried in the groceries, and put the gun back in its hiding place above the ceiling panel in my bedroom. That's where it belonged.

CHAPTER 16

The kid whose neck I had slashed open was still comatose. It had been two weeks since I treated Sal's battered lady.

I put on my brown glen plaid, tropical weight summer business suit and drove over toward Albany. It was my only suit. My name had been in the *Physician's Marketplace*, a monthly Want-Ad-Digest of practice opportunities for doctors, for months. An HMO called me for an interview. I wasn't particularly interested, but I decided to go anyway. I had something else to do in Albany.

I drove to the Albany Greyhound terminal with a pocketful of quarters. It was time to call back the criminal lawyer I'd found in New York City. I wanted to call from a random public phone booth nobody could trace to me. I found his name in *The New York Times* microfilms at the Berkshire Athenæum in Pittsfield. (The new Athenæum, that is.) The old one is an interesting old Gothic stone building on Park Square that now houses a lot of city offices instead of the library. I once spent a few afternoons in there with an assistant district attorney, helping him prepare his case against a drunken driver I'd treated. It's a nice building inside, high ceilings with old fashioned plaster moldings, rich oak woodwork, curved glass in the corner windows.

Anyway, the *Times* had said this lawyer had been involved in some big court cases involving the Mafia, had touted him as a prominent and successful criminal attorney. The first time I called, I couldn't get past the secretary, who said they don't give initial consultations to new clients over the phone. Certainly not to anonymous ones.

I had tipped my hand.

"If I mail you a five hundred dollar cash retainer, will he talk to me?"

Money talks, nobody walks.

I was sure the money would have arrived by the time I made the second call.

"I represent a young M.D. who is being forced by the Mob to take care of employees who 'get injured on the job.' Erratically he gets called at random hours by his Mob contact when he's needed. A rendezvous is arranged and the M.D. is transported where he's needed. My client presumes the reason that he's needed is because the injuries are suspicious, that they would be reported by an ER or a legitimate medical facility, or that perhaps the injured parties are on criminal probation. This M.D. has no interest in this involvement, only wants to keep his record clean and stay out of trouble without antagonizing the Mob. After each service he performs for them, he receives an unmarked letter containing five hundred dollars in used large bills. He does not want to be on their payroll or to appear to be in collusion with them. He has no desire to become an informant or to turn state witness, for fear of eventual reprisal. What my client wants to know is if you have any ideas about how to get out of the grasp of the Mob and resume a safe and legal life and career."

"The first thing you should know," replied the lawyer, "is that you should never bullshit your attorney. If only I had a dime for each time some nut called me up and said, 'Hey, I got this friend....' It sounds like you're in a lotta hot water. Lemme tell you a story. There was a guy in New York City who built up a successful business for himself from the ground up. Laundromats. Lots of cash, no receipts. Just what the Mob likes. He started small with a little Ma & Pa operation, worked hard, bought a few more outlets, kept growing, did all his own repairs until he had a chain of maybe a dozen Laundromats.

"One day two men paid him a visit and they offered him twice the market value of what his business was worth. The man said, 'Listen, I'm a putz for not taking your offer, but ya see, this business is like a child to me, I started it from nothing and I got dreams of having my kids run it when I retire. So, thanks a lot, but I'm not interested.' During the next week his repair truck and two of his Laundromats got blown up. The two men showed up again and bought the whole business for a fraction of what it was worth.

"The moral of the story is that the Mob is going to get what it wants, and if you stand in its way you're gonna get steamrolled. Like the guy with the Laundromats, you gotta realize that if they want you, they got you. If they went through all the trouble to find you, research you and check you out, they must've wanted you. And they'll take care of you. But don't think they'll take any crap from you if you try to break loose. They won't stand for any shit. Know what I mean? They'll blow you out like a match."

"So what should I do?"

"Stay with them for fifteen or twenty years. You're not a trusted commodity, right. You're not in the family. You never will be. After fifteen or twenty years, even if you're not officially in the family, you'll be their old pal, and they'll trust you if things've always been smooth. Be as cooperative as you can and keep your mouth shut. Don't let them know you talked to me, and don't even call me back again, because there's nothing else I can do for you or tell you. After fifteen or twenty years, you say to them, 'Hey, fellas, I'm getting too old for this, why don't you find somebody else?'"

"What about running away?" I asked.

"What're you, stupid? You think you can slip past them? What do you wanna do, be anonymous and wash dishes in the back of a diner in Kansas the rest of your life? Forget it. You run, you're dead."

I got in my car. I was disappointed. Again. Weeks ago I had called my old college pal, the ex-Green Beret, the ex-New York City cop. Surely he'd know what to do. Get a gun and a will, he'd said. Then I call a fat cat Manhattan lawyer who tells me to keep copacetic for twenty years and then retire. Some advice.

From the bus terminal I drove to the interview. The ride was a long string of tired, sweaty and hopeless adjectives pertaining to how dismal and despondent I felt. There would be no clear conscience, no peace of mind, no knowing when the phone wouldn't ring, and no move to some city for that nice quiet office practice. And then there was Patty.

When I got to the HMO, I saw that the landscaping was very neat and tidy. Neatly trimmed arborvitae hedges. A tidy lawn.

The lobby was also neat and tidy. So was the receptionist, who politely directed me to the administrative offices. There were several of us being interviewed for the position of general internist.

The medical director came and told us about this health maintenance organization and how it came to be. And about the twenty-three bathrooms, all in pastel colors. About what a fine area it was in, to live and work. About the fine patient population, all honest, hardworking, middle-class subscribers. He told us how well organized the fine medical records department was, and that all the charts were even color coded. They provide short white clinic jackets for their doctors to wear. (To present a neat and tidy image, no doubt).

We could have a half hour to do complete initial histories, physicals and consultations on people under fifty years old; and forty-five minutes if they were over fifty. We could have fifteen minutes for follow-up visits.

He rambled on about how the key to their success was cost containment by minimizing things like laboratory tests, hospitalizations.

He told us about the twenty-three pastel johns again.

They shared tiny little offices without windows or extra chairs. All very neat and tidy. I asked if there was an office where you could sit and talk with patients. He told me that they like their doctors to do their consultation with the patients in the exam rooms, which were even tinier than the offices, because it was faster that way.

Great. I could be an intern again. Now as an internist I could have a bunch of bean counters watching over my shoulder telling me when my number of minutes with a patient was up, making sure I wore my little white coat, making sure I didn't order too many urinalyses.

An exam room is a crappy place to talk to someone about an illness. It's hard to listen attentively when you're half undressed and lying down. People listen better when they're dressed and in a chair like a real person. They at least have the dignity of having their clothes on, and can listen to you explain things.

I turned down their offer.

I soothed my frustrations at the Viking Dairy Bar in East Greenbush. I ordered the biggest sundae on the menu. While I was trying to enjoy it, I remembered the last time I was there, which had been with Patty.

Then I spilled chocolate sauce on my suit. I'd just paid seven bucks to get it dry-cleaned. I wasn't very neat and tidy.

The only thing that felt good was thinking about Patty. I wanted in the worst way for things to go well. But Sal and I were having a power struggle. We both were trying to control me. Life was getting chaotic and uncontrollable. And unsafe.

CHAPTER 17

It was a quarter to five and eighty-eight sweaty degrees when I finally got back from Albany. I drove up the hill on Main Street in Dalton, past the Crane mansions, past Yankee Woolen Mills, O'Laughlins Pharmacy, the bank, the town hall, and turned left on Carson Avenue.

As I turned down my block, I was surprised and pleased to see Patty's car in my driveway. I pulled up and she waved.

She was sitting on the porch, tilted back on a chair, feet up on the rail, holding a bottle of beer.

I parked, grabbed my suit coat, and hurried to join her.

"Hello, dear, I'm home!" I said, as if we were an old married couple.

"Oh, good, dinner's almost ready," she said, equally trite. I leaned over her in the chair, and kissed her. Her lips were cool from the beer on that cranky hot summer afternoon. I sat down in a chair next to hers and as I turned I saw my front door was open. I wondered how she had gotten in.

"What brings you up this way?" I asked delicately.

"I came up to do some shopping in Pittsfield and I wondered if you were around. When I drove up, your uncle was here; he was just leaving."

"My uncle?" I asked bewildered.

"Your uncle Sal. He told me you were out for an interview, we chatted a few minutes and then he left. He's a nice man. So I stayed here to wait for you. I found some stuff in your kitchen and started supper."

"What was he doing here?" I asked incredulously.

"He said he was in town on business and stopped by to say hello. He said to tell you he'll call you tomorrow. I don't remember you mentioning him. How come you look so annoyed?"

"I'm not annoyed."

"You're doing a very good imitation of someone who's annoyed."

I tried to hide my annoyance by changing the subject. I told her about my interview. The one at the HMO, not the one with the New York criminal lawyer.

"What happened to your suit?" she asked.

"What? Where? Oh, here? I stopped at the Viking and had a sundae. I must've dripped some chocolate sauce," I admitted sheepishly.

"Some sauce? It looks like you dumped the whole dish!"

"Well, it needed cleaning anyway."

Shaking her head, she said, "Can dress him up, can't take him anywhere."

We sat there and I finished her beer.

"C'mon, let's go check the chicken," she said.

She had sautéed some chicken breasts, then covered them with a mixture of chopped onions, parsley, breadcrumbs, and not enough garlic. Then she put them under the broiler for a few minutes to brown. We had wild rice, green beans and beer.

I was distracted. I was also pissed. What was Sal doing here? Did he know everything I was doing? Did he find the gun? If my phone was still tapped, he could've known about the interview. He couldn't know about my call to the lawyer. And now he knows Patty.

Actually I'd been thinking of giving her a key to my apartment. I would do something corny like give her the house key and a skate key on a long white sneaker shoelace and say, "One is a key to my home and the other is a key to my heart." But that wouldn't be safe now.

We stopped at Kelly's Package Store, got a chilled bottle of Liebfraumilch, and drove up to Wahconah Falls. It was ten degrees cooler there. We waded in the pool and the brook and talked and nuzzled and sipped wine from the bottle.

CHAPTER 18

I needed to think. I needed a walk. I wished I had a dog. I drove to Monument Mountain in Great Barrington. It was a cool Berkshire morning. I parked, put on my knapsack and began walking up the trail. Had to try to think this out systematically.

Why is this a problem? Is it as big a problem as I think, or do I just choose to see this as a big problem? Is it just my attitude? Am I just whining because this is unconventional and doesn't fit into my schedule conveniently? Am I just pouting because Sal is making me do something and I resent not being asked, not having a choice? He is paying me well. Very well. But is it dirty money? Is it illegal? I don't know. Am I practicing illegally? Should I call up the Board of Registration in Medicine in Boston and explain the arrangement to them and ask if I'm still practicing within the ethics of the profession?

Sal takes me to see people who need care, but I may not be the most qualified person to give them care. I'm no trauma surgeon. If I didn't see them, would they get no care? Would they suffer or die if I didn't see them? In the real world if I do something to a patient that is beyond the scope of my skills, there is a big negligence issue. Am I immoral if I refuse to treat these people (not that I have much choice). Is it immoral for me to resent seeing these people? Could I loosen up and learn to accept this?

Wasn't there a doctor who unwittingly helped John Wilkes Booth with his broken ankle after he shot Lincoln? Wasn't he charged with aiding and abetting a fugitive even though he didn't know it? Didn't they hang him with the others?

What would happen if I went to the police? Would Sal and the others take retribution on my family? They have already made an implicit threat. Come to think of it, didn't he threaten Patty, too?

Didn't he say something like, "She's a real nice girl, Doc, you take care of her; it'd be a real shame if something happened to a real nice girl like her?"

At that point there was just one of me to suffer from my actions, but if things got out of hand, if I went to the police and Sal found out, or if the police didn't handle it securely, then there would be many loved ones who might suffer.

How safe or practical or effective is the Witness Protection Program? My relatives would not be pleased if they had to pack up in the middle of the night and leave their lives behind and move to Oz. We would all have to be reinvented. It is not as if I had lots of information that the feds would find valuable to prosecute organized crime and put bad guys behind bars. I did not have evidence about who inflicted the wounds I have treated. I would want the police to help me, but there would not be much in it for them. Would it be worth their while? Might they try only half-heartedly to help me? Or maybe the cops I go to turn out to be connected to the Mob.

Should I go to the FBI in Boston? My troubles might be beyond the scope of what the local municipal police deal with on a regular basis. First I would have to figure out how to do it so Sal wouldn't know. If I talk to the FBI and they offer me a plan, could I say, "Thanks, but no thanks, I was just looking"? And then just walk away? Not likely. Could I go away unidentified? Would they follow me? Would they identify me from fingerprints I might leave on a doorknob or desktop or coffee cup or piece of paper? But I've never been fingerprinted so they couldn't find me in a file. Oh, damn, I was fingerprinted when I applied for that damn gun license. *What am I doing with a gun?* Maybe if I went to a different state my prints wouldn't be available. Maybe I should go to New York. If I told the FBI my story and they tried to get me to tell them who I am, would they be able to intimidate it out of me? Very likely. If they gave me the third degree and had me handcuffed to a chair and shone a bright light in my eyes would I be able to say, "Hey, I gotta go now, if I don't get back soon Sal will get suspicious"? *Now I'm really getting nuts.*

Is it more foolish and reckless to cooperate with Sal, or to go to the feds? Am I courageous by cooperating with Sal, or by going to the police?

Am I already a criminal?

I came off the mountain with more questions than answers. Somewhere on this mountain was a ledge under which Herman Melville and Nathaniel Hawthorne sat out a thunderstorm. Maybe if I could find their ghosts, I could ask them some of these existential questions.

The legend is that some lovely Indian maiden was separated from her beloved and was in such despair that she threw herself off the heights of this mountain to enter the spirit world and escape her plight. I could keep that as an option.

I got back to my car and unlaced my stiff, heavy, sweaty hiking boots and put on my sneakers. I slung my knapsack into the back of the car, and my T-shirt was wet and cold with sweat where it had been under the pack. I got in and drove to the nearest bank and got a roll of quarters and drove to a pay phone and called Matt in Grand Rapids.

"Matt, this is Charlie, how are you?"

"Charlie, it's good to hear from you. I've been worried about you."

I told him what had gone on so far, essentially telling him a condensed story of what I had been writing in the notes in the bank vault. "Matt, if I went to the police or the FBI..." He interrupted me.

"Do not go to the police," he said in no uncertain terms. "Remember, I was one. They will not be able to help you. They are not good at helping or protecting people in a situation like yours. They are not good at keeping secrets. Too many people always get involved to keep secrets. Sal is taking good care of you. Be flexible. Adapt. I say again, do not go to the police or any other police agency. Did you get the gun?"

"Yes." *Why did I?*

"Don't shoot yourself with it."

I didn't tell him, but it was hidden above a suspended ceiling panel in my apartment. Someday, years from now, when my mysterious disappearance has been long forgotten, some new tenant will remodel and find a very scary and rusty gun in the ceiling.

"Charlie, be extremely careful. Be ridiculously careful. You never know when they'll be watching or monitoring you. One more thing."

"What's that?"

"Charlie, did you ever think of just doing a bad job for them? Just stand around with your thumb up your butt and say, 'Gee, Sal, I just don't know what to do in a situation like this.' Can you do that?"

"You know," I said softly, slowly, "I never even thought of that. It never even entered my mind. Not even remotely."

"Try it. Spit in a few wounds, get them all infected, see how quick he is to call you up another time."

"Gee, Matt," I paused, "I really don't think I could do that."

"I know, I know, I figured as much. There's that oath you took. It would be antithetical to your character. It was worth mentioning though. Worth considering. Remember, Hippocrates probably didn't anticipate you being in a situation like this."

"Matt, I need to get my life back."

"Charlie, be grateful you still have a life. I mean it. Don't make things worse for yourself. Good luck. I don't know how I can help you. I know that I cannot. Be careful."

"Bye, Matt, thanks for your advice." I hung up.

I called Michael, my lawyer friend in Albany. "Mike, I have some business errands to run in Albany this afternoon, wanna meet for supper?"

"Sure, where?"

"How about the Fountain on New Scotland Ave. for beer and pizza?"

"Sounds good, what time?"

"How about six?"

"Good."

"Do you have any simple fill-in-the-blank forms for a person to make out a will?"

"Lots. Is this for you?"

"Yeah."

"Then you are a potential client of my firm and I can court you on my expense account, and I will meet you not at the Fountain, but at Jack's Oyster House instead. How does that sound?"

"Very nice; I see the corporate world has its perks. See you then."

I didn't really have anything to do that afternoon in Albany so I went home, showered, cleaned the apartment, hung out for a while.

I met Michael at the lovely old landmark downtown restaurant just across the street from the palatial Delaware-Hudson Railroad building which had been abandoned and neglected for years and was now undergoing renovation. It was modeled after some government building in Belgium and was now being sandblasted, taking off decades of accumulated urban grime, to become offices for the state university system. It is a gorgeous building.

I got there before Michael and was well into my first gin and tonic by the time he arrived. He was very nicely dressed in a khaki summer suit, yellow oxford cloth shirt and a rep tie. He had a small leather attaché case that looked expensive.

Most of the waiters at Jack's are real professional, middle-aged or older, and appear to be real career waiters, always very deferential, efficient and formal in their starched and pressed white tuxedo shirts, black bowties, black vests, and white aprons tied around their waists. We asked what the specials were, and without referring to notes our waiter rattled them off. They all sounded delicious. Especially the sea bass. We asked what he would recommend and without an instant of hesitation told us what he thought. We ordered. We drank.

"As a rule, we always encourage our clients to go forward with whatever business with us we can cultivate. We are in business for business. It's sensible to have a will. But for a young single guy like you, with, I presume, not many assets and I presume some college debt and no dependents, is there a particular reason why you are thinking about wills now?"

Yes, there is, Michael, but I really can't tell you about it.

"Not really," I lied. "I met with my accountant a few months ago and asked him what aspects of my financial adulthood I needed to know about. What I need to know that I am too oblivious to realize. He told me about disability insurance, and about starting to save for retirement even now, what with the power of compound interest. He told me what receipts to be careful to keep all year to save for him for tax time, stuff like that. And he suggested I have a will. Here we are."

"OK. Makes sense. Here is a standard form. You can look it over and fill in the blanks. It is as simple as they come. Think about whom you want for your beneficiaries and your executor and remember things will change as time flies by. Eventually you'll probably get married, probably have children, you'll eventually lose your parents and so on. Remember to think long-range. Mail it back to me when you're ready and we'll go over it and make it real."

Soup came. Salad came. Dinner came, and then decaf coffee, and it was all very good and might have been delicious, but talking about the cold facts of death, my death, caused me to lose my appetite and I did not take much pleasure in the meal, and guessed I was not great company either.

I steered the conversation over to books. I told Mike I was reading a Mafia novel and there was a character who turned state witness and went into the Witness Protection Program. "Is there really such a thing?" I asked.

"Oh, yeah, it's been around for a while."

"How well does it work?"

"I don't know specifically, since I'm not involved with criminal law, but I'm sure it is an option of last resort for those people who enter it. I mean, it's either do that or wait to be assassinated. And they have to create a whole new identity and livelihood. And they have to sever every relationship completely with everyone they leave behind."

I finished deciding that I was not going to go to the police or FBI or anywhere else, and I still did not know if I was being wise or foolish.

CHAPTER 19

We had a date. We were going to "do the lawn" at Tanglewood. It was Patty's idea, and she had bought the tickets for the Sunday matinee performance. It started at two and I had to be at the ER at eight for my next shift. I wasn't happy about having to go to work. I was grumpy. I was crabby. The program was a nice assortment of five concert pieces including two I liked a lot – Mozart's "Eine Kleine Nachtmusik" and Beethoven's "Moonlight Sonata." Patty thought of that piece in particular with me in mind, since I torture a piano now and then.

Tanglewood is a huge facility in Lenox that had once been a grand estate at the turn of the century. That's when the ultra rich would spend summers here in magnificent huge homes they built to use for only a couple of months each year, which, with false modesty, they called "cottages."

The main shed at Tanglewood is a huge, covered, open-sided concert hall with a few thousand seats. Those are expensive. The shed is surrounded by "the lawn," which covers acres. Lawn seats are cheap. You brought your own. Far more people come to "do the lawn." Most people come with blankets, folding chairs and picnic coolers. Some come in formal attire with very elegant preparations and set up on the lawn with folding tables and chairs, linen, and dine on cold salmon served on china, with candelabra on the table.

It was the end of August, the concert season was winding down and the attendance was up. Seiji Ozawa was conducting the Boston Symphony Orchestra. It was being broadcast on National Public Radio. We drove through downtown Lenox, where there was a policeman directing traffic at the monument and the traffic down West St. toward Tanglewood was crawling slowly. As we were creeping along we were cut off a few times by ostentatious foreign luxury cars with out-of-state plates that cost more than I make in a year.

We finally got into the parking lot. It felt good to finally get out of the car and stretch. Patty looked really good in a tight red Izod sports shirt and white tennis shorts. I was dressed for work but without a tie. We gathered our things and joined the long line of people shuffling toward the entrance gates. Everybody was carrying something: coolers, blankets, chairs. It reminded me of all those Life Magazine photos of peasants evacuating their war torn village carrying all they could after their homes had been burned. Lots of people were carrying *The Sunday New York Times*. Most were older. Most were overweight. There were some women wearing the then fashionable moronic sunglasses with huge lenses the size of saucers, with their initials on the lower outer edge of the right lens.

Eventually we got through the gate, got our tickets torn in half and headed for the lawn, looking for some shade. We found a spot in deep left field and spread out our blanket and stuff. I could see the shed, but we were way too far away to see the orchestra. The outermost steel pillars of the shed had huge loudspeakers on them. Maybe next time I would use some of Sal's cash and splurge for good seats inside the shed.

Patty was chattering on again about the latest environmental debacle in the news, about yet another supertanker spilling oil somewhere or other, and I was still crabby and had heard it before and kept saying "Uhmm" every minute or two trying to sound interested. There were lots of people around us and most were talking too loud about nothing, just because they were in love with the sound of their own voice. I was in a sour mood.

I hated myself when I was like this. I hated it when I got intolerant of other people and what cars they drove and what kind of sunglasses they wore that they thought looked stylish with their initials and I thought looked stupid. I really woke up on the wrong side of the bed that day. I should've gone out for a run. Maybe I was overtired. Maybe I was getting overburdened by Sal and his demands.

The concert started and it took a few minutes for everyone on the lawn to finish their insipid conversations and shut up and listen to the music.

The concert began and it sounded like electronically amplified music. We sat and tried to quietly unwrap our food without making too much noise. Patty brought a package of pita bread and a few containers of hummus and tabouleh and melon. It was really very nice.

When the piano piece began, I stood up to look at the soloist and the orchestra, but they just looked like little ants so far away. I could've stayed home and picnicked in the backyard and listened to the simulcast on the radio and heard the same electronically amplified music. And not had to wait in a long line to go to the bathroom.

I stretched out on the blanket beside Patty and looked up at the clouds. The music went on, then there was an intermission, more music, and after the last piece there was the obligatory standing ovation. Or, as Neville Mariner was quoted as saying, a "standing evacuation," as people raced out to the parking lot to avoid getting stuck in traffic.

We lazily hung out on our blanket until the bulk of the mob had gone.

"How did you like the concert?" Patty asked.

"I did, I liked it a lot. And the food you brought was great too. Even though you didn't bring any Twinkies. And thanks for treating me for the tickets, too, that was nice of you. Good concert."

"How could you know," Patty said, sounding a little annoyed, "you slept through almost the whole thing!"

"I did?"

"Yeah. You kept snoring too. I had to bop you a few times to shut you up. You weren't in the same key as the orchestra. I feel sorry for whoever marries you and has to put up with your snoring."

She sounded a little more acrid than like playful teasing, so I didn't say anything. We walked back to the car and headed to Great Barrington. I suggested we stop and have some supper, so we went to Twenty Railroad Street, one of the favorite local restaurants and watering holes. We chatted, though without animation. We both ordered sandwiches, Patty had a beer, but I didn't, since I was going to work soon.

"Is something bothering you, Charlie?" Patty asked.

"Oh, I don't know. I guess I'm not in the mood to go to work."

"Has that been bothering you all day?"

"Oh, I don't know. Sometimes when I go to work I feel like a fighter going into the ring. I don't know what's going to come at me. I have to hope I can handle what comes at me. I have to hope I don't let anybody down. Like a patient. I have to get my courage up to step into the ring. I have to gird my loins. Sometimes it's hard to summon up the mental energy to do that."

"Wow. I never knew that. I always thought it was easy for you."

"It's never been easy. I'm not even sure if it's easy for Will, it might just be bluster and bravado," I said.

"What is it that might come up that you can't handle?" Patty asked.

"Oh, there's so many acute things that can become cataclysmic before you figure them out. Like not being able to put a tube in a guy's trachea. Not being able to figure out a guy's arrhythmia when he's in cardiogenic shock. Not knowing that a guy's shortness of breath is because he has collapsed lungs, and he decompensates before you get the X-ray. Someone with continuous seizures you can't stop and he cooks his brain. A Sudden Infant Death baby. A diabetic kid with ketoacidosis you can't pull out of it. I've got a million of them. An infant with epiglottitis."

"Wow. Are you worrying about these things all the time?"

"No. I'm probably aware of them most of the time."

"Can I ask if you've ever missed any of those things?"

"I've missed things. But I don't think anything in an irretrievable way, nothing awful. Diagnosis gets sharper, more honed down as time goes by, and you get more tests and data and the diagnosis declares itself. That's not the worrisome stuff."

"The acute ER stuff is."

"Yeah."

"Because you don't want to get sued?"

"No, not at all, because I don't want to lose someone who might be savable. Because when you're dead you're gonna be dead for a real long time. You only get one life. And, I don't wanna get sued. You get two eyes, ten fingers, two kidneys... You only get one life."

"Two ears," Patty added.

"Two ears," I agreed, "six ossicles."

"One dick," Patty added.

"Well, half of us." That surprised me. I laughed. Her levity cracked the seriousness of the conversation.

We finished our dinner and I drove Patty home. She turned and kissed me, gathered her things from the backseat, and walked up the walk to her front porch. She got to her door and waved. I waved back, but didn't drive off until she went into the house and I lost sight of her.

I drove to Fairview and parked in the back, walked in and said hello to the nurses as I headed back to the doctor's room to wash up and put on my necktie.

It was a long, slow night and the time went by so slowly. Being the end of a weekend there were a couple of the usual alcohol-related incidents. The most memorable was a big beefy drunk in a blue flannel shirt, jeans, biker boots, who was drunk as a skunk. Evidently a ruckus began in the bar he was in, probably started by him, and he must've gotten his comeuppance when someone appropriately smacked this guy around, split his lip and tore his ear an eighth of the way off. I sewed it back on. Like so many drunks, he was a big belligerent baby and whined through the whole thing, especially when I was needling his ear to numb it up.

Afterwards he was going to drive himself home. I told him "no way," he had a blood alcohol of 0.160, better call a friend to come and get him. He told me to fuck off, no one's gonna tell him what he should do. I asked him what he was driving. A Ford F-150 pickup. What color? Blue. I said good luck, drive slow, get your stitches out in a week.

Then I went into my room and called the Great Barrington Police Department and told them it was "Deep Throat" calling, like the Watergate informer, and they should be on the lookout for a blue Ford F-150 pickup, leaving Fairview with a drunk shit head in it with a bandage on his left ear, and a fat lip. I loved doing stuff like that.

By the time the nurse and I had the place cleaned up, it was two a.m. We sat and chatted and drank coffee for a while. Then the security guard ambled by and joined us. I really like this guy. He was a retired guy who did this a few days a week. He came on at eleven, always freshly showered and shaved, his hair smelling of Vitalis hair tonic and aftershave. He was always energetic, jolly. He used to be a game warden. We talked about bird hunting and fishing.

Around three I went in to lie down on the fold-a-bed in the doctor's room. Around four I got called to see a patient. A forty-year-old paper mill worker with a toothache. For a week.

"Why are you coming here now?"

"There's no dentist here?"

"No." He had no fever, he had no redness or swelling, or lymph node swelling under his tongue, in his neck, or around his ear. The tooth hurt when I tapped it with a tongue depressor and a rubber reflex hammer. I gave him Penicillin, and codeine if he needed it, and told him to call a dentist in the morning.

There was no point in going back to bed. Will would be here in a couple of hours. The sun would come up, people would come into the building, another night fighting in the trenches would be over. It was always entertaining to see Will work the crowd in the coffee room.

I hung out with the gang, had a few cups of coffee. One of the EMTs came in with a box of doughnuts. Will was in good form, made us laugh. After a little while I packed up, said goodbye and headed home.

On the way north out of town I stopped at Patty's pharmacy to say hello and apologize for not having been the best company yesterday. But she was busy at her counter with some customers and I didn't want to embarrass myself in front of them, so I just said hello.

"Hello, how was your night?" she said, sounding officious in her professional mode and setting, as she glanced up at me from her work.

"Long," I said.

"Then you should go home and get some sleep," she said, still working.

"OK. I'll talk to you soon," I said. She smiled and nodded, still counting out pills.

I drove home to Dalton and went to bed.

CHAPTER 20

Several days later, Sal called me at work and arranged for a rendezvous at the usual place. This would be the second job of the week.

The first job was an easy one. It was a man who'd been stabbed in the ass with an ice pick. Though he had a lot of muscle soreness, he hadn't hit any major nerves or blood vessels. I doubted that the pick could have penetrated as far as the pelvic cavity. But the little bit of doubt I had made me uncomfortable. I flushed out the hole as best I could. They were surprised that I didn't sew the hole closed. You can't sew up a puncture wound because you can't be sure you cleaned it out well enough. To sew it would bury the germs. They condescended to accept my judgment.

"I wish I had a tetanus shot to give him," I said. "Do you think you could have him go to one of those walk-in health centers and get a tetanus shot?" I asked Sal.

"Not, probably," Sal said.

"Why not?" I asked.

"They'd probably ask him why he wants one, did he get a wound?"

"How about the next time you have me come here, have this guy come and I'll vaccinate him?"

"Sure. Right. Whatever you say," Sal said.

"Are you BSing me?"

"You can say bullshit, you're among friends," Sal said.

"Sure. Right. Whatever you say," I said.

"You're trying too hard, Doc."

"Trying too hard to do what?"

"Trying too hard to take excellent care of these people. Half decent is good enough, better than they deserve."

"How much should I do for you if you get sick, Sal?"

"Everything."

"Why is that?"

"Because I deserve it," Sal answered.

"And they don't?" I asked.

"No," Sal said tersely.

"Care to elaborate on that?"

"No."

Go figure.

Sal drove me home and we had another one of our fireside chats in the van. He told me he thought Patty was "swell."

"Doc, I read in *Newsweek* how expensive it is to go to medical school these days."

"Yeah, I'm astonished too. It doesn't make any sense. I got out just in time."

"How much did it cost when you went?"

"When I was accepted it was $3,200 a year, I think. That was 1979. That's just for tuition. And then before I got there, they sent me a letter saying they were increasing it to $4,000. By the time I got out it was $7,200."

"Wow."

"Wow is right, and now it's over thirteen grand. It's one of the most expensive med schools in the country."

"How come it's so expensive?"

"I don't know. I have some ideas, but they're probably just pet peeves and not very insightful."

"Like what?"

"For instance, I thought the place was very poorly administrated. The bursar was an M.D. who was a professor with no business training, no MBA or anything, and he got elevated to his level of incompetence as bursar.

"The faculty was so much bigger than I thought made sense. There were professors who were on the faculty, doing research, and might only give us a couple of token lectures a year! And at that they were usually lousy. There were only a very small number of professors who were effective teachers. They had all this deadwood there, doing esoteric research so they could publish papers and the institution could gain prestige."

"That doesn't make sense."

"You know, the first two years are the ones that are like school, with lectures, and labs, and dissection, and a lot of microscope work. But the second two are on-the-job training; we're usually not even in the med school building. We're in the hospitals getting taught from the residents, and the private M.D.s, and only very few of the med school M.D.s. Most of them didn't get paid for the teaching."

"I know research has to get done," Sal said, "and medical students need to learn the basics. But I don't see why basics and research gotta be under the same roof and screw up the same budget."

"That's the way I feel," I said, but I didn't think I could have said it as well.

"I know that there's a lot more to it," I added, "that has to do with federal and state contributions per student. Capitation, they call it, which has been cut way back recently. All that funding stuff changes so often I can't keep up with it, let alone understand it."

"Me either," replied Sal.

"Anyway, I used to like to think about how much money I didn't make. Between college and med school, I spent eight years working eighty hours a week at least, paying tuition, making no salary or overtime. Then I graduated and I got to be an intern and work a hundred hours a week for twelve thousand a year. It's depressing to think how much better off I'd be if I put all that time and effort into a trade."

"But you get a lot of respect as a doctor."

"Oh, I don't know. You get targeted as someone to sue, someone the garage mechanic can charge more. I don't mean to sound so cynical about it. I like it. It has its pros and cons. There is a lot of worry and stress."

"It's harder for you because you care so much."

How does he know me that well?

That was the first job of the week, and when I got off work tonight we'd go on our second job. I had a few other points to mention to Sal pursuant to the discussion we'd had. Strange that I'd be looking forward to talking to this hood. But he was such a nice hood.

It was almost the end of my shift, and as bad luck would have it, there was a call on the ambulance radio that they were in transit with a woman in a full arrest who collapsed in the bathroom of a restaurant. I joined the staff in the cardiac room getting everything ready. We alerted all the techs from the lab, EKG and X-ray. I stood at the head of the bed with laryngoscope in one hand and endotracheal tube in the other. I heard the beep-beep-beep warning signal as the ambulance backed up to the doors, the swish as the automatic doors opened, and the bustle of the big men as they hurriedly rolled the lady toward me.

One man was doing the chest compressions as he sidestepped along with the stretcher, another giving oxygen, holding a squeeze bag in one hand and face mask in place with the other. They rolled her alongside the ER bed and quickly slid her off the flimsy collapsible stretcher onto ours. They continued CPR as I prepared to intubate her trachea. As I tilted her head backwards, I inserted the laryngoscope, trying to see the vocal cords through which I'd pass the breathing tube.

Suddenly she vomited, and I caught a spray of hot acrid liquid on my glasses and forehead as I peered down her throat. Without asking, the nurse handed me the suction catheter and I quickly sucked out the vomitus. Her neck and throat muscles were tight and it was hard to use the awkward laryngoscope. I saw the vocal cords. Bingo, the tube went right in the first time I passed it, something that always seemed as much luck as skill. They taped the tube in place and attached the green plastic "Ambu" bag to the tube, squeezing oxygen into her between every fifth compression of her chest by the husky EMT sweatily leaning over her.

The nurses were having difficulty getting our IV line started in the lady's arm. I called for a subclavian vein catheter setup and, while I gloved, a nurse poured Betadine antiseptic over the lady's right collarbone. Straight from the gallon jug. No time for neat and tidy. She was hooked up to the electrocardiogram by now, and it only showed the results of the chest compressions. With my left index finger on the top of her breastbone as a marker, I snaked a large, long needle toward it, from under the middle of her collarbone. When I entered the large subclavian vein there was a gush of black blood that soaked my sleeve. I quickly slipped the long, thin plastic tube through the needle.

I removed the needle and taped the whole assembly in place. Through this tube we could give the fluids and medicines that hopefully might revive her. Getting this line in quickly was also good luck.

"No blood pressure, doctor," said a nurse.

"Normal saline through the subclavian, wide open," I ordered calmly. Fake calm. It took so much effort to try to be calm.

"What do you see on the EKG monitor?" I asked as I was listening to her chest for breath sounds.

"Not much, there's a lot of static."

I looked at the oscilloscope on the cardiac monitor and saw electrocardiographic gibberish. There must have been a bad wire or contact somewhere.

"An amp of sodium bicarb, please, slowly," I ordered, while looking at the wires. One of the wire leads was caught around the jacket of the guy doing CPR, and every movement caused a flurry of static on the screen. I untangled it, looked at the EKG monitor, and saw that the lady was in ventricular fibrillation.

"She's in V. Fib," I said, "please give her an amp of epinephrine followed by a hundred mg of Xylocaine. We'll let that slosh around for a minute while we warm up the mighty Wurlitzer. Then we'll defibrillate her. Charge it for two hundred joules." That was my pet name for the defibrillator, and this was my standard act during a Code Blue; which most of the staff have heard before. Slowly the pattern on the oscilloscope enlarged in amplitude as the ventricular fibrillation pattern coarsened. I placed the defibrillator paddles, each with its jelly pad, on her chest.

"Everybody clear?" I looked around while everybody stepped quickly away from the bed.

When I pressed the buttons on the paddles there was a pop as the machine discharged. The lady's body shuddered and her arms were flung upwards and I could smell the ozone from the spark. My brother used to have electric trains that smelled like that.

"Better living through electricity." Another standard line.

The monitor showed a better rhythm that looked like one called ventricular tachycardia.

"Can anybody feel a pulse?" I asked. I could feel none as I searched for the femoral artery in the groin, nor could I hear the sounds of the heart valves closing as I listened to her chest with my stethoscope.

"Rhythm but no pulse means she has electromechanical dissociation, right? Keep pumping. OK, let's try to get her out of V. Tach now. Charge the defibber to fifty. Let's draw blood for the usual labs, get an arterial blood gas. Have X-ray get ready for a chest film to check the tracheal tube placement. Please start Xylocaine infusion at two through a piggyback on the subclavian line. Please give half an amp of calcium chloride slowly."

It didn't look good for her. Thankfully, the endo tube and subclavian line went in, or she'd have no chance at all. Which she probably didn't have anyway.

"Dr. Davids, Dr. Connor is here and wants to know if you need him," said a nurse who had just poked her head in through the door.

"No, thanks, he might want to catch up on the people who've been waiting." Once I start one of these things I think it's better to see it through.

I was doing fine. Intense, but calm. Not really calm, but controlled. I tried to run a calm, quiet "LeBoyer" code.

As I was going to use the paddles to convert her to a yet more stable rhythm, I saw the monitor show some aberrant beats, and then slip back into the V. Fib she'd been in before.

"Up the charge to two hundred," I instructed. When it was up there, I repeated the defibrillation, the lady jolted again, the ozone smell again. V. Tach again.

But not for long.

"Bretyllium five hundred mg IV, please," I said, always trying to sound calm and polite. Grace under pressure. The Hemingway hero. If this medicine didn't work, nothing would. Usually it didn't work.

It didn't.

"Keep pumping. Does anybody know anything about this lady, is there family here? Should we get a priest?"

A nurse said she'd take care of it and went out of the room.

I began to systematically examine her, going from head to toe, while the EMT wearily continued CPR. Her pupils were wide and didn't react to my penlight. Her face was blue. I couldn't hear heart sounds. We were moving air in both lungs. Her belly was distended with air.

"The bretyllium is in, doctor, and here is the blood gas result."

Her blood was too acid, from too little oxygen for too long. She was as good as gone.

"Another amp of bicarb please, follow it with an amp of epi."

I waited a moment after those drugs were squirted from their pre-filled syringes into the subclavian line, hoping they would soak into the heart tissues and render them more responsive to the hefty jolt of electricity I was about to administer.

"Everybody clear?"

Zap.

No soap.

"Doctor, this lady's husband is here, can you come out and talk to him?"

"Charge it to four hundred joules. Keep pumping."

The defibrillator beeped while charging, and buzzed when charged.

It buzzed.

"Stand clear!"

Zap.

No improvement. Four hundred joules is the highest setting. That's all there is and there ain't no mo'.

"Keep pumping. Where is her husband?" I asked. I had controlled myself down to an intense, numb automation. I felt too warm in my long white lab coat, wool tie and strangling stethoscope. I might still have had vomit spray on my forehead. Maybe that's what the speckles were on my glasses.

"Please continue CPR, I'll be back shortly." I started toward the door. "You're all doing a fine job, very smooth, I thank you," I added. Important to support morale under all this tension. *Who's supporting mine?* Before I went into the waiting room a nurse told me to take off my lab coat with its bloody sleeves.

I'd done this many times before. I knew only one best way to do it. And that is to do it. Short and sweet, pull no punches, don't beat around the bush. Numb thyself.

"Dr. Davids, this is Mr. Angelo. I called the priest," said a nurse, beckoning me toward a small man sitting nervously in the corner.

"Hello, Mr. Angelo, I am Dr. Davids," I said softly to him, and I stood close to him.

"Dr. Davids, how is my wife?" he said to me with an old Italian immigrant's accent.

"I'm sorry to say that she is very, very sick, sir." I paused to give him a chance to respond. Like ask a question. Or shout. Or cry. Or faint. "We are doing everything there is to do." I paused.

"I know you are. Thank you doctor."

"But it does not seem to be working, and I am afraid she is almost gone," I said very softly, slowly.

"Oh, Mother of Christ, oh, doctor, oh doctor, can I see her?"

I should've known he'd ask that. I didn't want him to see her with all the ugliness and violence of a resuscitation.

"Soon," I said.

"Thank you, doctor." So polite. I got up and he leaned back in his chair.

"Sir, her heart is not able to pump blood on its own now, and we are helping it pump with CPR. Do you know what that is?"

"Like on television."

"Yes. But it's not helping. I think it is time for the chaplain to help us now. OK?"

"Yes, doctor, thank you."

"I will get you as soon as it's OK for you to come in."

"Thank you, doctor."

The priest was at the head of the bed with his prayer stole and bottle of oil, speaking quietly. The EMT was still pumping, soaked with sweat. All the extra nurses had left, those that remained looked disappointed. The monitor showed only a lazy wavy line.

The priest finished, he looked at me, nodded and left. I nodded back.

"Thank you very much, all of you," I said, somberly, as I turned off the monitor.

Relieved, the big EMT ceased his efforts. "It's Miller time for you, Doug." Another of my standard lines. They don't get chuckles anymore.

"Let's clean her up so her husband can see her," I said to the nurse. I removed all the tubes and wires and things, covered her up to her neck with a sheet and blanket.

When I got to the waiting room, the priest was with Mr. Angelo. I nodded at them. He already knew. He mumbled something silently to me, and head in hands, followed the priest into the room.

My part was done. Except for the paperwork. I had already said Kaddish.

That done, I washed up, said good night to Will. On my way out the door I glanced at the clock in the waiting room. It was ten p.m.

I'd completely forgotten that I was supposed to meet Sal over an hour ago. I checked my new beeper, which was in my knapsack all day. There was no message on it. Sal hadn't tried to call me on the ER phone line, either.

I raced to the meeting place, but the blue van was not there. I ran up and down the lanes of the parking lot, checked out the back and side of the building, looked behind the enormous dumpster, as big as semi truck. Nowhere. I stood in front of the supermarket, keeping the parking lot and the road behind it under attentive scouting. They didn't come back. Maybe they thought I got tied up at work and decided to take in some Dunkin' Donuts and check back for me later. These things happen to doctors, you know. Unavoidable. I always wondered what would happen if I didn't show up.

I stood there a long time. A lot of the late night shoppers eyed me oddly.

Sal didn't return. At midnight I shrugged with resignation, headed home, had a beer and went to sleep. I hoped the guy Sal wanted me to see would make out OK.

CHAPTER 21

It was my turn to work the weekend so I headed south. It seemed like autumn was on its way. It was chilly when I walked out of the house in shirtsleeves, and there was a film of dew on the windshield. As I drove down Holmes Road past the Canoe Meadows Wildlife reserve, I saw traces of red, yellow and orange in the trees. Mostly in sick-looking trees, that is; they always seem to turn first in the fall. The infirm of the tree world, unable to last as long in the oncoming harshness of fall. Too nice a day to spend indoors.

When I arrived at work it was an hour later and almost thirty miles south and it seemed more like late summer again. Still too nice a day to spend indoors. Everybody should be outside on days like this, having fun, being careful, not getting hurt, and staying out of the emergency room.

Things were quiet and I made my weekly call home to my folks on the WATS line. They lived about four hours away, in a New York City suburb. My father was still asleep and I chatted with my mother. Not much was new, she got me caught up on what was going on with all the family, friends, and relatives.

"And, oh, by the way, we got broken into again."

"No kidding, when?" They'd been broken into one or two times in recent years, by petty thieves, probably kids. This was not uncommon in the neighborhood.

"Four days, no three days ago. Wednesday, that's it."

"What did they take? They didn't tear the house apart did they?"

"No, they didn't do much. The police said it was probably kids. They just kicked the back door in. Dad had to replace it. They turned over a lot of drawers looking for cash, I guess."

"A real sloppy job, huh?"

"Yeah. Very unprofessional. They took that small portable TV in the den, they took Daddy's portable radio. Hey, do you wanna know what else they took? The took your brother's painting of the roses, the one he did in high school that was hanging in the living room. Isn't that funny?"

"That is funny. I wonder why they took it. I'm sure Robert would be very flattered to know someone thought enough of his artwork to break in and steal it. That's almost an honor. Hey, why don't you tell him they didn't take anything else at all, they just busted the door in, walked past cash and silver and cameras, didn't touch a nickel, but they just left the scene with his painting? I'm sure he'd be thrilled!"

"That's a good idea. I think I'll tell him."

"Listen, Ma, say hello to Dad, I've got to get back to work." Always easy to end a conversation at work.

"OK, sweetie, be good to yourself. G'bye."

"So long, I'll call you next week."

I was thinking about the break-in as I went to see my first patient. He was a big, beefy guy dressed up in work boots, jeans, a flannel shirt so old it had no nap left. He had the deep red tan of an outdoor laborer. He'd started working on his woodpile this morning and got a big splinter in the palm of his hand. Yes, fall is here for sure. The woodcutters are out, piling up logs to fuel their stoves through the endless Berkshire winter. The avocation of woodcutting has its own assortment of injuries. Splinters. Broken toes from dropping logs on them. Getting cut on their saws. Ragged chain saw lacerations. Wood chips in the eye. People pounding wedges with sledges, occasionally sending shrapnel-like flakes of metal from the mushroomed edges deeply into shins and calves.

Fairview made a fair bit of money from its woodcutting clientele.

As the day went on it got busier, with a lot of the usual. Twisted ankles, colds, kids with earaches, back pain, minor lacerations. A couple more woodcutting-related injuries.

During a lull I thought about calling Sal to find out what happened to his patient, but of course, I had no way to contact him.

I was in the doctor's room stretched out on the fold-a-bed trying to snooze. It had been a slow afternoon. I had the new issue of the New England Journal of Medicine on my chest so if anyone walked by I would look studious. One of the nurses was stocking supplies and the other two were talking about girl stuff at the nurses' station. No one was in the coffee room.

Will walked in.

"What are you doing here? Aren't you on tonight?" I asked.

"I came in to get my paycheck so I can get it in the bank before they close today. Yeah, I'm on tonight."

"What's up?" I asked.

"Nothing. You?" He sat on a chair backwards, crossed his arms on the top of the chair back. He put his chin on his arms and looked at me.

"What?" I asked after a moment.

"What's going on with you, Charlie?"

"Nothing. Why?"

"There's got to be something going on. You're acting a lot differently lately. You're tired all the time. The staff says you don't hang out with them anymore. You're withdrawn. It's very unlike you to ever be late for the start of a shift. You've been very out of character.

"I thought you were tired all the time because you were burning the candle at both ends working here and playing hide the salami all the time with Patty. But I called her and she said you don't see her as much anymore and she sees you're different too. And you've stood her up a few times for dates. How could you do that to a piece like her?"

I didn't know what to tell him. I was aching inside from frustration because I really did want to tell him. I wanted to tell someone. I wanted advice. I wanted someone to sympathize with me. I was stuck in this trap all by myself and nobody knew it and I couldn't even tell the people who cared about me the most.

"Nothing's going on. I promise," I said.

"Charlie, you are not a good liar." Will paused. "Is there any way I can help you?"

"No, Will, thank you for offering. I just have a lot on my mind." I got up off the couch and headed to the bathroom to get away from him and to end the conversation.

"Is anything wrong with your family?" Will asked, turning and watching me as I moved across the room.

"No, Will, they're fine, thanks for asking," I replied. "I'll see you at eight." I sat down in the bathroom and waited until I heard him leave.

After Will left I moped for a while and then called Berkshire Medical Center to see what was going on with the kid I trached. Some progress in his respiratory status, he was almost fully weaned from his mechanical ventilator and soon would be able to breathe on his own. But he wouldn't be at all aware of it. Neurologically he was still comatose, not interacting with his environment at all. What a shame.

I tried calling Patty, but she wasn't at home or at the pharmacy.

And so the weekend went. A lot of little stuff. Fortunately nothing very tragic happened, nothing that would much change the course of anyone's lives. Just the way I like it. But nothing very interesting. Nothing I needed to be an internist to deal with. There's the paradox-- it is a definite risk factor for a patient to be an "interesting case." I don't like diseases. They're the bad guys. Even when studying pathology as a first-year med student, I winced to learn about all those bad afflictions people could suffer. Some doctors like patients and hate diseases, other doctors like diseases and hate patients.

After working Saturday and Sunday eight a.m. to eight p.m., I was glad to get out of the hospital and head home. I deserved an ice cream cone on the way home, probably Friendly's double chocolate.

It had gotten chilly again when I arrived home, which made my bladder feel more full, especially after a forty-five-minute ride. I didn't get any ice cream on me. I must tell Patty that. I dropped my knapsack on the floor at the top of the stairs and en route to the bathroom I stopped in my tracks in the living room.

Propped up on the couch was my brother's painting of the roses. Scraped in the crusted oil paint were the words, "Don't be late again."

Every muscle in my body clenched and I stood there vibrating, my shoulders up, my fists clenched by my sides, steam coming out of my ears.

I shouted.

"Goddamn it all, Sal, keep my Goddamn family out of this!"

I didn't know or care if the neighbors were in downstairs. I didn't care if they could hear me.

"What the fuck did you have to do that for? Where do I work? Did you ever think there might be an emergency, you idiot! You big fat thug!"

Phew. I shouted. Loud. I hadn't shouted in years. I could feel it in my throat. I thought, I hoped the house was still bugged. If he put that picture there to get a reaction out of me, he'd probably want to hear it. He would've heard it.

"You really crossed the fuckin' line, Sal!" I added, shouting for emphasis.

I calmed down. I drank a Genny Cream Ale. Quickly. All along I didn't want any trouble. And now he threatens my parents. He could've phoned me at the hospital or beeped me. He had no need to overreact like that. I tried to explain this to Sal the next time I saw him but he brushed it off. He listened but he was unreceptive to my apology, as he had been to my first infraction when I stayed overnight in Boston. If this was his response to strike two, I didn't want to know about strike three. Machiavellian.

CHAPTER 22

"So, how do you figure this stuff out?" Sal asked.

"What stuff?" I asked. We were on the Mass Pike. The autumn colors were at their peak. We were passing through Blandford, near where you could sometimes see two oxen outside a small barn. He was driving, I was in the passenger seat. I guess I graduated. No longer did I have to travel blindly in the back of a dark van. I must now have higher Mob security clearance. Sal had a nice Buick LeSabre and it was a comfortable ride. Except it smelled of cigarette smoke. I was surprised to see an Etch-A-Sketch and a Barbie doll on the backseat. Probably Bob's. I wondered why he didn't have a big, black Cadillac with tinted windows. Or at least a Lincoln Town Car. Though we were getting pretty comfortable with each other I didn't want to ask and risk the sarcasm. Though he was nice for a mobster, he was still a mobster.

Sal was an excellent driver. He kept a steady speed, a few miles above the speed limit. He never got annoyed when some other driver cut him off or wove in and out of traffic. He was considerate of other drivers, signaled his lane changes, gave people plenty of room as ramps merged onto the Pike.

"How do you figure out what's wrong with people, you know, when they're sick?"

"Sometimes it's easy, sometimes it's hard. How much of an answer would you like? This could be a very long discussion."

Sometimes I tried to get Sal back by giving such a long answer he'd be sorry he asked a question.

"Well, Doc, we'll be driving for a while anyway," Sal replied.

"Well, if someone said he was walking down the street, stepped off the curb and landed on his foot wrong and he rolled his ankle, heard a snap, fell down and now it's black and blue and hurts a lot, then he probably broke his ankle. That one would be pretty easy."

"Yeah, I got that one," Sal said.

"But you still have to take an X-ray and see which bones are broken and if there is displacement and stuff like that. And to see if anything else is going on."

"Like what?"

"There's a thing called a pathologic fracture. Which means the bone was diseased or had a tumor in it or something, causing a weak spot and it was sitting there ready to break given an overload."

"You can see that on an X-ray?"

"Yeah, but I'd want a radiologist to read it, it might be subtle."

"I didn't know something like that could happen," Sal said.

"I only saw it once. The guy turned out to have metastatic prostate cancer. So now it's cold and flu season. All day at work we see people with headaches and fevers and sore throats and aches and pains and cough and sneezes. They come in with any combination of these things, and with fatigue and malaise."

"People come to the ER because they have colds?" Sal interrupted.

"Oh, yeah, all the time," I said.

"Isn't that kind of a piddly thing to go to the ER for?" Sal asked.

"Yeah. You'd be amazed at the nonsense people come in for. 'I have a mosquito bite and I can't sleep.' A lady comes in with her three kids and says, 'This one has an earache, the other two are fine but I want them all checked out.'"

"Does that bother you?"

"Not really. At least they have access to care. What bothers me is thinking about all the people who need access to care but don't have insurance or can't afford it. How many women aren't getting their Pap smears and mammograms. How many kids aren't getting vaccinated. How many old people can't afford their meds."

And thinking about the patients Sal takes me to see who really should be going to an ER. I wasn't going to say that out loud to him.

147

"So, anyway, we're back to people with colds and flu. And they all have a different assortment of symptoms from the local viruses going around lately. So you take their history and do an exam and look at their throat and ears and feel their lymph nodes and listen to their chest and all that stuff. And, in the back of every doctor's mind is the knowledge that one of these people, sooner or later, won't be there because of a virus but because they have acute leukemia, or they're septic with a raging bloodstream infection. That's the guy you wanna catch, that's not the guy you want to send home telling him to take two aspirin and call in the morning, because this is the guy who could be dead in the morning."

"How would you pick that guy out from all the others?" Sal asked.

I paused. "I don't know."

"What do you mean 'you don't know'?"

"That's the hard part," I said. "It's the intangibles. You have to remember that each patient is unique. Separate. Just because you saw colds and flu all morning doesn't mean the next similar one will be the same. Common things are common but you have to notice the uncommon."

"You gotta keep your edge?"

"Like that. What are the most likely diagnoses, but if you're wrong, what's the most dangerous diagnosis? There's an old saying in medicine: 'if you hear hoofbeats, it's probably a horse, not a zebra,' but there are a few zebras out there."

"What's that mean?" Sal asked.

"The same thing. Common things are common, but you still have to be prepared for the uncommon. But sometimes there are doctors who are always striving to make some great obscure diagnosis, we say they're always looking for zebras, for them nobody ever has anything common. Those guys are a pain."

"Do you ever have a sick patient and you can't figure out what's wrong with them?"

I turned and looked at Sal's profile as he sat in the driver's seat. I put my hand softly on his shoulder. "Sal," I said, slowly and deliberately, "more often than you want to know."

"So what do you do then?" Sal asked.

"I guess that's one of the obscure parts of doctorhood. What to do when you don't know what to do. What kind of problem solving do you do, Sal? That you can tell me. Do you work on cars? Do you do your bookkeeping? You have a logical system of things to check when your bank statement doesn't match your checkbook ledger. You have a system of checking the car's components when it isn't running right. You go through the system checking those things that are likely and easy to check and keep digging deeper until you figure it out."

"What does differential diagnosis mean?" Sal asked.

"Just what we've been talking about. It's the last step in this system of figuring things out. You collect all the information you can, think it through, and make a list of the most likely diagnoses. Then you need to develop reasons to support your best diagnosis and reasons to exclude your other tentative ones. Do you remember learning the scientific method when you were a kid in school?"

"No, Doc, that was like maybe a hundred years ago."

I was going to give him more information than he'd ever want. It would be revenge for me in a small way.

"The scientific method is a four-step process used to try to figure something out. First is to shape the question into a hypothesis, a theory that you want to prove. Second is to devise an experiment to test this theory. That's usually the hard part. Third, you do the testing and collect the data. Fourth, you analyze the data and make a conclusion. This usually involves a lot of math and statistics."

"Give me a for instance," Sal said.

"Do you remember Robert Koch and his postulates?" I asked.

Sal turned and looked at me for several seconds as hundreds of yards of road flew by without him looking. "You know I don't remember Robert Koch and his postulates."

"Robert Koch was a country doctor in Germany in the middle 1800s. He got interested in bacteriology. He figured out the cause of anthrax that killed so many sheep. Then he found the cause of tuberculosis."

"You're telling me this because...?" Sal interrupted.

"You asked for an example of scientific method in action and I'm giving you one." Sheesh. "So, he came up with four postulates. First the germ has to be present in every animal with the disease. Second, he wanted to be able to grow the germ in the laboratory. I don't remember the third one. Oh. After the germ is grown in the laboratory for a few generations it must still be able to cause the same disease in the test animal. The fourth step is that the germ has to be present in the sickened test animal. Isn't that logical?"

"Doc, you're wearing me out," Sal said.

"How do you think I feel?" I said. It worked. I got him back. I tilted my head back against the rest and closed my eyes.

We got to the house in Springfield. Sal parked in the driveway and we went in the side door, Sal first, and went down the stairs. Bob met us at the bottom of the stairs.

"He's doing worse now, he's really out of it," Bob said to Sal, for me to hear.

"What's the story?" I asked.

I didn't usually get very good information. They didn't want to tell me what had really happened. I needed background information; they never gave me any. It made it hard to be thorough. Sal always said I was thorough enough. When I'd complain, Sal would say, "You're doing a great job, Doc, they're getting much better care than they deserve." That didn't make me feel any better. It was a funny contrast between the level of care that I was able to give in this basement for Sal compared to the level of care in the ER. Different worlds. In this basement Sal says good enough, Doc, good enough, these are bad people Doc, this is more than they deserve. I'm not allowed to make value judgments like that. At work I have to provide the best, and often that is not enough.

"What's the story with this guy?" I asked again.

"He hit his head," Sal responded.

We went into the bedroom and I turned on all the lights. He was a middle-aged man, heavy set with a beer gut, receding short black curly hair with gray on the sides, with a crude bandage of washcloths on his head. He was sweaty, his skin was cool, pasty in color. His breathing was stentorian. Fast and loud. His left pupil was midsize, the right was wide open. His hands were up on his chest, his hands in fists, curled forward at the wrists. His feet were extended down as if he were on tiptoes. We read Plum and Posner's classic text in medical school, called "Stupor and Coma." It was so boring it could put you in a coma. This guy was showing decorticate posturing, meaning he had a very serious brain injury, with bleeding inside his skull that was building up under pressure and pushing his brainstem down through the hole in the bottom of the skull, the foramen magnum, through which the spinal cord exited.

"This guy is in bad shape, Sal. He needs a CAT scan and a neurosurgeon."

"That's not gonna happen, Doc."

Oh, come on. Can't you give in to me just once?

"He's bleeding into his brain and the pressure is squeezing his brain through the hole at the base of the skull. He might have a chance," I pleaded.

"Then he doesn't anymore," Sal said.

I decided to try the holier than thou approach. I put my hands on Sal's shoulders. Slowly. No fast movements near Sal's person, please. My hands were two feet apart. I looked up straight into his eyes. I said, "Thou shalt not stand idle while thy neighbor bleeds."

"I hear what you're saying, Doc. But if you knew the circumstances, you'd understand."

Resignedly I took my hands off him and backed up and went over to the patient. I continued to examine him. He had all the signs. Hyperactive deep tendon reflexes. Downgoing toes. There really was nothing to do. I doubted he would have been salvageable even with a neurosurgeon. I sat down at the bedside. I wondered what really happened to this guy. I'd keep him company while he died. Probably only a few hours away. At least there was someone here who wanted to help him. I was tired.

Sal stood in the doorway. He also filled the doorway. He looked at me, then at the guy on the bed. "What's up, Doc?"

I don't think he intended it to be funny.

"Nothing," I said. "I just thought I'd sit with him a while."

He looked at me. "OK. Lemme know when you're ready and I'll take you back." He left the room.

I wondered what would happen to the corpse. If he was too hot to handle in a conventional medical system, where would he go? Could he go back to his family? Would they bury him in some shallow unmarked grave? Would they take him for a nice boat ride in the Long Island Sound? Could I ask Sal these questions? I didn't think so. We had some very carefully kept boundaries of propriety between us.

Were these victims guys who were on Sal's side of the Mob? If so, how come, with all his contacts and networking, he could not get them more formal care than me? If they were from the wrong side of the Mob, why did they bother to help these guys at all? It didn't make any sense to me. I couldn't figure it out. Did I dare ask Sal to explain this stuff to me?

I sat on the side of the bed, holding this victim's hand. I just stared into the corner of the room, my mind drifting. Another deathbed. As time went by the pattern of breathing changed and he developed a crescendo-decrescendo pattern of breathing also called Cheyne-Stokes breathing, which was a signal of further central nervous system collapse. The guy was like a pithed frog now.

After a while, Bob walked into the room. "Hey, Doc, as long as you're here, can I ask you something?"

"Sure."

"I got a rash. Could you take a look at it?" Bob asked.

"Sure, but I'm not very good at dermatology."

"How come? I thought you were good at everything," Bob said.

"I wish that were true. Skin disease is tough to learn. There is so much stuff that all looks alike that's different. You really need to be a dermatologist to understand that stuff, to be able to split the hairs. But I'd be glad to take a look."

He lifted up his shirt and I looked at his back. He had scattered pink and red spots, some with a little bit of scaliness, and some of them formed vague lines and most of them didn't.

"Gee, Bob. This is one of those tough ones. It could be so many things," I said.

"How come they don't teach you dermatology?"

"I don't know. There's barely enough time to teach enough about heart attacks and cancer and diabetes and stuff. I guess we focus on the more dangerous stuff," I said.

"Doesn't make sense that they don't teach you enough simple everyday stuff," Bob replied.

"You're right. You're absolutely right."

"So what do you think this could be?" he asked.

"Geez, It could be anything from psoriasis to pityriasis to secondary syphilis," I said.

"Syphilis?" Bob repeated in alarm. "This could be syphilis? I'm gonna kill that bitch!" he ranted, his voice rising in pitch.

"No, no, no." I tried to calm him down. "That's just like saying it could be anything from A to Z, I don't have any real suspicion that it's syphilis. It's just a saying, you know, psoriasis to syphilis, it kind of rhymes, don't get all upset," I soothed. *What did I get myself into. Next thing I'll be seeing his girlfriend as a patient.*

"No, really, Doc, do you really think there's even a chance it could be syphilis?"

"No, I really don't."

"What about gonorrhea?"

"No, not that either. Why, does it hurt when you pee?"

"No, I'm just asking. Can you give me something for this rash?"

"It would be easier if I knew what it was. You're supposed to have a diagnosis before you plan a treatment. We could always try a cortisone cream. Want me to write you a prescription?" I reached for my knapsack to find a prescription pad. "What's your name?"

"You know I can't tell you my name. Why don't you just write it out and leave my name blank and I'll fill it in later?"

At that point Sal came into the room. We looked at him. I was sitting on the bed, still, which was littered with my stethoscope, ophthalmoscope, reflex hammer, penlight, tools of my trade.

Sal said, "Bob, how's about you leave the doc alone. Can't you see he's got a lot on his mind with this man dying in front of him. Go outside and have a smoke." It was an order, not a suggestion. Bob got up and left without another word.

I looked at the patient. He was on the down slope of his breathing pattern. I held his wrist. His pulse was getting thready. Sal leaned against the doorjamb, looking at us. I shrugged. In a few seconds he quietly turned and left the room.

The time passed slowly. Every little while Sal would pace into the room. As the time went by the guy's pulse got softer and softer, and with my stethoscope I could only barely hear his heartbeat, and his breathing became weaker and weaker, and then he died.

"He's gone," I said to Sal. I looked at my watch. It was a habit. "Would you excuse us for a minute?" I said softly.

"What do you mean?" Sal asked.

"Would you please step out of the room for a few minutes?" I asked quietly.

"What're you gonna do, Doc?" Sal asked, his voice just above a whisper.

I reached out and gently closed the guy's eyelids. Like in the movies. I didn't really want to tell Sal, just like I didn't want to tell Will. "I just want to say a little prayer, Sal."

"Sure, go ahead," he said quickly, and turned on his heel and closed the door behind him.

I dug the little Kaddish card out of my knapsack, stood and read the Hebrew. I stood there a little while looking at the guy. I sighed. I wondered who he really was, what had happened to him, if he deserved what he got. Who loved him, whom did he love, are there some now-fatherless kids out there? What was important to him? I'd never know. I packed up my things and went out of the bedroom to where Sal was waiting to take me back.

On the drive home, Sal did not ask me anything about medicine or statistics or differential diagnosis. We were quiet in the car. Eventually Sal said, "I didn't know you were religious, Doc."

"I'm not," I replied. *Hadn't I just had this conversation? Oh, yeah, with Will.*

"But you said a prayer for that dead man," Sal added.

"That doesn't mean I'm religious," I said.

"Ah, come on, Doc," Sal urged.

"If you sneezed and I said God bless you, would that make me religious?" I countered. Sal mumbled something I didn't understand, and the conversation ended.

A while later, miles down the Pike, I asked, "How come you picked me for this job? An internist. Why didn't you pick a surgeon?"

After a moment, Sal said, "Surgeons are tough. First off, they always wanna be in charge. Everything with them is an argument. And they really aren't any good without an operating room around them. They want to fix everything by cutting everything. You, you know a lot. All the surgery that can be done in the basement, an ER doc like you can do. You know some neurology. You know how to detox an addict. You know some gynecology. You know your way around sick people who don't need an operation. You can help the old people with their joints."

Funny. Sometimes I felt the same way about surgeons. "We have some funny sayings about surgeons, you know, Sal."

"Yeah? Like what?" Sal asked.

"Like, the way to heal is with cold steel. When in doubt, cut it out. A chance to cut is a chance to cure." Sal chuckled once and kept driving.

He was wearing his navy suit with a spotted paisley tie knotted loosely at his collar. He had not shaved very carefully around his Adam's apple that morning.

Sal said, "Last month a guy I know felt sick. He went to his doctor's and they did some tests but they didn't find anything. A few weeks later he still felt sick and they repeated some of the tests and did some more and found out he had cancer. How come it didn't show up the first time?"

"That has to do with testing theory," I said.

"Testing theory," Sal said, "I bet you're gonna make this complicated."

"I don't like for these things to be so complicated, either. Do you know how hard it was to learn this stuff?" I said.

"If it was easy then everyone would be doin' it, right, Doc?" Sal said. "OK, Doc, I bite, what's testing theory?"

"OK. So. You're a kid in grade school and you take tests. In the tests you grow up with they ask you a question and then you give an answer and it's either right or wrong. Black or white. True or false. The light switch is either on or off. Your car either passes inspection or it doesn't. Your wheel alignment is either OK, a little off, or way out-of-whack."

"OK, I get the idea," Sal interrupted.

"Those are the questions you get used to because they are easy questions. But there are a lot of questions that don't have such an easy answer. Instead of saying true or false, you might want to say, 'it depends'. Some tests are not looking for such a clear-cut answer. You may be asking a question for which there is no easy test. You may be searching for the presence of a characteristic that may often, but not always, be present in a certain disease you are considering."

"Like what?"

"Make believe that I disappear from the face of the earth. After a few weeks someone notices my absence and they tell the police. The police ask a whole lot of questions about characteristics they could use to identify me. Then a few weeks later a body washes up on the shore of Long Island Sound. There's a .45 caliber bullet hole behind the left ear. The body goes to the morgue and they wonder if it could be me. The body is five feet eight. They know that I was five feet eleven. Could this body be me?"

"No," said Sal.

"Of course not. So in this case the height test excludes the body from being me. Right?"

"Right."

"Could the body belong to someone else?"

"Of course," said Sal.

"Then who does the body belong to?" I asked.

"Who knows? There's not enough information," said Sal.

"Exactly. The height test didn't tell you very much, did it? Now suppose another body washes up. This one doesn't have a bullet hole. After they finish chiseling off the cement galoshes…"

"Oh, Doc, with cement galoshes, bodies don't wash up on shore, they stay right where you dump them. But it's been years since we've done stuff like that, anyway."

I turned and looked at Sal, and in a few seconds a smile crept across his face. He reached over and patted me on the knee and said, "Just kiddin' Doc," followed by a throaty chortle. Of all the hoods in the world, at least I got mixed up with one with a sense of humor.

"So after they get the concrete off they measure the guy and he's five foot eleven. Does that mean he's me?" I asked.

"No, but he could be you," Sal responded.

"Exactly right. The test for height can state that it might be me, cannot be me, but cannot specifically state that it *is* me. This test casts a net that will catch everyone my height, will exclude everyone not my height. Therefore it is sensitive for picking up guys my height, but is not specific for Charlie Davids. Follow me?"

"I follow you."

"So we might know that a certain disease will likely show a certain characteristic, usually but not always, and we can test to see if that characteristic is present or not to either add certainty or doubt to a diagnosis, to help whittle down the list of possibilities. OK. So that was the concept of sensitivity and specificity. Now we have to talk about false negatives and positives, and positive and negative predictive values." I hoped this would turn him off.

"Uh, Doc, I think I've had about enough testing theory for one day. Thanks, though, it was good."

"But the reason this stuff is so important is because without understanding these things you don't have the tools to evaluate a study or a claim and see if it holds water. Then you can be a victim of how the newspapers and big companies distort the information to manipulate your thinking. This is how myths get perpetuated. This is why people still want Penicillin when they have a viral cold, and why doctors don't want to give it. This is why people take vitamin C to cure a cold even though the studies don't support it. People don't want to look at something analytically, they just are grasping for something that someone said will make them feel better. And there is always another fad. These days everyone thinks if it's natural, it must be good for them. Ever hear of poisonous mushrooms? They're natural. So are uranium and poison ivy. It's from this ignorance that people want to take laetrile made from peach pits to cure their cancer."

This kept Sal quiet for a while. We drove along the Mass Pike going west. We drove over the Woronoco bridge over the Westfield River.

"I hear eating oatmeal lowers your cholesterol," Sal said. I groaned and put my face in my hands.

"What?" Sal asked.

"That was such a bad study," I said.

"What do you mean?" Sal said.

"You ready?" I said.

"This another long story?"

"Not too long," I said.

"OK."

"OK. So they took, say, five hundred people, and measured their cholesterol. And every day for breakfast they ate a bowl of a cold breakfast cereal made of oat flour. And a month later all their cholesterol levels were repeated and they averaged about ten points lower. Sound good?" I asked.

"Sounds good to me. That's why I've been having oatmeal for breakfast." *Yeah, but you still smoke, and you're still overweight and I doubt you exercise.*

"Remember what I told you about the scientific method and the importance of study design to remove bias?"

"Yeah."

"Well, all these five hundred people were now having oatmeal for breakfast. A lot of them used to have bacon and eggs and sausages and pancakes for breakfast. Now they only have oatmeal. Did the cholesterol go down because of the oatmeal, or because they weren't having the bacon and eggs?" I asked.

"But on the box of oatmeal it says it lowers cholesterol," Sal pleaded.

"If you sold oatmeal, wouldn't you print that on your boxes too?" I countered.

"So I don't have to eat oatmeal?"

"Oatmeal is good for you. It's benign. It gives you some protein and some roughage. But the value is that you're not having the eggs and bacon."

"Doc, you're taking a lot of the fun out of things," he said.

"Look who's talking," I said. "Besides, the public focuses on such minutiae. People obsess about whether to choose whole wheat or white bread only to smear mayonnaise on it with their lean turkey and cheese. They focus on the little picture and ignore the big picture by being sedentary, overweight, and by smoking...."

"Oh please don't start in about smoking," Sal said plaintively. "Geez, Doc, I'm sorry I brought this up. You're not giving an inch."

Geez, Sal, you ain't no picnic, neither.

CHAPTER 23

During the fall, Sal and I went on more and more trips together.

Nothing much changed at Fairview.

I turned down another job.

It got cooler, especially at night.

Sometimes I would drive over Benedict Road, in Pittsfield, up the hill so I could park and look north at Mt. Greylock and the nearby hills. The fall foliage was even more spectacular than usual this year. If you got up Benedict Road early enough and looked across the General Electric Athletic Club's golf course toward Greylock, when there was still frost on the mountain and the sun was just right, you had a view to tell your grandchildren about. If you get to live long enough to have grandchildren.

Sal arranged our trips to alternate very neatly with my time off from Fairview. This resulted in my being forced to break more than a few dates with Patty. She didn't like that very much. She didn't like my vague excuses very much either. Nor could she understand why I didn't want to give her a key to my apartment.

Sometimes he'd pick me up after work, as we did in the beginning. Sometimes I would come home, see his car out front and find him waiting for me on my living room couch, smoking a cigar and reading *The Berkshire Eagle*.

Another thing that was different was that my practice had expanded. I was no longer just taking care of beat-up people in the middle of the night. In addition to that, once a week or so, Sal would line up a half dozen people for me to see in the basement with various common legitimate problems. A man with chronic low back pain. A lady plagued with frequent sinus infections. A tiny silver-haired Italian grandmother dressed in black complaining of arthritis. I felt like a general practitioner in Sicily.

Sal always supervised me. He and the patients always thanked me. We continued to have our fireside chats.

Sal was making it a busy fall for me. It was early November, the trees were bare. I got out and ran in the annual Richmond Fall Foliage Run, placing #192 out of a field of 350. Not too bad for thirty years old. Other than that, I'd done nothing. I hadn't hiked at all. The Appalachian Trail runs through Dalton a half-mile from my apartment, and I hadn't seen it since last year. The leaf watchers were gone, and I wouldn't see anymore city people at Fairview until the snow brought the skiers. I didn't get to see enough of Patty. When I did see her, it wasn't like it had been before.

The kid in a coma at Berkshire Medical Center suddenly got bilateral pneumonia, was put on the ventilator again, and died.

Sal kept me pretty busy. I didn't like what I was doing. Between my two jobs, I was always tired. I didn't like being made to work for him, having to be available whenever he called. It was ruining my relationship with Patty. That was the most upsetting of all. I didn't like him limiting the care his people could get. I couldn't get used to it.

I didn't like having my family threatened. Every time I saw what he'd done to my brother's painting, it made my skin burn. I finally took it to the dump and threw it away.

I couldn't do anything I wanted to.

I resented coming home and finding Sal and his adipose comfortably ensconced in my living room, my three-hundred-dollar burglar alarm quietly and stupidly waiting for someone to break in.

CHAPTER 24

I was sitting at the desk in the nurses' station fooling with the triple-hole loose-leaf punch as I listened to Patty's telephone ringing. Each time I pressed the hole-punch lever down a little and let it snap back up, the whole gadget jumped forward an inch.

"Hello?" Patty finally answered.

"Hello, Patty, this is Dr. Wonderful."

"No shit? I thought you were Mister Mediocre."

"You really know how to hurt a guy," I said.

"They say the truth hurts. What's doing Charlie?"

"Nothing. I'm here at work, it's two in the afternoon on a Saturday and I'm thinking about you and your smiling face and your shiny hair and I'm off in six hours."

"And...."

"And, I'd like to know if we can get together after work."

"What do you wanna do?"

"Oh. Have a beer and talk and stuff. Mostly stuff."

"Mostly stuff. You are so juvenile," she scolded.

"I know and you love it," I retorted.

"OK. Call me when you're done. Bye."

That was quick. She must've been doing something.

"Charlie, you have a call on line two," said the secretary. I picked it up.

"Hi Doc, sorry to bother you, this is Sal."

Oh, no. My spine went rigid. *Don't tell me you need me tonight. I can't stand her up again tonight.* I pressed the hole-punch handle all the way down this time and let it go and the thing snapped almost halfway over.

"What's up, Sal?"

"I need to pick you up after work tonight, Doc."

"Shoot," I said.

"Shit, is what you mean. Wrong vowel. Whatsa matter, you had plans?"

"Yeah. Just made them."

"Break them," Sal said.

"I don't want to break them."

"Break them anyway." I snapped the lever again, the hole punch flipped over and all the little paper dots spilled out all over the place. With one hand on the phone I used the other to collect all the dots and put them in my pocket.

"What've you got?" I asked.

"You know I'm not gonna tell you on the phone," Sal said.

"Why does it always have to be a surprise? If I had an idea of what was up I could prepare and get some supplies. Why do I always have to guess what's behind door number three? What am I gonna tell Patty?"

"Did you have plans with her tonight?"

"Yeah, can I bring her along?" I asked.

"No. Very funny. You want me to take care of it?"

"No," I said.

"See you later," Sal said.

Now what am I going to do? What am I going to tell her? I waited until seven-thirty and called her and asked for a rain check. I told her it was pretty chaotic at work and I was stressed out and wanted to go home to bed.

"Charlie, why are you doing this to me again?"

"I'm sorry, Patty, I'm disappointed, too, I just don't feel up to it. I wouldn't be good company."

"Charlie, just come over. I already went out and got some nice wine and cheese and munchies. Come on over and maybe I can think of a way to help you relax."

"Patty, please let me off the hook. Give me a rain check," I pleaded.

"You suck, Charlie. Call me tomorrow." Click.

Sal and I were driving down the Mass Pike in the dark. I was in the front seat. He didn't know it but I was sprinkling little paper dots all over the interior of his car.

"So, what do we have tonight?" I asked Sal.

"We've got a drunk with the DTs we need you to detox."

"Oh, shoot," I said.

"Wrong vowel again, Doc. What's wrong?"

"I hate detoxing people. It's hard, it's hard on the patient, there's so much that can happen, it's messy, it takes a long time. Why couldn't you tell me that on the phone?"

"Don't you know anything about security, Doc?"

When we got there, the guy was in pretty rough shape. Bob said he'd been vomiting. Of course, no one would give me any history. I wanted to know if it was drugs or alcohol, or both. Just alcohol, they said.

I examined him. His autonomic signs were all messed up. His blood pressure was high, his pulse was up, his respirations were shallow and rapid. He was hyper-alert, agitated, unable to sustain a conversation. His pupils were too wide and he was sweaty. His tongue was dry and coated.

I discussed all this with Sal and Bob. There's such a big spectrum within the alcohol withdrawal syndrome. There's the tremulous type, hallucinatory type, epileptic (the Rum Fits), and then worst of all, full blown delirium tremens. A patient can go from one type to another. They can die. They need a lot of attention, a lot of nursing care. I couldn't really see Sal and Bob changing this guy's sheets or feeding him. I had never treated someone for this outside a hospital, without IV fluids and blood tests. I couldn't depend on Sal and Bob to take his pulse, blood pressure and respirations every half-hour.

"I don't suppose we can send this guy to the hospital?" I asked.

"Nope."

"Why don't we just let him start drinking again and he'll feel so much better. Then you could send him to Alcoholics Anonymous and get off it gradually."

"Nope. They want him dried out."

"This can take a long time," I said.

Sal rolled his eyes and nodded.

I looked in the supply closet. There wasn't anything there that I needed. I made a list of drugs, both oral and injectable. This included Librium, paraldehyde and Aldomet. Syringes. Gatorade.

"Will they have these at a regular pharmacy?" Sal asked.

"Maybe. Maybe not the injectables."

"How am I going to get it?" Sal asked.

"I suppose you must have your ways," I said.

Sal said quietly, under his breath, "I suppose I must."

"Where am I going to find a drug store this late at night?" Sal asked.

"I don't know, Sal, where are you? Maybe if you had told me what was going on I could've brought something?"

"Where would you get it?"

"From the drug closet at work." *Did I just say that? Did I just say I'd swipe drugs from work?*

"You can't be swiping drugs from work!" he said.

"Sal, we'll also need a rubber sheet for the bed, and extra bed sheets. Is there a washer and dryer in this house?" I asked.

Sal and Bob went off and talked for a few minutes. Sal gave Bob my list. He gave Bob the car keys and Bob left.

Until he came back with the meds, all I could do was try to comfort the guy and try to get him to take sips of water.

A couple of hours later Bob came back with a few packages. He put them on the table and I began going through it.

Bob asked, "Hey Sal, how come there's all this confetti stuff all over the inside of your car?"

Sal looked at Bob for a few seconds. "Vacuum them up," he mumbled.

"Huh?" Bob said.

"I said, vacuum them up," Sal barked. Bob left the room.

Sal looked at me for a minute. As he turned to walk away he said, "very funny," under his breath.

I took some of the supplies I needed and went into the patient's bedroom. He couldn't reliably swallow pills for me. I gave him a nice intravenous dose of Librium. The driest martini in town. Then I gave him some Aldomet IV. I kept checking his vital signs. He settled down a little. Spoonful by spoonful I got a cupful of Gatorade in him.

It was now four in the morning. Sal and Bob were sitting together at the kitchen table in the basement apartment, leaning back, arms and legs crossed, with a bottle of whiskey in front of them. They looked tired.

"Doc, you want a snort?"

"Sal, I've got a problem."

"What's that?"

"This kind of patient, it could take days."

"OK. Tell us what to do."

I can't. I can't rely on them.

"I can't. There's too much that can happen. He could go into a coma, or have a seizure or... lots of things. I need to be here. I need to do it myself. I shouldn't leave him."

"OK. If you have to stay, then stay," Sal said, looking at Bob for agreement.

"But I'm supposed to work Monday."

"Then call in sick."

"I can't. It isn't done. That would be dumping on the other docs. It isn't done. We don't call in sick unless we have a 104 degree temperature and a positive blood culture."

"I can take care of it," Sal said. "I'll call them for you."

I paused. "You can't take care of it. I'll do it myself. I'm one of them. If you take care of it, then I'm one of you. I don't wanna be one of you. I don't wanna be here at all. This guy should be in the hospital."

"So, what's so bad about being one of us?" Sal asked, as if his feelings were hurt.

"You mean, other than that you're thugs?" I asked.

"Thugs?" Sal asked, mouthing the word as if it was something distasteful in his mouth. "You think of us as thugs?"

Now his feelings really were hurt.

I got some catnaps in the armchair in the room with the patient. Around eight a.m. I smelled coffee and I went out into the living room.

"How's your patient?" Bob asked.

"Much quieter. Stable. But really dehydrated, he hasn't peed once since I got here. Still disoriented." The three of us sat at the table drinking coffee and eating doughnuts.

At nine in the morning I called Will. I begged him to take my shift for me. He said he would. The hard problem wasn't getting him to agree, it was explaining why I was asking.

"See, Doc, you got that problem out of the way," Sal said.

"Sal, I've got a problem," I said.

"What now?"

"I promised Patty I'd call her today and we'd try to get together. I broke our date last night, she wasn't too happy about it."

"Tell her there's an illness in the family. Just don't say which family," Sal said, laughing louder and louder at his own joke, slapping the table with his hand. *Now I bet he thinks he's cute.*

"No, huh?" Sal said.

"Look, Doc," Sal continued, "if you call her up to break the date she's gonna want an explanation. You'd have to make one up and lie to her. You're no good at that. You want me to call her for you?"

"No!" I said.

"Then you're better off not calling at all."

I took good care of my patient. By the evening he was taking his pills by mouth pretty well and I didn't have to keep fussing with IV injections. I could get him to take sips from a cup and finally began to get some decent volume into him and he finally urinated for the first time. He'd been so dehydrated. He was no longer so tremulous but still quite obtunded, which made him easy to deal with. I kept checking his vital signs but now only once an hour. I wondered who this guy was and why he was important enough to the organization to merit this level of attention.

Sal and Bob would come and go and usually came back with food. One of them was always there with me. On the afternoon of the second day I was getting pretty stir crazy.

"Hey, Sal, think I could walk around the block for ten minutes, get some air?" I asked.

Sal thought about it for a few seconds, looking at Bob.

"Sure, Doc, that's a good idea. I'll come with you." We put on our coats and went up the basement stairs. You can get starved for natural light in a basement. We went out the side door, down the driveway to the sidewalk, turned right and slowly ambled down the block. An older man, a younger man, out for an early evening constitutional, like a father and son. We chitchatted about nothing in particular.

When we got back Bob was busy in the kitchen of the basement apartment and it smelled wonderful.

"Oh, Doc, you're a lucky guy, you're gonna eat good tonight; look what Sal's wife sent over for us." Someone had dropped it off while we were walking. Bob was putting a big casserole of stuffed green peppers in tomato sauce with cheese on top into the oven. He emptied out a big paper bag onto the small counter and the kitchen table. There was a container of marinated olives, one of an eggplant campanata spread, a big, dark loaf of Italian bread, almost black, so hard you could stand on it. The inside was still warm and moist, the crust so crunchy. I wished Patty were there.

"You like red wine, Doc?" Bob asked.

"Yeah, I do, but I never drink when I'm on the job," I joked.

"This here's a Barolo, it's real nice and thick."

Sal and Bob took care of the kitchen detail while I went into the bedroom and ministered to my patient. His vital signs were normal, he was dopey but arousable on all the Librium I'd given him, and over twenty minutes I cajoled him into getting down another two cups of Gatorade. I got a big bowl of warm soapy water and washcloth and stripped him down and gave him a sponge bath. I changed his bed sheets and got him into a clean pair of pajamas.

"Hey, Doc, you almost ready?" Sal asked.

I went out into the kitchen/living room of the basement apartment. What a transformation! There was a red and white checked tablecloth on the kitchen table with three place settings. There was a lit candle in a raffia-wrapped Chianti bottle on the middle of the table. Things were bubbling on the stove and it smelled delicious.

"C'mon, Doc, come and sit down."

"Lemme wash up first." I had just washed down a patient, and I'd been in the same clothes for two days. I went into the bathroom, took off my shirt and T-shirt, and now gave myself a sponge bath. In my knapsack I had a little bathroom kit with a toothbrush and comb and razor and stuff. A shower and fresh clothes would've been nice. I joined them at the table.

"Make yourself comfortable, Doc," Sal said. I did.

He picked up a large bowl, and with a wooden spoon, ladled some pasta onto my plate.

"What kind of sauce is this, it smells wonderful," I asked.

"Ollie-o," Bob said.

"What is it?" I asked.

"It's a very simple sauce. Peasant food. It's aglio and olio. When you say it fast it's ollie-o. Aglio e olio. Garlic and oil. But we fancy it up a little with just a little bit of minced black olives, bacon and pepperoncini." It was delicious.

Sal filled our wine glasses. Barolo. Deep red and delicious. Sal raised his glass. "To you Doc," he toasted. "You're a good man. You're a good doctor."

"To you, Doc," Bob said, his glass raised. We touched our glasses all around. While I was detoxing an alcoholic in the next room.

Sal kept carving slices of the big loaf of bread and handing them around. Both Sal and Bob were in their relaxed mode, with their suit jackets off, their shirtsleeves rolled halfway up their big hairy forearms. Bob had a big pistol in the holster at the small of his back. Sal's was on his right hip. They acted as though they weren't there, but it rattled me.

After the pasta dish came the entrée. I was full already. The peppers, breaded veal cutlets pounded thin, sautéed with a mushroom white wine sauce with capers. Sal's wife made it; Bob reheated it. Delicious. I should've called Patty and had her join us.

As we finished the veal, Sal mopped up the rest of the gravy on his plate with a small piece of bread and popped it into his mouth. He chewed slowly and his eyes smiled. He swallowed, then took a deep breath and let it out. He looked left to Bob, right to me, then up at the ceiling. He tilted back on the rear legs of his chair and stretched his arms out wide. Slowly his arms came back and found their place on his big belly, which he patted affectionately.

"La pancia é grande. Ho mangiato tanto," he said, smiling. "You know what that means, Doc?"

"Something about good food," I guessed.

"My stomach is large. I ate a lot," Sal translated.

I tried it. "La panza grande. Yo mangato tanto."

"Close, Doc," Bob said, "but you gotta lean back and pat your stomach when you say it."

I tried again, following his stage directions.

"You got it now, Doc," Bob said, and Sal agreed.

We all got up to stretch and clear the table. Then they set a cardboard box and a bottle of limoncello and three glasses on the table. We sat down again. In the box were delicious little delicate pastries that looked like light brown clamshells, filled with a light, slightly sweet, lemony cheese filling. So light and crunchy.

"What are these called?" I asked.

"Zvooyadell," Bob said. "You gotta get 'em fresh. The next day they lose their crunch. Like the bread."

"How do you spell that?" I asked.

"I think it's s-f-o-g-l-i-a-t-e-l-l-e," said Bob.

"They're wonderful. Hey, if we're gonna eat like this tomorrow night, can I invite my girlfriend?"

They chuckled and Bob said, "Nice try, Doc, you can't eat like this every night, you'd get as big as Sal. No, tomorrow night it's take-out Chinese food."

An hour had gone by and I went to check my patient. Then I helped clean up the kitchen. I was full, happy and lethargic.

We cleared the table. Sal threw a deck of cards down and said, "OK Doc, now it's time to play poker."

"Sorry, Sal, I'm not much of a card player," I said.

"OK, I'll teach you. It's the best thing I learned in the Army."

The Army. The military. The government. The country. Patriotism. OK, I had a full belly, felt a little loose from the wine, hadn't slept much in the last couple of days and was willing to be a little testy and risk being obnoxious.

"So," I asked, "what kind of a job do you think Reagan is doing?"

"I think he's doing OK, gotta cut the taxes down," he said while shuffling the deck.

"Going to be hard to do that with all the spending he wants to do on the Star Wars missile defense system. Did you vote for him?" I asked.

"Yeah," said Sal, "I always vote Republican."

"And you?" I asked Bob.

"Yeah, I think I voted for him too."

"Do you guys always vote in every election?" I asked.

"Oh, yeah. Always. Usually," Sal said, dealing cards.

I lost another hand at cards. Clumsily.

"Are you guys proud to be Americans?" I asked.

"Damn right," Sal said. "This is the best country in the whole world."

"How come?" I asked.

"Look what this country's done. Look how we've become the leader of the free world. Look how we saved Europe from Hitler. Look how we put Japan in her place."

Look what we did in Korea. Look what we did in Vietnam. I didn't say it. I didn't want to step on Sal's patriotism.

"Look at the opportunity that this country gives people. Look what we do with education and health care. Look what we produce. Look what we invent. We just spend too much money on little pissant countries overseas. Let them take care of themselves, do it the hard way, by themselves. We just hafta keep Russia under control. Too much welfare."

"Bob?"

"Yeah, me too. I love our country. I almost cried when JFK got killed."

"Liberty and justice for all. Life, liberty and the pursuit of happiness? All that stuff?" I asked.

"All that stuff."

"But what about all the kinds of stuff you guys get involved in?" I daringly asked.

"That doesn't apply," Sal said.

"Why not?" I asked.

"Different rules," Sal said.

"Do you think JFK would've thought you were good citizens?"

"Of course. Why wouldn't he?"

"Don't you guys bend the rules a little?"

"No, not Bob and me. We're straight as an arrow. Pure as the driven snow."

"Of course, what was I thinking?" I said while I thunked myself in the forehead with the heel of my palm. "You guys are regular Florence Nightingales."

"We get a warm fuzzy feeling helping you take care of these people and their medical problems. We're just glad all over, being here, helping you take care of that sad ass in the next room."

"Except for the ones who need more than I can give them and you won't let me get them to a hospital, and they die, when they could've been saved."

"You see, Doc, sometimes there are complications that I don't want you to know about, to make it safer for you, and easier for you."

"What about your other, uh, associates, who are not as lily white as you, who are involved in things that might be not legal, that might get people hurt?"

"You see, Doc, everything in the world has its place. There are predators, there is prey, there are scavengers, there are parasites. Anybody can be taken advantage of. But predators usually make out better than prey. If someone comes up to us and wants something from us, we're gonna see what we can get from them. People leave us alone, we leave them alone. If we see a way to make a profit, we'll take it. If someone makes a mistake and we can turn it around to our advantage, we will. That's the way the world works."

I shook my head, not comprehending.

"What?" Sal asked.

"How can there be different sets of rules?"

Sal looked at me for a minute. "Doc, not to be disrespectful, but isn't that a little naïve? There's lots of different sets of rules. There's a lot of different rules down south for white people and black people. There's lots of different rules for men and women. Remember women couldn't even vote once. And there were different rules for Japanese-Americans during World War II. And an educated white guy like you would get more breaks than a Puerto Rican dropout in bad clothes. Look at the different rules there were for your Jewish people in Europe."

"Yes, but things are getting better. Society as a whole is trying to get closer to one set of rules. Blacks are doing better than they were. There are women senators now. Slowly society is becoming more fair, just bit by bit by decade. Shouldn't we be making our own little efforts to repair the world, to shape the world into a more fair place, a more level playing field?"

"Sorry, Doc, I don't think you're realistic. Remember, I went through the college of hard knocks. I've spent too much time in the street to have such big ideas; I'm from a different generation. You sound like those hippies."

"Didn't you say if people leave you alone then you leave them alone?" I asked.

"Yeah."

"What about me?"

"What do you mean?"

"I was minding my own business. I didn't ask to work for you. My life, liberty and pursuit of happiness are being interfered with."

"Aw, come on, Doc. Aren't we taking good care of you? Didn't we just have a nice meal?"

"Sal, Bob, you two are the nicest couple of thugs I would ever want to meet. I'm having a ball with you this evening."

Sal turned to Bob, grinning. "There he goes, calling us thugs again."

"But you did interact with us. You took care of one of our guys in the ER."

"Oh, yeah. By the way, who was that?"

"He was the tall, skinny guy who was a line judge at the race track who got punched in the nose during the Great Barrington Fair. He told us about you."

I thought for a minute. "Oh, yeah, I remember him. But I didn't choose to interact with him. He interacted with me. It was passive. He came to me."

"Aw, come on, Doc, same difference. Besides, we needed you."

"By the way, whatever happened to the guy who was doing this stuff before you got me?"

No answer. That was worrisome.

"So, you do believe in liberty and justice for all, as long as it doesn't inconvenience you, right?"

"Sorry, Doc. I guess we aren't as socially progressive as you are." Sal folded the cards and looked at his watch.

"Well, it's ten o'clock. I'll get going. Bob'll keep you company tonight. I'll bring us a nice breakfast in the morning. Your patient's still doing OK?"

"Yeah, he is. I think he is."

"Good. Good." He patted me on the shoulder. "We're grateful to you. I mean it. But, you're a lousy poker player."

"I didn't mean to give you a hard time in that conversation. I just want to see how you see things."

"No, not at all. I figured sooner or later you'd want to ask some questions." He had his coat on and went up the stairs and left the house.

Bob and I looked at each other.

I shrugged. "You wanna learn how to take vital signs and we can take turns all night? I'll teach you how to take someone's blood pressure."

"I'd rather teach you to play poker better. You're damn lucky we weren't playing for money!"

The patient continued to improve, and the next night Sal and Bob took me home.

CHAPTER 25

I had a day off, and after getting some chores and errands done in the morning, Patty met me at my apartment in Dalton. She also had the day off, and drove up from Great Barrington. We were going to go to Williamstown to the Clark Institute of Art, one of my favorite places. We hadn't been together for a few weeks.

It was a thirty-minute drive north on Route 7 to Williamstown. I always liked this drive; it had interesting things to look at. As you enter South Williamstown the road is on the shoulder of a high open ridge, and to the right, downhill is a beautiful bucolic scene of fields and farms and barns and wood lots worthy of a Currier and Ives print. All of the leaves were off the trees.

The extremely wealthy Clarks, from the Singer sewing machine fortune, established this museum for their collection in the 1950s. The original was a smallish, white, classical stone building, and more recently it had been much enlarged by a larger modern addition. It is in a very lovely setting on the edge of town, just beyond the stately brick Williams College campus buildings, and the Victorian mansions that now serve as fraternity houses. They look very stately from the outside but probably smell like stale beer on the inside.

I often took people to the Clark when they visited me in the Berkshires. What a collection. They were always so surprised to find such a collection in the 'middle of nowhere'. It rivals collections in big city museums, they say. I know nothing about art. I just like to look at things that are pretty. Especially if they tell stories. The Clark has a lot of Winslow Homer paintings and they really tell a story.

I wanted to see their new temporary exhibit of nineteenth- century daguerreotypes of the Yosemite Valley by some photographer long ago whose name escapes me.

I also wanted to show Patty this wonderful museum. She'd not been there before. It is so nice, when you have something you like that is special, to introduce someone you like to it, so they can enjoy it too, and it doubles your own joy to see them catch the spark.

I also needed to give her a lot of attention because I'd been neglecting her. I'd been busy at work as always, which always drains me right down. Also, Sal had been needing me a lot lately, and there were a number of times when I had plans to be with Patty and I had to call it off at the last minute because of Sal. How angry that would make me. When I would call her to beg off, I felt that my excuses were lame and that if I were her, I'd have a hard time believing me. This was so difficult. I really, really wanted this woman in my life, and forces way beyond my control were interfering.

We left her car at my house and drove in my Subaru. We talked about stopping at one of the classy Williamstown restaurants for an early dinner after the museum.

We had some shop talk about medicine and pharmacology and one of the new cardiac anti-arrhythmic drugs that came out, and did she fill any prescriptions for it yet. We spoke about one of the new non-steroidal arthritis medicines. She was funny. Funny strange, not funny funny. She didn't much keep up her end of the conversation. In our months together I had noticed two modes. Most of the time she was funny, sarcastic, ready to tease and hit me hard with one-liners. Sometimes she was quiet, a little withdrawn. Not moody or depressed, just a little distant. But not chilly.

We went through the museum. The daguerreotypes were interesting to me for about five minutes and then they were pretty repetitious. There were about a dozen muddy brown pictures of Half Dome, all from slightly different angles. Also there were pictures of the Yosemite Falls, and tourists dressed in the formal clothing of the era standing in the foreground against Yosemite Valley in the background.

The Cézannes and Renoirs and Monets were just where I left them. Oh, those peaches. Those sunny country homes and flowery fields, Renoir's pretty girl asleep in a chair with a cat in her lap. *Do you think they'd miss one? There are so many paintings here, don't you think I could have just one of them?* At each of my favorites I turned to look at Patty to see if she was smiling. It was subtle.

We went to see two others that I liked, both by Boldini. One was a miniature of a fish market scene, photographic almost; you could see miniscule features and expressions on the tiny figures' faces. In the same corridor, the other painting, Impressionist, was of a pretty young woman in Victorian garb crossing a street on a drizzly day in Paris, carrying a bouquet of pink roses wrapped in paper, reflecting a pinker blush on her pink cheeks. A long legged, high-cheekboned, pretty woman. Like Patty. I wondered what Patty would look like with her hair up like that.

Both by Boldini; one rural and photographic, the other urban and Impressionist; a versatile artist.

We saw the Winslow Homers and the John Singer Sargents and the Monet water lilies from Giverny, and the Degas little dancers.

I like museums, but an hour and a half is enough. Patty felt the same way. The museum has a nice shop, and we browsed there. I asked Patty if there was a print she liked that I could buy for her, for her new bungalow. She turned to me and her eyes looked tight and she smiled for an instant. "Yes," she said, "I'd like that."

Patty picked out a two-by-three-foot poster of Monet's water lilies. She said it looked so peaceful, with the water and the soft muted pink and green tones of the plants. It would go well in her living room. She picked up a rolled copy of the print in a cardboard tube.

As we headed to the cashier I saw on display the same print mounted in a frame, behind glass.

"Let's get that nice mounted one," I said.

We went over and looked at it.

"It's much more expensive," Patty said.

"Yeah, but it will look a lot nicer hanging in that frame on your wall than being held up with thumbtacks."

I paid for the framed print. We left the museum and went to the car in the parking lot. I put the print in the back. Patty stood outside the car, staring into the distance. Beyond the parking area were some large old trees with an outdoor sculpture garden.

"Let's go look at the sculpture," Patty said.

I closed up the car and we walked over. There was a little gravel path that wound through the parklike grassy area under the trees. There were large modern welded metal sculptures all painted white that seemed so much in vogue lately but really meant nothing to me. I did not see anything representational or graceful in them. I have trouble with abstract art. Sometimes it just looks like a welding project. Patty was quiet. She was staring at the sculptures. She was holding a finger to her lip. I thought I saw her lip quiver. We strolled along, not talking. I was watching her. We came to a park bench. Patty stopped. She looked right, then left. There was no one around. She took a deep breath.

"Charlie, please sit down. We need to talk." *Uh oh.*

"Charlie, I can't live like this. I don't understand what's going on with you. You're not like the same guy you were when we met. You're tired. You're distracted. You aren't relaxed and funny anymore. I still don't know why you carry a beeper. Are you selling drugs?"

"No. You're the pharmacist," I volleyed, thinking I was clever.

"I don't know where you disappear to. I don't know why you have to cancel our plans so often. I don't know why our relationship isn't moving forward. I don't understand why you aren't comfortable having me stay at your house. I don't understand why you aren't comfortable staying over at my house. Boyfriends are supposed to like to do that. I don't know if you have another girlfriend. You tell me you don't. I ask you what's wrong and you say it's nothing, you're just preoccupied. It must be something and you have your reason to not tell me. I need more openness if this relationship is going to work. I spoke with Will about you and he says the same thing. He notices you're different, preoccupied, less interactive and you won't say why."

I started to say something.

"Please let me finish, I have to get this out. Charlie, I never told you this, but I was engaged once. He was a guy I dated for about a year and I was surprised when he proposed to me. I wasn't expecting it at all. He got me a nice ring. We had an OK relationship. Maybe it was good. But it wasn't very good. I hesitated when he asked me to marry him. Finally, I said, 'OK, let's be engaged, but lets not set a date yet.' I thought if I accepted it would be a stimulus for our relationship to grow and deepen. But it didn't. It didn't get better. I felt sick all the time. I had to break it off. I knew it wasn't going to work. I had an ache in the pit of my stomach all the time. It was awful. It's a long story. But it's not about him, it's about us.

"I've had a great time with you, Charlie; you're twice the person Alan was, and I really thought we might have a future together. But it isn't working anymore. You've put walls up. I don't know if you just lost interest in me, or if it's because you have your own secret problems. I walk around now with the same ache in my stomach I did when I was going through all that with Alan, and I just can't do that to myself again. I need to take a break from you, Charlie. I hate to do it, but I need to, I have to do it. This is just a bad place for me to be in. I've been here before."

She was sitting there on the bench, tense, her face pinched, her eyes almost closed, looking at the middle space between us. She was leaning forward, her forearms on her knees, her hands together, her ankles tucked under the bench. She was in knots.

She was right. Completely right and I agreed with her. She needed to protect herself. I wanted to protect her. I wanted her to be safe and happy and secure, but if I told her what was really going on, she would be less safe. I needed to say something but I didn't know what. I wanted this woman in my life. If only I could tell her about Sal and all. If only I could explain to her, if only I could confide in ·her, in anybody, about this vise I was squeezed in. Secrets are hard to keep and once out you can never reclaim them, and I had no idea what consequences might follow.

"Patty, I think I understand how you feel," I said, expecting her to say, "No, you don't."

"I am sorry that these past months I haven't been myself and I haven't been there for you." Pause. "Do you think you could bear with me for a few more months?" *As if I thought something might get better in a few months.*

"No, Charlie, I'm sorry, no. It's been more than a few months already. I'm already past my maximum. Charlie, could we please skip dinner? Would you please take me back? I want to go home." Her head was now in her hands and I saw her fingers glisten with tears. I took her back to her car.

CHAPTER 26

The next days were not ones for the scrapbook. I was devastated. Crushed. Deflated. Rejected and dejected. Depressed, detached and disconsolate. Pretty shitty.

I was always tired, but once in bed, too restless to sleep. I was hungry, but had little interest in eating. I wanted to be half drunk all the time, but I didn't want to emulate Fairview's midnight clientele. I sat around my apartment and moped. I felt cold. Not cold as in chilly, but cold as in numb. Without feeling. Without vitality. As if the warmth in my body had suddenly been puffed away in an icy Berkshire breeze.

Maybe I should give up. Stop thinking so much. It would be easier. Join them because I cannot beat them. Let them work me, keep me busy and distracted so I will forget the emptiness. Let them continue to push me around like a chess piece, let me become an automaton. I can barely care.

Thanksgiving came and went. I heard nothing from Patty. When I wasn't working at Fairview or with Sal, I sat around at home. I took a lot of naps, and I watched television.

My pants got looser. Sometimes my legs would tingle when I sat on a hard chair too long. My butt had less padding.

One of the nurses asked me how come I looked tired all the time. Another asked, "Hey, Dr. Davids, how come you don't tell dirty jokes with us anymore?"

One of the doctors noted my recent weight loss and asked if I was on chemotherapy. I would have to keep up a better front.

Being an automaton made some things easier. I didn't care about anything. Vacant days passed quickly. I didn't mind. After a few weeks, I became disgusted with myself.

On the first page of the second section of *The Berkshire Eagle* one December morning was a small article about a murder in Hartford, Connecticut. Hartford was an hour and a half away. A forty-seven-year-old man, a reputed mobster, was found shot to death in front of his $200,000 suburban home. He was shot in the head with a single, small caliber bullet. Investigators called it a gangland-style slaying and said that it was under investigation by state and federal authorities.

I hoped that business wouldn't pick up.

It did. I started getting more calls from Sal and he didn't come by himself anymore. We rode in the van again, and I had to lie on the cot so I couldn't see where we were going. And now there were always several other men along for the ride. All of them big. And nervous looking. They often kept their hands in their pockets. We didn't go to the usual basement apartment anymore. Sometimes we would drive around in circles for a long time before pulling up somewhere. Sometimes we'd wait in the van for a long time before getting out. I thought about taking my gun along, but didn't. A few of the people they took me to see had gunshot wounds. I could not provide them all the care they needed.

They were no longer so considerate of my schedule at Fairview. Several times I didn't get back in for the start of my shift. This was met with great consternation by the staff, especially by the guy I was supposed to relieve.

It was very unlike me to suddenly become so habitually tardy, they said. I became disinterested and distant. And always tired.

One day my boss gave me the benefit of the doubt and asked if anything was wrong. I said there wasn't, and he went on to say that the staff had brought to his attention the fact that I'd been behaving differently, coming in late, not interacting as well as I had. Implying that if there was really nothing wrong, I had better clean up my act.

On Christmas Day, the boys picked me up at the usual place, and I took my usual place on the cot in the van. I'd learned to dress very warmly for these trips; it was always freezing back there. They drove me to the back of a liquor store. There were several men waiting for us. My patient was the unconscious one in the storeroom. He was a young man. His straight brown hair was matted with dried blood that had oozed from his left ear.

"What happened?" I asked.

"What do you think?"

"Sal, I need to know," I volleyed with annoyance.

"He got hit."

"With what? A stick, a fist, a bullet?"

"I don't know. Maybe all three."

"When did this happen?"

"A couple hours ago."

I could see I wasn't going to get much information, once again. I examined the man's head. There were swellings and bruises from being hit, but I didn't see anything that could pass for a bullet hole. On his head or anywhere else. His pulse felt thready, but his blood pressure was OK. He was in a light coma. He did respond to painful stimuli on both sides. His pupils were of normal size and reacted to light. Yet another head injury. We'd been seeing lots of them.

"Sal, we gotta take this guy to a hospital."

"How come?"

"He's bleeding inside his skull, it's putting pressure on his brain and that's why he's in coma. Not as bad as that guy a few months ago."

"So?"

"What do you mean, so? He has to have surgery. They open him up, tie off the bleeder, and suck out the clot. Takes twenty minutes and he could be good as new."

Sal looked at me and swallowed hard.

"Forget it," he replied quietly.

"What do you mean, forget it?" I asked incredulously.

"It can't be done."

"Why the hell not? He's a young, strong man and some simple surgery could save his life!" I was getting exasperated. "You owe him that, Sal. To deny him, that is murder!"

"His blood's not on our hands," said one of the other men.

"Bullshit," I exploded. "You're just as murderous as the bastard that hit him! I'm sick of this stuff."

"Now, Doc, don't get so excited," commanded Sal sternly.

"Don't tell me not to get excited! Sal, you're just gonna let another poor bastard die? Give me a break. Give him a break. Just for once, let me take this guy to the hospital. I'm begging you!"

"Now, Doc, settle down. You just don't understand. This man is a bad man, he's done a lot of bad things to people in his life. Awful things. You can take it from me, society would be a lot better off without this guy."

"Who the hell do you think you are, passing judgment like that?" I shouted.

"Doc..."

"You're pretty fuckin' blasé about human life aren't you?"

"Doc!"

"Listen, there's this oath I took that says..."

"Take him away," Sal commanded.

The goons sandwiched me, pinned my arms against my sides and carried me off. As I left the room, I caught a glimpse of Sal standing in the storeroom, his hand over the left side of his chest, his face pinched. He was looking down at the dying man on the floor.

The next time, I would do something. It was time. I really wasn't living anyway. I had nothing to lose. I would try.

CHAPTER 27

Sal and his friends didn't know it, but I was following right behind them, driving through the slushy Springfield streets during a freak January thaw. I went out on a case with them and they dropped me off at my car in the supermarket parking lot. I started up and drove a block to where I'd left the small Plymouth I'd rented. I parked my Subaru and headed off in the Plymouth toward the Mass Pike. Two miles beyond the tollbooth I spotted them ahead of me in the left lane. It was midnight and they were speeding.

I had changed into a ratty old army coat. That was my disguise They would never recognize me in that, in a different car. Not a clean-cut young doctor. With me I had my Smith & Wesson fourteen shot Angel of Death. I also brought extra cartridges, a flashlight, my Dictaphone, binoculars, cord, a hammer, pliers and a heavy screwdriver. I was equipped for anything, loaded for bear. I was riding behind them, smiling, their license plate number well memorized. I had no idea what I was doing, but I was going to do it. It didn't matter. I didn't know what information I might find. Maybe when I found it, I would know what to do with it. It didn't really matter to me. I had nothing to lose, and I smiled as I drove behind them. I wasn't tired at all.

I tried not to follow them closely. We drove into the familiar Springfield neighborhood. Finally the van stopped in front of a small, neat, two-story brick house with Sal's LeSabre in the driveway. Sal got out and went into the house. He flashed the porch light, the van pulled away.

Should I watch Sal, or follow the van? I followed the van. We drove into a more rundown-looking neighborhood and the van let off another passenger, who quickly disappeared into a dark doorway. I drove past slowly in the darkness, trying to fix the image and address in my mind.

I continued following the van, until just the driver was left. It was getting boring, and I thought I would head back to Sal's.

On the way, I got a little lost, but in my wanderings I passed the spot where one of the other men had been let off. I drove past, took a right, and found a parking spot a block away. In the unfamiliar car, I found you had to press a little button on the steering column to get your key out. I got out from the warmth of the car into the damp cold of the January night. The stars were out, there was no wind and you could smell the city in the air. I walked around the block the long way, my hands in my pockets, cradling the butt of my weapon. I chuckled as it occurred to me that it was the only butt I'd cradled in a while. *What am I doing with a gun?* I wanted to look around where the guy had been dropped off. Maybe I'd learn something. Get a name off a letterbox. What would Humphrey Bogart's character, Sam Spade, do? I wished my feet didn't make so much noise in the slush as I walked, my ears now thoroughly cold.

I looked for the doorway that had footprints in the slush going toward it in the right direction from the curb. The doorway I decided on had no mailboxes or doorbells. I tried the door of the tenement. It opened to a stairway. It was much warmer inside, but it was dark and I'd left my flashlight in the car. I wasn't in the mood to go back for it.

I did, anyway. Might as well be thorough and do what I came to do.

Back at the car I got in and turned on the heater to thaw out my ears. I changed my mind about the tenement and I worked my way back to Sal's house. I parked a few blocks past it, headed away, with the driver's door unlocked. The getaway car. Tonight I was thinking of everything. Real slick.

I walked back to Sal's house and studied it from across the street. Brick on the first story, white shingles on the second. A driveway, and ten feet separating it from the next house on the left, ten feet and a driveway to the next house on the right. All three looked the same. A bay window off the living room on the front of the house. A side door opening to a stoop, and the driveway on the left side. Evergreen shrubs laden with wet snow. The house on the right still had a modest string of Christmas lights burning, even at one-thirty in the morning. I thought I saw a string of unlit lights under Sal's eve. I noted he did not have an electric Chanukah menorah in the window, as I still had.

I stared at the house, waiting for sleuthful inspiration. Disappointed, I pulled up my collar, shrugged my shoulders up to protect my ears from the cold wind that had picked up. The slush was freezing. I sunk my hands into the large pockets of the old army coat, my right hand wrapped around the gun; turned, and set off to walk around the block. I wanted to look at Sal's house from the other side. Check out all the angles.

As I reached the corner, I left the protective bulk of the houses, which had shielded me from the wind. It made me even colder, but tonight was my night and I wouldn't let a little cold wind get to me. The blocks were set up like checkerboards, all streets met at right angles. I took a left, passed two houses, took another left, counting houses as I walked. Sal's house was the eighth from the corner, one street over.

I stood opposite the eighth house from the corner on this block. It was very similar to Sal's house; all of them were similar. A station wagon was in the driveway and a snowman stood pathetically deteriorating on the front lawn.

I crossed the street and stood on the sidewalk. I went to the driveway and peered down it. In front of me was the station wagon, beyond that the garage. To the right, I could see the backyard in shadows of cold moonlight. A picnic table, a swing set. It was a small yard, bordered in back by a four-foot-high chain link fence that separated it from Sal's yard. It was two in the morning and there was a light on at Sal's house. Back room, ground floor.

Having thoroughly checked out the lay of the land, I was ready for action. I continued circling the block, not wanting anyone in a house I'd passed to remember seeing me walking back and forth. As I was walking, I saw headlights coming toward me, several blocks ahead of me. I ducked down beside a parked car so I wouldn't be seen, but it made a right turn ahead of me, down the street I'd be walking on when I reached the corner.

When I finally got to Sal's house, I stopped and looked up at the stars, and filled my lungs with the clean, cold winter night air. Star light, star bright, I wish I get out of this mess tonight.

I walked very slowly, placing each foot carefully and quietly. What had been slush on the ground had frozen into uneven ice. I slowly walked down the shoveled driveway toward the rear of the house. I passed the side door and stoop, past the garbage cans. I came to the back corner of Sal's house and huddled against it. As I slowly peered around the corner, I caught the wind in my face again and it made me swallow involuntarily. The lighted window was above me. It was five feet in from the corner of the house and the bottom of it was six feet above the ground. There was light coming through a translucent knit curtain of yellows, oranges and browns. From my awkward angle, I couldn't see inside. I crept beneath the window, checking the ground to make sure I didn't trip. I stood quietly, listening, but all I could hear was the hiss of the winter wind and the rattling of branches in the bushes and trees. I stepped about three feet from the wall and looked up, but all I could see was part of the ceiling of the room.

I went back to the wall and crouched down. I stared into the yard waiting for my eyes to readjust to the darkness after looking at the window.

Slowly I crept over the frozen snow toward the garage. From there I might better be able to see inside the window. I was doing great. Very quiet, very stealthy. I took my time and made it to the garage without a slip. I leaned against the side of it and looked around. The window was twenty or twenty-five feet in front of me. The fence between the two yards was twenty feet behind me. Sal's yard was empty. I wanted to check out the terrain before looking at the window and losing my night vision. I was being so skillful.

I could see in the window, but nothing was clear because of the gauzy knit curtain. I could see a dark rectangle that was probably a piece of furniture, or a picture on the wall. I leaned against the garage, waiting to see something in the room.

The minutes went by. I heard a dog bark once, a few houses away. Sal's neighbor's bathroom light went on for a moment, then off.

I fantasized that the hoods were having an executive staff meeting in the house. I would sneak in and suddenly come crashing through the door, my Smith & Wesson holding them all at bay. I would deliver my ultimatum. If they accepted it, we would all drink a toast of Grappa to our new understanding, and they would applaud my strength and daring courage.

If they refused, or if they underestimated my skill, I would leave the house littered with bleeding bodies and smoking spent shell cases.

Walter Mitty had nothing on me.

A movement in the room brought me back from my daydream. A shadow moved across the curtain. Judging from the size of the shadow, it must have been Sal. Then the light went out. An upstairs light went on for a few minutes, and then off.

Great. I had gone through all this trouble and surveillance to watch Sal stay up late and then turn out the light to go to sleep. Suddenly I felt cold. The excitement, now gone, had kept me warm. I decided to stay where I was for fifteen or twenty minutes so Sal could fall asleep before I snuck out of his yard.

The next five minutes took a long time to pass. I stood there in the cold, looking at my watch, suspecting it was running slow. It was cold, I was tired, it was time to go home and go to bed. Enough sleuthing for one night. I kept reminding myself not to stamp my feet.

After another five long, boring minutes, I decided I would go to the back of Sal's yard, hop the fence, and exit through the rear neighbor's yard. I wanted to leave Sal's place as directly as I could.

I turned and walked slowly to the fence, planting each rubber sole firmly downward on the glazed snow. I put both of my hands atop the fence, bent my knees, sprung up and neatly vaulted over, legs together in the finest form, landing quietly on my toes on the other side.

I was getting away. Confidently, I walked through the yard along the garage, heading for the driveway. As I passed the front of the garage, I stopped short as a large form suddenly appeared in the shadows, an arm's length in front of me. Before I knew what had happened, his battering ram of a fist hit me in the stomach. My arms reflexively crossed over my abdomen as I bent over in pain, as if broken in the middle, gasping, breathless. An instant later his knee came up and struck me in the face. It snapped my head up and I straightened up, my right cheek and nose feeling crushed, my eyes squeezed closed in pain. He threw a punch to my left eye and another to the right side of my jaw. They were explosive bursts of pain, complete with stars and sparks, leaving me dazed. He kicked me in the groin, and my arms dropped from my face to my crotch as an excruciating ache spread through me, followed in an instant by nausea.

I heard movement behind me, but I was powerless and too disinterested to look. I felt a firm, but painless, tap on the back of my head, began feeling a comfortable, restful warmth pervade my body. I fell forward into the snow.

CHAPTER 28

When I awoke, I was sitting on a hard, metal folding chair. My neck ached as I picked my head up off my chest. As my mind cleared, I became aware of throbbing and constant pains. I tried to say "ow" and felt a red-hot ice pick pain in my right jaw joint. I could taste blood in my mouth.

I could see only out of my right eye. My left eye was swollen closed. That's why I thought I couldn't see out of it. I couldn't touch it to see if it was. My hands were tied tightly to the chair behind me. So were my legs. I was alone in a cold dark room. The floor and walls were gray concrete and the windows were few and up high, so it probably was a basement. Across the room, hanging from the ceiling, was some clothesline running beneath the joists.

It hurt to move, to turn my head. I could only breathe in shallow breaths. I wanted to throw up. My whole face was throbbing. The back of my head hurt.

I sat there, slowly remembering what had happened. I had really blown it. I wished they had killed me so I wouldn't be here, feeling this bad. I would have accepted getting killed when I set out on this thing. I had nothing to lose and all to gain. Getting beaten up wasn't one of the options I'd agreed to. Maybe they'd finish me off.

Sometime later, I heard something to my right. I heard someone coming downstairs. Turning to look gave me a jolt of pain that made me clench my teeth, triggering another jolt of pain in my jaw. When the man moved into view of my right eye, I saw it was Sal. I nodded.

"Doc. Doc, Doc, Doc." His quiet, lazy tones.

"What did you have to go and do this for?" He began to wince. He walked over and got another folding chair from the darkness. He set it near me and sat down.

"Huh, Doc? What did you have to do this for?"

I didn't answer. I looked down.

"You look like shit, Doc. They really did a job on you. How come you came here snoopin' around with a gun in your pocket like some kinda secret agent? What the hell are you doing with a gun? Doc, I warned you once, I warned you twice. You really shouldn't have done this. How come?"

I tried to speak, but it hurt too much.

"I just wanted to find a way out," I finally managed to say.

"Why? How come, Doc? Didn't I pay you enough? Did I mistreat you?"

"Because it's dangerous. It's illegal. It's immoral. I can't live like this. I need a life."

"Doc, it's too bad you feel this way. It's too bad this had to happen. Goodbye, Doc." He turned and left, his right hand going under his left lapel.

Goodbye? What did he mean, goodbye? Sal slowly went up the stairs. A moment later I heard lighter, quicker footsteps coming down the stairs. It was one of the big young goons who had often accompanied Sal on our rounds. He walked over to me and stood directly in front of me. Six feet away. I looked up at him. He was expressionless. He was stuffing tissue paper into his ears.

"Doc, you got sixty seconds to pray," he said, gesturing at me with his right hand. In the hand, to my horror, was a gun. My gun. Pointing at me. With a great big hole in the end of the barrel. I was stunned. Casually he looked at the watch on his left wrist as if he was waiting for a bus.

He was going to kill me. I closed my eyes tight, my nose began to run and my eyes watered as I realized my last seconds were ticking by. *Oh God, I am not ready to die, I'm only thirty, there are so many things I haven't done yet. Don't waste me because of these criminals. I have just begun to live, I have just begun to love. Don't kill me, please. Or kill me but leave my family alone. Don't hurt them, don't do this to them. How did I even get sucked into this mess?*

I was in silent panic when the gun went off. An immense explosion, a concussive atmospheric force jolting my body, breaking my ears. A bright flash of orange flame visible even through closed eyes. A megaton sledgehammer slamming me, throwing me backwards onto the concrete floor, my hands mashed beneath the chair, my eyes closed, my mouth and sphincters open, new pain from many places, the echoes reverberating in the concrete cellar.

I fought to catch my breath. I lay on the floor, still tied to the chair. I was not dead. Why, why did they not kill me, and end all this? It could've been over now.

They let me lie there for a long time, soaked in tears and blood and urine. My left thigh was the source of a new agony. My left wrist was pinned beneath the metal edge of the chair's seat beneath me. I couldn't rock myself to free my wrist. They let me lie there a long time to think about the gloom of death, the sweetness of life. It was confusing. Of submission, of resistance. Of discipline. Of morals, of survival. Of experts, of novices. Of wisdom and fools.

CHAPTER 29

I could see panels of early morning gray through the cellar's casement windows. Two of them, the young ones, came down and untied me from the chair, overturned on the floor. One on each side, they lifted me to my feet. With the change in posture, the throbbing in my leg became colossal, and I weakened, light-headed, faltering. Silently, they half carried me across the basement, creating a breeze that made my soaked trousers feel cold against the fire in my leg.

They set me on a hard bench. One of them went upstairs as the other turned on a light and put a large cardboard box beside me. I felt drugged and the room spun. Drunkenly I looked in the box and saw a bunch of medical supplies spinning within it. Then the man who had gone upstairs was putting a big mug of black coffee in my hand. My left hand didn't work right.

The hot coffee burned my split and swollen lip, it ran down my chin onto my chest.

Temperatures, temperatures. The orange hot flare from the gun, my seared thigh, the cold damp cellar. The cold wet of my pants. The rough heat of the coffee.

"Try to drink it," one of them said.

Easy for him to say. I tried again to sip, my jaw joint screaming protest. It was good. I sipped. The warmth spread. I kept sipping. My jaw loosened up.

They refilled the mug. Strong black coffee. Hot, with sugar.

I was waking up. I felt warm. Things began to look less fuzzy.

What I was leaning against as I sat on the bench was the side of an old stained soapstone laundry sink.

The throbbing in my leg was steady. I resisted looking down because it made my bruised face throb, but I wanted to see my leg.

Yes, it was still there. The brown corduroys were soaked black. There was a large clot looking like jelly covering the groove the bullet had made on the side of my thigh, oozing down my leg. There were singe marks on the torn edges of the corduroy.

I undid my belt and opened my pants. The dried blood stuck and hurt and the jelly clot disgustingly oozed as I peeled my pants down to my knees.

I took some gauze from the box and painfully reached to the sink to wet it. One of the boys turned the tarnished brass faucet. How kind.

I dabbed at the blood on the side of my leg, trying to find where the wound was. It was much easier to do this to someone else. I found it. It was a six- or seven-inch long diagonal groove. It must have been an inch wide, split like an overcooked frankfurter. I was glad the gun salesman hadn't sold me hollow points.

It hurt too much to try to clean it any more. My efforts had renewed some bleeding.

I put some packing over it and bandaged it, wrapping it around and around and around.

The boys stepped forward and helped me to my feet. I almost screamed when my pants pressed against the bulky dressing.

They helped me up the stairs. I could almost support myself. We went out the side door. They put me in the little Plymouth.

And I drove away.

I was looking for a big tree to drive into. But I wouldn't have been able to get up enough speed in residential Springfield to do it right. I got onto the Mass Pike, headed west.

As I drove, I clenched my teeth and I enjoyed the pain each time. *Why did they do this to me? Why couldn't they have had the decency to finish the job?* It was hard to drive with one eye open.

Every time I saw a good solid abutment for an overpass coming up, I saw the perfect opportunity to become a blazing fireball. But each time I approached, there were damned guardrails cleverly placed to guide me away from the concrete.

The Westfield River was coming up and that seemed like a good prospect. But there was a three-foot retaining wall on the right side of the bridge. Maybe if I went real fast in the left lane and then pulled the wheel sharply to the right I might hit the wall with enough force to roll the car over it. By the time I figured this out, the river was a mile behind me. Damn. Nothing was going my way.

After an endless drive, I finally pulled into my own slushy driveway. I lusted for my bed. Attempting to get out of the car, I found that my shot leg had stiffened up. It didn't like bearing weight, it liked bending even less. Throb, throb, throb.

I half hopped my way onto the porch, fumbled with the lock, and managed to crawl up the stairs on all threes.

There were several things I had to do before I could collapse. I had to call the rental agency to come and pick up the car. I hoped I hadn't left any suspicious maroon addition to the maroon upholstery. I needed to make up some lame excuse, call Fairview and tell them I needed a leave of absence.

That done, I dragged myself into the bathroom, leaned on the sink and looked at my face in the mirror. I was dizzy. It was now after ten in the morning. I looked as if I'd had a rough night.

Gently I washed my bruised and swollen face, and rummaged through the medicine chest. I took two codeine pills left over from a bicycle wreck a few summers before. I started to undo my bandage, but it hurt too much. I put some ice against it in a plastic bag and wormed my way into bed.

It was dark when I awoke, and I was disappointed I wasn't dead. The leg was still throbbing, even more than before. I couldn't bear weight on it. I wanted to cry, but the tears wouldn't come. The pain was just a small part of it. Everything, everything was such a mess. My nice neat little world had been blown apart and it didn't seem worth trying to rebuild it. If only I could cry, it would be such a small but welcome outlet for my frustration. I made it to the bathroom, swallowed more codeine, ran the tub and got in with my pants still on. I soaked for a long time. After my leg had gotten used to its new position, I undressed. Piece by piece, I flung my sopping clothes into the far corner of the room. I undid the bandage and let the warm water soften the crusted blood.

I dozed. When I awoke, the water was cold. I needed more codeine. While I ran more hot water, I crawled out and took two more pills, emptying the bottle. I soaked the carpet as I stood, and I hurt no less than before. As I moved back into the tub, the soaked gauze finally fell off, landing with a splat. The hot water felt bad on the wound and good on the rest of me and I remembered to turn it off before falling asleep again.

When I next awoke, the tub was barely warm. The long soak had softened the wound and the bath water was tinged pink. Good thing there were no sharks.

The leg was black and blue and purple. The wound edges were swollen open and an inflamed purple-blue. Within the wound I could see the yellow-red globular texture of the subcutaneous fatty tissue, and the fascia beneath. The bullet only barely grooved the muscle. The high velocity bullet caused a hydraulic shock wave that shattered the tissue, blood vessels and lymph channels, causing deep bruising and swelling for several inches all around.

Not being as well supplied as Sal, I covered it with a washcloth, made a new ice pack, grabbed a liquor bottle and crawled back to bed.

And so it went. I would sit in bed and drink until the pain lessened, and sleep until it reappeared. I could drink away some of the pain, but not the disgust. When I would awaken, the ice would be melted and I would limp around the apartment using a ski pole for a cane in my right hand. My left hand had no grip strength. Three things to do: Urinate; get more ice; get another bottle.

Several days must have gone by this way. I drank my way through the good stuff and was left with only cooking sherry. While lying in bed one time waiting to fall asleep, I noticed the pain in my leg was almost tolerable. I continued drinking to continue sleeping, which was the next best thing to being dead. Except that dead men probably don't dream. Dreams made sleep an imperfect escape.

I lay in bed, aware only of my leg and a new gnawing in my belly. As I rubbed my sunken stomach, I realized I had not eaten in days. My throat was dry and my lips were peeling. Each time I hobbled around the apartment with my ski pole, I was more and more light-headed. With great effort, I prepared some Kraft macaroni and cheese and ate it. It felt good and I ate too much. Too fast. My abused stomach protested and I vomited in the kitchen sink.

Later, I ate again, more slowly, and it stayed down. I took another bath. The wound looked better. Less swelling, less red, less raw. I could put more weight on it and I had more mobility.

I began to take care of myself. I continued eating. I stopped drinking. My black eye began to open up and fade. I slept a lot, though less than before. The gash on my leg began to close. I could now hobble, almost comfortably, my ski pole and me.

It seemed like I would be a survivor, but I was not sure if that was a good thing.

I wasted time in front of the TV watching idiot soap operas. I opened a book but could not concentrate. I had not thought at all about what I was going to do. It was easier to just ignore it. They might as well have shot me dead, because that's the way I felt.

I was sitting on the couch, in the same spot, in fact, that Sal sat the night we first met. I was watching some stupid game show and I heard steps at the front porch.

I kept watching the show.

The doorbell rang. I ignored it. The TV was on but I wasn't paying attention. Whoever was at the door was stomping the snow off his feet, and it made a loud drumming sound on the wooden porch floor. In a minute the doorbell rang again. I hoped whoever it was would just go away. It rang a third time and then whoever it was jiggled the doorknob. I heard the door push open. I guess I didn't click it closed all the way.

"Hello?" It was Will's voice.

"Hello? Charlie?" I heard footsteps up the stairs.

"Hi, Will," I said. It was the first time I'd heard my voice in days. He came into the living room from the hallway, where I sat on the couch, in pajamas, wool socks and an ancient blue terry cloth bathrobe and my ski pole crutch beside me.

He stood there looking at me for a minute, his expression blank. "Charlie, you look like shit." I'm sure I did.

"When I heard that you took a leave of absence I tried calling to find out what was going on but there was never any answer."

I didn't say anything. He hadn't asked a question. Yet.

"We're in a little bit of a lurch finding people to fill your shifts."

I didn't say anything. I did feel badly about letting them down, but what could I have done? I didn't ask to get shot. I hoped he wouldn't see the bandaging material on the counter in the kitchen. Or the bloody gauze in the bathroom trash pail.

Will walked around the apartment. First he went into the kitchen. I heard the refrigerator open. There was almost nothing in it. He opened the freezer door. He must have seen the dishes in the sink, the liquor bottles in the kitchen trash, the bandages. He went into the bathroom.

He walked past me in the living room to my bedroom, which was messy and had bottles and glasses in it, too.

He came back to the living room and sat across from me. He looked at me for a few moments without speaking.

"So, here is my analysis. You're in trouble. You got beat up. It would have to be big trouble for you to let it interfere with your work. Clearly you didn't take a leave of absence to run off to Vegas with some floozy. Clearly you didn't blow us off to take a better job. You didn't win the lottery and sail off for the Caribbean. There's no Porsche out in your driveway. If you'd had surgery or an accident you would not need to be secretive about it, unless you'd had a penile implant or a sex change. So you must have been badly hurt. You're in trouble and you're scared and you're trying to be an alcoholic and you won't tell me anything because you're afraid or embarrassed to bring me into it. Knowing you, I can't imagine you'd be stupid enough to get involved in anything illegal unless you got framed or strong-armed. Did you welch on some gambling debts? I don't see an extravagant lifestyle. I don't think you have a drug habit. I don't think you're a gambler. I get the sense this is situational and not a major depressive episode. You wouldn't be afraid to get psychiatric help if you needed it."

"Will, you are a very bright and insightful man and I'm very grateful for your concern and loyalty," I said slowly and softly, almost in a whisper.

Will sat and stared at me.

"OK. I've made my offers to help. I don't know what else to do. If you change your mind, you can call me. I won't bring it up again. Good luck." He zipped up his coat, stood, came over and shook my hand, and walked out. I heard him go down the stairs. The door opened and closed.

I sat there.

An hour later the door opened. Someone came up the stairs. It was Will. He didn't say anything. He had a supermarket bag in one hand and a gallon of milk in the other. He went straight into the kitchen. I heard the refrigerator open and close. Then he walked through the living room again, looked at me as he walked by, without stopping, and went out the front door. I heard the door open and close, and then he jiggled the knob until it clicked.

CHAPTER 30

Days later, a person came up the stairs and into the living room. It was Sal.

"Hello, Doc."

I nodded.

"I was worried about you, I called every day. You never answered."

I said nothing.

"How are you feeling?"

"I'll live," I answered flatly. My voice was frail.

"Is your leg better?"

"Getting better," I said, alternating my glance between Sal and the game show.

"I'm sorry this had to happen," said Sal, in a voice so sincere he sounded truly apologetic.

Me, too.

"It would have been nicer if you killed me," I decided to say. I felt my throat close and I expected tears. They still couldn't come.

"Now, Doc, deep down I don't think you really mean that. I can understand why you feel that way now. This may sound brutal, but you made us do what we did. You took a very grave risk, you did a very stupid, dangerous thing. Following us, with a gun in your pocket. We're into each other too deep." He lit another cigarette and looked around for an ashtray. "You see, Doc, if you let it, it could be very easy for you. I have a need for you. And you would be well taken care of, and thanked, and protected. You should realize this, and relax. Cooperate. Do you hear what I'm saying?"

I heard what he said. It was difficult to concentrate. But what was clear was that I was conquered. I could only do as he directed. He had brought me to the edge of death, and in terror he turned me inside out. I had felt no true will since, nor could I again.

"Yeah," I said, nodding, in a whisper.

Sal suggested that we drink a toast to our new understanding. He was surprised when I told him that I didn't drink anymore, and that there was no booze left in the house.

"That's OK. I'll bring something else."

He went into the kitchen and soon returned with a glass of orange juice for each of us. He touched the two glasses together in a toast, and handed me mine.

"L'chaim," he said. "Hebrew for life."

I know.

I was silent.

He sat across from me in my living room, sipping his drink, smoking, and chatting. I wasn't paying much attention. The game show was over and the four o'clock movie was starting.

"Mind if I turn that off?" asked Sal.

I shook my head.

"When you get to be my age, background noise can be distracting. It's an early sign of deafness, you know."

I know.

"Doc, how soon do you think you'll be able to work again?" he asked, rubbing his left shoulder, his hand under his jacket.

I should have been outraged. I should have thrown my glass at him and swore. I couldn't muster the malice. Without even annoyance in my voice, I said, "I can only barely walk. My wrist is messed up."

"Yeah, those flesh wounds can be sore for a while. But when they start to get better, they get better fast. You'll be up and around soon. I got wounded myself, you know. In the war."

"Where?" I asked, not really interested.

"In my ass. I got some shrapnel in my ass."

Served him right. But that wasn't what I'd meant.

"No, where were you?"

"Oh. France. They gave me a Purple Heart and sent me home a hero. Still have some in there."

Sal finished his drink and sat back in his chair looking at me, rattling the ice cubes in his glass.

"Y'know, Doc, a lot of people are gonna be very happy to have you back. You did a lot of nice work on all those, ah, accident patients."

"Thanks," I said softly. *Yeah. As much as he let me.*

"And all the neighborhood people you treated, too, they really liked you. The old woman with the arthritis is much better. She always asks about you."

"That's nice."

"You know, Doc, Jews and Italians always get along like this," he said, holding up two crossed fingers. "You know, similar values."

I thought of a different finger gesture I could show him, but I didn't bother.

"Well, Doc, I shouldn't stay too long. They say you shouldn't visit a patient too long the first time." He lit a cigarette. "I'll come by and see you tomorrow."

He left.

I turned the television back on.

CHAPTER 31

Sal returned the next morning. He came huffing and puffing up the stairs, carrying a brown paper bag.

"Good morning Doc, how ya' doin' today? You been sitting there since last night?" he asked as he walked into the kitchen.

I was sitting on the couch in the living room watching the *Today Show*.

"I brought you some fresh milk and bread and things." He came into the living room and unbuttoned his old topcoat. He was jolly. He was wearing another of his drab and worn suits. He lit a cigarette.

"So how are you today?" he asked again.

I cleared my throat. "I'm OK." I hadn't bathed and inspected my wound yet. I hadn't eaten yet either. I was getting pretty thin.

"You gonna watch the Super Bowl on Sunday?" he asked.

"I guess so."

"If you wanna place any bets, just let me know."

"OK."

"Doc, you mind my asking you a medical question?"

"No."

"I haven't been feeling too good lately. I get outta breath real easy. Sometimes when I get breathing heavy my chest hurts. What's that, bronchitis or pleurisy or something?" He was sitting forward on his chair, looking at me intensely, waving around a cigarette as he spoke.

"What's the pain like?"

"It's not really a pain, it's a, it's a discomfort, an ache."

"What's it like?"

"It's a heavy feeling, it's tight."

"Where do you get it?"

"Right here." He made a loose fist with his right hand and tapped it over his sternum.

"Does it last long?"

"Nah. If I quit what I'm doing it goes away in a minute."

I noticed that I was starting to feel funny. I felt a little dizzy, a little floaty. I didn't have to think about what to say or ask, I just said it. It was automatic. I sat there listening to myself talk to Sal.

"Have you ever had any trouble with your heart?"

"My heart? You think it's my heart? I thought maybe I was just smoking too much."

"I don't know yet. That's what I'm trying to find out."

It was a weird feeling I had. I could sit back and listen while my mouth did the talking. I felt like I was sitting a little behind myself, watching myself interact with Sal. Like I was Edgar Bergen and I had my Charlie McCarthy dummy. Except mine was a Charlie Davids dummy. It was that depersonalization thing, like when I was a sleep deprived intern.

"How much do you smoke?"

"Pack, pack-and-a-half a day."

"Eat a lot of fatty foods?"

"Doc, I eat a lot of everything."

It was like I was on autopilot. The front of me was talking and interacting and the back of me was just watching and listening.

I told Sal to take off his coat and shirt, and limped off to get my medical knapsack. It was funny, seeing myself when I came back, weak, pale and skinny in old flannel pajamas and bathrobe. I needed a shave, and I had a black eye.

Fat Sal was sitting there, bare-chested, with his big gut spilling onto his lap.

I took Sal's blood pressure. It was high.

"When's the last time you saw a doctor?" Charlie asked.

"Long time."

I watched myself as I examined Sal. I was very thorough. I looked in his eyes, felt his neck. I took a long listen to Sal's lungs and heart, in different positions.

I wasn't split in two, but I was like two within one. Part of me did all the work while the rest of me just kind of watched and was amused with the whole thing.

The Charlie who was working looked frail and puny from all he'd been through lately, but I was feeling better every minute. I stood tall and strong on two good legs. I felt powerful. When I looked down at Sal, my contempt and disgust for him rose like phlegm in my throat, rising to be spat out. I had a big wide grin.

Charlie told Sal to go up and down the stairs a few times to see if it could bring on the sensation. He told Sal he wanted to see if his heart sounds would change.

While Sal was on the stairs, Charlie took a glass vial of adrenalin from the bee sting kit in his knapsack. He snapped off the top and drew up the fluid in a small syringe. I knew what my other half was going to do and I silently laughed out loud. I was split in two. I was Jekyll and Hyde both at the same time.

Sal came back into the living room panting. He had broken a light sweat.

"I got the ache now, Doc. There's a little pressure, too."

The Dr. Jekyll told him to lie down on the couch and we both went over to take a listen.

Then Charlie said, "I'm going to give you a little pill that you just let dissolve under your tongue, then I'm going to give you a little injection. This will make you feel better."

Charlie dropped the little nitroglycerin pellet under Sal's tongue. In the minute it would take for the pill to work, Charlie explained what was going on. He explained how a lifetime of smoking and overeating and inactivity had caused the arteries in his heart to become clogged. They didn't always allow enough blood to get to the heart muscle. When the heart muscle was more active with exertion and needed more blood, it couldn't get it. When the heart was starved for blood like this, it caused the symptoms Sal complained of.

"It's called angina pectoris," Charlie said.

"I've heard of that," Sal replied.

"Do you feel any better?" Charlie asked.

"Yeah, I am feeling a little better."

I just listened to myself go through all this, inwardly laughing.

Sal was still lying on the couch, and we were sitting beside him on the coffee table.

"So what happens now, Doc?"

"Well, what this means is that you've been walking around on the brink of a heart attack. For one thing, you've got to stop smoking. Also, there are medicines you can take to make things easier on your heart."

"You really mean I've been on the brink of a heart attack?"

"There really isn't any question about it. Let me give you that injection now." My voice sounded a little deeper, and a little stronger than usual.

Charlie wiped Sal's shoulder with alcohol and gave him the injection of adrenaline.

"This will make you feel better."

Charlie began to explain that Sal needed a proper doctor's appointment with blood tests, electrocardiogram, the works.

I don't know how I could keep a straight face because I was cracking up inside. The adrenaline wouldn't make him feel better at all. It could kill him. It would make his arteries tighten, his pulse quicken. His blood pressure would soar even higher and he'd get jittery. It would give him severe chest pain.

"Feeling better?" we asked.

"No. I'm feeling a little worse. Can I have another one of those pills?"

"No, just give the injection a chance to work."

Charlie took Sal's blood pressure again and it was up to one-eighty over one-fifteen, pulse one-oh-five. Sal was breaking out in a cold sweat.

"Doc, it's really getting bad."

We put the stethoscope on his chest, listening to nothing in particular, just stalling while the pain got worse. Sal was breathing heavily. Inside I was jumping up and down, cheering for our side.

"Listen," Charlie said, with an incredibly straight face, "your heart sounds have changed. If that injection didn't help you, the pills probably won't either. Here, I'll give you one anyway." I dropped another nitroglycerin pellet under his tongue. "I believe you're on the brink of having heart damage right now, with pain this severe. Whatever you do, don't move, don't even raise your arm, just relax and breathe slow and steady."

"Mother of Jesus," Sal said.

I fished another vial out of my knapsack and snapped off the glass nipple. I sucked the propranolol up into another syringe. I turned from the coffee table back toward Sal, the syringe in my hand between us.

"What's that stuff?" he asked, wiping sweat from his forehead.

"It's a beta blocker. It'll lower the RPMs in your heart so it won't work so hard, won't hurt so much. Put your hand down, don't exert yourself or you'll make things worse." I poked the needle into a vein in his elbow and gave him a milligram.

In a minute Sal said it was easing off.

"OK, Sal," I said. "Here's what we can do. This is a legitimate medical problem. Is there any need to treat you in secret like we've done with all those other people?"

Sal shook his head, no. I had my finger on his wrist, following his pulse.

"I can call an ambulance and have you at Berkshire Medical Center in minutes," I said, doing my best to appear concerned, caring, compassionate.

"OK, Doc, let's go."

"OK. Let me check your pulse again." I reached for his neck, to feel the carotid artery. I felt his pulse in it and I massaged it, which might stimulate his vagus nerve to further lower his pulse and make him nauseated.

I looked at the two half-empty syringes sitting on my coffee table. He was ready for a little more adrenaline.

Back and forth, up and down, fast and slow, accelerator and brake.

"Sal, try and relax, I'm going to give you a little more of this." I gave him 0.1 cc of adrenaline, just a little bit. His pulse went up.

"I'm feeling that tightness again."

"Just try to relax, loosen up, don't exert yourself at all, that would be the worst thing to do," I said.

I dropped another nitroglycerin under his tongue a minute later.

I put my fingertips on his neck again. I hadn't trimmed my fingernails in a while. My focus became normal again. I felt crazed. My hand was on his neck. I thought hard about strangling him. I thought hard about not strangling him. Decisions, decisions. The muscles in my good right arm were ready, tight, tingling. My thumb was on one side of his neck, my fingers on the other. I could tear out his larynx in an instant.

"What are you doing?" Sal asked sheepishly. I had been staring vacantly at his face.

"Has it eased off? Is it a little better? Yes? Be sure not to move or to exert yourself," I said sweetly, in a slow, deep voice.

"Sal, you're on the brink now. No, don't tighten up. I can call an ambulance now. But, you've destroyed my life. Shall I destroy yours now?" My fingers tightened a tiny bit on his neck, just to get his attention.

"I could call an ambulance now, but maybe I won't. You're a bad man, Sal. I'll bet you've done lots of bad things in your life. The hospital might be better care than you deserve. Take it from me, Sal, society would be better off without you." I seethed menace. By now I was almost shouting, and as I spoke we both watched little specks of spittle fly from my mouth and hit him on the face. I was crazed.

"You're on the brink of dying right now. This sofa could be your deathbed any minute. You want me to help you, you want me to save your life, you're gonna have to bargain for it. You tried to kill me last week and now I'm offering to save you. Or else, you're on your own fucking deathbed right now. All you have to do is get out of my life. Make me an oath that you'll leave me alone forever and then I'll help you. But, you'll have to convince me.

"You can choose life or death. I recommend you choose life. How hard do you want me to try to help you?" I seethed.

CHAPTER 32

I was sitting on Patty's stoop. It was cold. It was snowing. It was dark. The streetlights were on. The wooden stoop was hard. My hands were in my pockets. I was leaning forward. In my lap, between my chest and my knees, was a bouquet of yellow roses wrapped in paper. It was a few minutes after five o'clock. Patty's shift was over at five and I hoped she'd be coming straight home. Alone. If she stopped at the grocery or had errands to run I might be frozen by the time she returned. I wanted to be there sitting on the stoop. I didn't want to be sitting in my car when she drove up. Putting up with the cold was good for me. It filled up my senses. I had hope. I had anxiety, I had love, I had remorse. I had butterflies, I had the cold. I could feel my pulse in my thigh wound. My wrist ached. It would be embarrassing if she drove up with a new boyfriend and saw me sitting there.

It was dark. Every time I saw headlights turn down the street I got my hopes up it would be her. I didn't know what I was going to say. I imagined smiles and open arms and being inside her warm house and out of the cold.

There was a half-inch of snow on my coat sleeves, my arms crossed in front of me on my knees. I was catching a little snow between the end of my sleeves and the top of my gloves. It was cold on my wrists and felt good. The snowflakes were small and dry and fell slowly. There was almost no breeze and the snow piled up vertically on all the branches and phone lines like little aerial walls. Someone walked down the other side of the street, walking a dog. The dog noticed me first. Then the person looked at me but did not break stride. I couldn't tell if the bundled up person was male or female.

Did Patty still live here? I didn't look at my watch. I didn't want to disturb the snow on my coat. I wanted to see how high it could get. Some of the snow on my bare wrists melted and became bitingly cold. I didn't need to know how long I'd been sitting. She'd come eventually. Another set of lights turned my way but did not slow down as they came near. Not her. The car's wheels made a funny squeaky sound on the fresh, dry, fine snow. I took a deep breath and saw the fog when I exhaled. The cold made my eyes water a little, which made my nose run a little. It was cold but not bitter cold.

I kept thinking of her coming home, as if I could plan it out like the screenplay in a movie. I still didn't know what I was going to say. How much of my story should I tell her?

Sitting next to me on the stoop was a shopping bag with the dinner I hoped to share with her. It was almost the same dinner we'd had together on that warm summer evening on the island in Goose Pond. That seemed so long ago. It was like a warm, peaceful, relaxed dream. The memory seemed so unreal to me now. So much had happened since then. It was that night on the lake that I first realized that I loved her; when I began to realize that she might be the one. *Oh, I hope I can get her back.*

When I first sat down on her porch that night I caught an occasional steamy whiff of the lemon herb rotisserie chicken in the box in the bag next to me. It must've cooled off by now; I couldn't smell it.

As I sat there, I passed the time daydreaming disjointedly. I tried to remember each of my times with Patty in chronological order, thinking about how our relationship grew and deepened and developed, like one of those time-lapse movies of a flower going from bud to blossom to flower.

It had been about three months since our parting conversation at the art museum. I had tried to keep some contact with her. I called her every week or two to say hello and I hoped to keep myself in her thoughts. The phone calls were awkward and short and uncomfortable. I had stopped calling a couple of months before. The calls weren't making anything better. I still had walls up. Now the walls were down. I needed to show her that. I hoped she would give me a chance to show her that. I needed this woman in my life.

I could wait. I wasn't in a hurry anymore for her to come home. The cold was good. I still didn't know yet what I was going to say. The cold was cleansing. This period of sitting here was good. It was a separation, a border, a margin between my ugly recent past and my new and hopeful future. That's if the story would unfold like my screenplay. Sitting here was a cleansing restoring preparation, between my troubles with Sal and what I hoped would be my new life with Patty.

A car came down toward me. Very slowly in the few inches of snow. I could only see the lights, not the car. It approached. It was Patty's car. She slowly turned into the driveway and her headlight beams swept across me. I stood up, erupting from the cocoon of snow that I had collected. I was stiff. My left leg was asleep, and as I stood and put weight on it, it buckled and I fell to the ground. I landed on my left thigh and left wrist on the hard frozen ground. The snow didn't cushion my fall. Both my injured places were screaming and I rolled on my back, teeth clenched, waiting for the pain to stop. I clambered to my feet.

"Charlie, is that you?" Patty asked.

"It's me. Was I graceful?" I asked. "I'm back, Patty. The old me is back. The walls are gone. My problems are over. Please, Patty, can we pick up where we left off?" I just blurted out.

We stood there looking at each other five feet apart on the snowy driveway. Abruptly I bent down and picked up the bouquet. "These are for you." I stepped forward.

"Oh, Charlie," she said, stepping forward, and she gave me a snowy hug. "Come in the house." I hobbled to her front door and picked up the bag of food.

"I brought dinner, if you haven't eaten."

"Oh, Charlie, let's dust you off. You're covered. How long have you been sitting here?"

"Since five or so," I said.

"Charlie, you've been sitting out there for two hours? You must be freezing!"

The door opened. We stepped into her foyer. She turned on the light. I went back out the door to stamp the snow off my shoes, shake more snow off. I took off my knit cap and shook it. I went back into the foyer and closed the door. I opened my coat. It was happening. She had greeted me warmly and hugged me and took me into her house.

She was hanging up her coat as I took mine off. She really looked good in her work clothes. Classy. She had on a pewter gray lambs' wool sweater and dressy, tight black slacks.

After she hung up her coat she turned to me and looked at me in the light. The smiling expression dropped from her face and her mouth opened.

"Charlie, you look like shit," she said. I paused, looking at her. I handed her the food bag and bent over to untie my shoes.

"I need to tell you what happened," I said. I thought my black eye wasn't that noticeable any more. It still throbbed when I bent over.

I stood up and stepped out of my shoes. She was standing there looking at me, frowning. She hugged me again.

"Charlie, you're freezing. And you're wet. Come with me, I'll make you some tea." We walked in our stocking feet through the darkened house to the kitchen. She turned on the kettle and I was sitting at her kitchen table. My leg and wrist were throbbing. It was so good to see her. It was so good to be with her in her kitchen.

"Patty, I am so glad to be here. You don't know how glad I am to be here. I need to tell you what happened," I said again. She began to unpack the food bag. She laid out the cheese, the bread, the plastic container of macaroni salad. She took out the chicken and smelled it. No tennis ball cans.

"It smells so good." She unwrapped it and put it in the oven to warm. She took out the bottle of white wine and looked for an opener.

"Would you like some?" she asked, turning to look at me.

"No, thanks, not now, I'll wait for the tea." The kettle was steaming. She put a teabag in a thick ceramic mug and poured water into it. She put it in front of me. She stood looking at me.

"My God, Charlie, you got so skinny."

"I need to tell you what happened," I said. I reached for the mug but I fumbled it with my left hand. No grip strength. I picked it up with my right. After all that time in the snow, it wasn't until now that I began to shiver.

She walked across the kitchen and opened a cupboard. On tiptoes she reached up to the top shelf to get wineglasses. As she stretched, her gray sweater separated from her black slacks, and I could see four inches of the concave curve of her lean, pale flank. She poured herself some wine.

"Come into the living room." I got up and followed her. She turned on a lamp. She watched me limp. She'd pruned the dieffenbachia.

"Sit here. Put this around you." I sat on the couch, and she wrapped an afghan around me. "I'll be right back." I heard her in the kitchen. She came back and sat down beside me. "Alright. Tell me what happened."

"Can you keep a secret?" I asked.

"Yes."

"I mean this with the utmost seriousness. This story can go nowhere. Hold my hand and promise me," I said, nearly in a whisper.

With a confused look on her face she reached for my hand and said, "I promise."

"Thank you," I said.

"Remember Uncle Sal?"

"Yes."

"He's not my uncle."

"Who is he?"

"He is with organized crime in Springfield. Last year I treated a guy in the ER who later told Sal about me. They needed a doctor to take care of injured people secretly, people whose injuries, in a conventional setting, would need to be reported."

"So you sewed up bullet holes and stuff?" she asked.

"And stuff." I told her more details.

"So for all these months, they'd beep you, tell you they need you, pick you up, drive you somewhere to see a patient and then drive you home, and in a few days mail you money?"

"Yes."

"So you were on call for the Mob?" she asked.

"Yes."

She looked at me for a few seconds, leaned away, and then she said, not smiling, "That sounds like the biggest cock-and-bull story I ever heard." Admittedly, it was hard to believe.

"Can I show you something?" I asked. She nodded. "It's on my thigh." She nodded. I stood up and opened my belt and undid my trousers to my knees. She saw the big bandage on my thigh. I sat on the edge of the couch and peeled back the bandage. It must've started bleeding a little when I fell. There was a scab over the entrance hole in front, and a bigger scab on the exit hole in back, and a long blue-black area connecting the two, which was the roof of the tunnel connecting the two, and it was yellow and green all over.

"What happened?" Patty asked in a whisper, her eyes wide.

"I got shot."

"Oh, my God, Charlie." I hinged the dressing back in place and pulled my soggy pants back up.

"Will you be alright? Will it heal up OK? It looks so awful."

"It's a lot better already," I said.

"So is it over now? Are you really all done with them now?" she asked.

"Yes. I'm done with them. I couldn't have come back here to you if I wasn't sure it was safe."

"How do you know?"

"Well, to make a long story short, Sal had a heart attack. In my apartment." I wasn't going to tell her how I tried to provoke it. "I stabilized him, called 911, went with him in the ambulance to BMC. They worked him up, admitted him. He went up to CCU. He had, fortunately, a small inferior wall MI. His enzymes weren't very high. He did well. When I visited him a few days later in the hospital he was really very funny."

"What did he say?"

"First, he greeted me very warmly. He asked if he could call me Charlie instead of Doc. Then he asked me if I remembered the Aesop's fable about the mouse who pulled the thorn out of the lion's paw. He said that I'd done that for him. He said he was very grateful for helping him with his heart attack, that he saw the cardiologist that morning and he had a good prognosis. He'd already had his last cigarette, was going to lose weight and enter a cardiac rehab exercise program in Springfield. He thanked me for taking care of all those people we worked with. He was very complimentary. He apologized for what happened to me that night I got shot. He said I was free now, I was released, he would develop someone else to take over what I'd been doing."

I was standing at his bedside in CCU.

Sal said, "Charlie, sit down. Listen. I wanna tell you something. About me. You realize I never told you very much about myself. For safety reasons.

"Charlie, you're a nice boy. You are a good person. You are a person who likes to live by the rules. You have strong feelings about what's right and what's wrong. You try hard to be strict with them and I think sometimes you make life harder for yourself because of it. You have your rules for taking care of patients, rules you follow to be thorough and careful and to think things through, and rules about being nice to people and being respectful. Even though you say you're not religious, you really are, and I can see those rules mixed in with you, too. You are a sensitive person and I know that you suffer for it and that sensitive guys like you always find the sharpest picket fences to sit on. I know it's been hard for you to work with me all these months, but you've done good, careful, caring work, and I'm grateful to you for it. And I'm grateful for all you've explained to me, and for helping me get through this heart attack. You're off the hook. You'll be protected," he said.

"I never told you anything about me before because of the kind of business we're in. But lemme tell you something now. My wife and me, we had a son. If he was still alive, he'd be about your age now. Maybe a little younger. You remind me of him. He was sensitive like you are. He didn't like me, he didn't like what I do for a living. He rebelled. All I wanted was to love him. When he finished high school he joined the Peace Corps. He went to Africa to teach English and help build modern huts out of mud brick. He was gone for two years and then he came home once for Christmas. We had a great visit. He went back to Africa, and when they were flying him back to his little village in a little plane, it crashed. That was it. Dead. He was kinda like you. He wanted to save the world, or at least a little bit of it. He would've liked you. He would've looked up to you. My wife hasn't been the same since."

I was speechless. "Wow," I said. It was all I could say. "I'm so sorry to hear of your tragedy. Do you have any other children?"

"I do. And two grandchildren. My daughter's," Sal answered.

"That's great," I said.

"OK, Charlie. I thank you. You and me are done. I'm gonna find some other doctor to harass now. Got any ideas?"

"How about a surgeon?"

"No! No, no surgeons. I told you no surgeons." He smiled.

"Wow," Patty said.

"Wow is right." She was next to me under the afghan now. On my left. We were shoulder-to-shoulder and thigh-to-thigh. I turned to look at her face in profile. A few long strands of brown hair were caught in her earring. The freckles on her nose had faded in the winter months, since I last saw her. In the tangential lighting I could see the almost invisible golden baby hairs on her cheek. She shifted, and bumped my bandage. I winced.

"Oh. Sorry."

I nodded.

"How do you know there are no strings attached?" she asked.

"I asked him the same question. When I asked, he chuckled and said, `Don't worry about it. You and I are done with this. Go back and get that little girl of yours.'"

"I'm not little," she said.

"Compared to Sal, we're all little." The wind had picked up and it was snowing harder.

"So all this time you were working two jobs?"

"It wasn't constant. Sometimes it would be a few trips each week. Sometimes not at all for a few weeks."

"So you'd work your twelve hours in the ER, then he'd pick you up and you'd work for him, and then maybe sleep a couple of hours and then go back to the ER."

"Sometimes."

I began telling her more of the story. How they scared the crap out of me when I came home and found them in my living room. About the phone tap. About how scared I was the first time they picked me up that spring night in the supermarket parking lot. I hadn't known what to expect. I told her about all the awful head injuries I saw and how they wouldn't let me take them to the hospital, and how they died in front of me. I told her about the abused women I saw, and the one who'd been so brutally beaten.

I told her how I missed a pick-up once because I was tied up in the ER with a cardiac arrest and Sal sent his goons to trash my parents' house.

I told her about the drug addicts with hepatitis, and the three days I spent detoxing an alcoholic.

Patty was just listening, wide-eyed, without saying anything.

I told her about the wonderful meal I had with Sal and Bob in that basement apartment and how I asked them if I could invite her.

"I would've come," she said.

I went on and on, telling her about the little skirmish between different Mob factions, and the half dozen men I saw with gunshot wounds. One with a sucking chest wound and a collapsed lung, which I vented, and he pulled through. Another with an upper arm wound with nerve damage to the brachial plexus, who wouldn't do much with that hand again. All this with no backup, no X-ray, no labs. And Sal made me do it all because he refused to let them go to a hospital. One time with a guy with an intracerebral bleed, I begged him to get him to a hospital but he refused, and I started yelling and then his thugs carried me off. Bodily.

"Patty, I was so scared. I was always so scared."

"For them or for you?"

"That's a good question. For them I guess. I was the only chance they had."

"That's a lot of pressure to be under. And you couldn't tell me about it. You couldn't tell Will about it. Did you ever think about going to the police about it?" I told her what I'd researched and what I'd considered, and about my conversations with Michael, with Matt, and with the criminal lawyer in New York City. I didn't tell her about the gun. I told her Matt's suggestion to do bad work for them.

She asked how it happened that I got shot. I sighed, and said I wasn't ready to talk about that. Yet.

"So, was I smart or was I stupid?" I asked.

Patty sipped her wine. "You were trapped. You didn't know what to do. You were never in a situation like that before. You tried to get all the information you could but it didn't do you any good.

"All you know how to do is to be nice to people and to help people and to engage them personally and try to comfort them. You were probably born that way. And it led you to your career.

"You cling to your values. The value and sanctity of life. In all of the violence Sal took you to, you clung to it like a life raft. I couldn't see you fighting back or hurting or threatening anybody to get away from Sal. That would be so out of character for you. You'd have to become deranged or crazed before you'd ever threaten or hurt someone, even to escape a monster like Sal. Besides, they were experts in violence, and you wouldn't have had a chance."

She was right. I'd been crazy. That's the only way I could've done what I did to Sal. I didn't tell Patty that part. That secret I'll keep to myself.

"But in the end, you survived. And it's over. And you're back. And I'm glad."

"It's over." I sighed. I tipped my head back against the couch. The framed Monet we got at the museum was on the opposite wall. I looked at it. It looked so peaceful. I closed my eyes.

"That is an amazing story, Charlie." I nodded, eyes closed.

"I'm gonna set the table." I nodded. Patty got up.

"Patty, I should go. I'm really not hungry and I can't keep my eyes open," I said.

She was standing there looking at me. "No," she said. "No way. I'm not letting you drive all the way to Dalton on a night like this. In the condition you're in. You're staying here. In my bed. With me. Come," she said. She took my hand and led me to the bedroom.

"Take off your wet clothes and I'll put them in the dryer." I did. She watched me.

"My God, Charlie, you got so skinny," she said again, her finger going to her lip. I didn't think I looked that bad.

"Oh," I said, "I have one more thing to show you." I took my corduroys back from her and pulled an envelope out of a pocket. I handed it to her. As she opened it I said, "Royal Caribbean Cruise lines. Tickets for two. We can leave next week."

The wind howled outside and we could hear the snow on the window glass. We stood a foot-and-a-half apart. I was in boxers. I was shivering. She was holding the tickets between her hands, up against her chest, under her chin. She was smiling dreamily. Her eyes were watery. She leaned forward and kissed me. She put her arms around my neck and pulled me to her. She was warm. We stood there.

"You're back," she whispered in my ear.

"I am," I said.

"Get under the covers," she said.